# Chocolate Chocolate Moons

### Jackie Kingon

D1400552

Copyright © 2012 Jackie Kingon

All rights reserved.

ISBN-10: 1477561803

EAN-13: 9781477561805

Library of Congress Control Number: 2011919692

CreateSpace, North Charleston, SC

TO AL
FOR HIS SUPPORT AND LOVE

1

These words change my life:

"Congratulations, plus-size student! Based on your cholesterol readings, body-fat ratio, Fibonacci number sequence for digesting chocolate, and high school cafeteria records, you have won the Good and Plenty Scholarship for two at Neil Armstrong University on the Moon. Call this toll-free number to collect your prize."

Until this moment, my life has been filled with diets, promises to diet, failed diets, exercise, therapies, nutritionists, acupuncture, hypnosis and memories of falling over the marbles rolled in my path at school as my classmates laughed and yelled, "Molly Marbles, round as a marble, fat as a moon."

I suck in my breath, pull up my bra straps, push my hair behind my moon-shaped face, crack each finger and toe, and call the number. Then I call my boyfriend, Drew Barron, who is far heavier than I am.

"Pack your bags, sweetheart. We're joining the class of 2333 at Neil Armstrong University on the Moon where the gravity is light, the classes are right, and the livin' is gonna be easy."

One month later Drew and I sit on the Earth–Moon shuttle feeding each other our favorite candy, Chocolate Moons. We savor its rich dark chocolate coating for as long as we can before our tongues slip into the dense truffle center. We pucker our lips, kiss, and swallow. I lean back wide-eyed and look at Drew.

"These are so delicious," I sigh, "they should be called Chocolate Chocolate Moons."

"You're right," Drew says, closing his eyes and letting the last sweet morsel slide down his throat. "Can't have too much of a good thing."

I turn toward the window on my left. When I crane my neck I can see the Moon coming very close. Drew leans in to get a better look. Its glowing gray surface is slowly covering the window until it is the only thing we can see. I sit silently and wonder if I made the right choice, my excitement masking my nervousness. Suddenly a red light above blinks "Warning: Gravity Change" and under that, blinking green, "Seat Belt Release."

We yank to attention.

"So soon," I murmur.

Drew pales and white-knuckles his armrest.

"It's time," I say, prying his sweaty fingers free.

We stand, shift from foot to foot, and shuffle with the others toward the door.

My damp palms flutter like little birds. I spread my arms, lower them to the smooth cool railing, and slide forward until I stand at the threshold's flashing lights. I descend a few steps, extend a toe and step on to the Lunar Port's silver-and-black tiled floor.

My body looks the same, the soft skin jiggling beneath my arms, my butt reaching way beyond its proper place, forming a humongous Z with my tummy, but I feel as light as a whipped egg white in a floating island dessert. I leap, higher than I thought I could, toward a sign that says "Weighing Area," step on a large round circle embedded in the floor, and read the numbers floating before me. My 287 Earth pounds are 47.6 Moon pounds. I raise my arms in triumph. I throw my head back and shriek, "Miracle! Miracle! It's a miracle!"

Drew hesitates in the doorway. "Outta my way, fat boy!" snarls a man shoving him through. Drew quivers, and then he bounces like a ball on springs toward the weighing area laughing out loud ignoring the stares. His 385 pounds are 65.

A flight attendant shakes her sleek blond hair, frowns into the confusion of sights and sounds surrounding her, and mutters to no one in particular, "You can always tell the new arrivals." She waves her luggage chip over a bag and scoots to the slide-run.

I squint through the high clear dome that protects us from the vacuum outside and gasp at the billions of unblinking diamond sharp stars against black velvet space. Without an atmosphere the familiar words *twinkle twinkle little star* are now as meaningless as my former weight.

Drew slows and jelly-rolls near me, pushes his dark curly hair from his eyes, and gives me a serious look. He straightens and stands; his elephantine shape stops jiggling. He walks toward me on legs that look like hundred-year-old oak trees. I grab his hand. My voice cracks. "You know, we're never going to see a blue sky if we stay on the Moon."

Drew grins and pulls me close. "But, sweetheart," he says and laughs, "we never have to see a scale either."

Part frontier town, part research center, every café and market in Armstrong City crackles with the energy buzzing from scientists, architects, engineers, and more miners than those who finally dug the hole from some kid's backyard in North America to China.

My scholarship for writing the winning essay, "The Joy of Salami," pays the rent on a small condo in a crater near the university. It is the first school either of us has attended where we look average and fit right in. Everyone jokes that the Moon is made not of green cheese but full-fat mozzarella. We hold hands and march around singing, "When the Moon hits your eye like a big pizza pie, that's amore."

Drew studies media and marketing. I major in culinary arts and, which I thought was a whim, minor in criminology. It was a strange combination of classes that overlapped when studying chemical compositions of foods, and poisonous reactions on worlds with different gravities and atmospheric pressures. I also learned techniques for observation that come in handy sooner rather than later.

Like college students everywhere, we party hard and drink the local moonshine that tastes a lot like beer. We eat and dance, eat and make love, and have heated philosophical discussions like if Eve made apple pies from the forbidden apple tree in the Garden of Eden, would God let her and Adam remain so they could open a bakery? And, if not, is there a God?

Several times a week we swim at the university's pool floating like balloons in bathing suits we were too embarrassed to wear on Earth. Shopping is divine: everything fits or has to be taken in.

It doesn't matter that Earth's light shining on the Moon doesn't look as romantic as moonlight shining on the Earth; I'm happier than I have ever been in my life.

But, alas, my happiness is briefer than a frozen margarita on a hot summer day.

One morning when soap slips from my hand and slides to the floor, I bend to pick it up and find a half-empty bottle of vanilla birth control pills stashed under the bathroom sink.

Mine are chocolate!

Three weeks pass. The mystery of the vanilla pills is solved at the Man in the Moon costume ball. Wearing my salad costume, in memory of all my former diets, I watch as Drew is called onstage. Dressed as a ball of green cheese encased in a floating onion ring, he receives the Best Costume award from last year's winner, a student named Colorful Copies. CC, as she likes to be called, is a plain-looking girl with brown hair and brown eyes. She is heavier than I am, wears a 50DD bra, and dyes her brown eyebrows rainbow colors. Her fondue-pot costume with its multicolored fork headdress is stylish if you like that kind of thing.

When I see CC inch closer to Drew and swoon, I toss inside my salad costume. I hear "Your green cheese would feel so good in my pot." Then she bends and sinks her teeth so deeply into Drew's onion ring that it spins.

Suddenly I feel like a pizza cut into more than eight slices, more stunned than if I saw the prophet Elijah actually show up at a seder table, more grated than a Parmesan cheese. How could love have made me blind? Like those nights Drew came home late not hungry for anything. Anything! And me chalking it up to hard work and ambition, which as it turns out, depending on definitions, was in fact technically true.

CC and Drew dance the first dance. They circle near me. "Drew, sweetheart," she says in a loud voice so I can hear, "you are the best melted cheese I ever ate."

Hearing that, I yank the green peas that hang like cultured pearls around my neck and hurl them at Drew.

"Ouch," he winces holding up his hands to ward them off. "Cut it out, Molly."

Several peas land in CC's fondue pot. "I hate vegetable fondue," she hisses in a spiteful baby thin voice, the kind of jeering voice that makes me want to push a chocolate cream pie into her face but I would never because I couldn't disrespect and ruin all that chocolate.

Instead, using what's at hand I rip the carrot sticks off my shoulders; free the tomatoes from my chest, sever the corn dangling from my waist, tear the curly endive wrapped around my hips, and hurl everything at them. *Splat!*

CC's light goes out under her fondue pot. She reaches up for a fondue fork.

I glare at Drew.

Drew looks at CC. She lowers her arm and narrows her eyes. He wipes tomato pieces from his face.

CC glowers at me.

I look back at Drew.

None of us say anything. We all know what it means.

On our way home Drew and I are more rumpled than empty candy wrappers. Finally, in bed, as my head hits the pillow, he murmurs, "Night." It was not good.

The next morning before I can say *granola*, Drew's bags are packed and he announces that he is moving in with CC.

"What does she have that I don't have?" I sob to a friend. "Is she prettier than me?"

"Nope."

"Is she smarter than me?"

"No way."

"Have a better personality? Is more charming?"

"No to the first and no to the second. I can't believe you don't know. Everybody knows."

"Knows what?"

"CC is the daughter of Carbon Copies, owner of Carbon Copies Media, the Moon's largest media conglomerate. And CC is his heir apparent."

# 2

DREW'S AFFAIR WITH CC DOESN'T LAST. He and CC have such differences that they can't even agree on how many filets in a mignon, something the average school child knows. But when they went head to toe about what's beyond the bed and the bath, a topic Drew had given many hours of serious thought, he knew he made a mistake. Nor did the job CC promised that her father would give him materialize. Not after Drew reached over Carbon Copies's desk to shake his hand and knocked to the floor and shattered his rare autopen-signed photo of George from Washington with his arm draped around redheaded Cherry Tree lying about.

After enduring two weeks of the silent treatment from CC, and trying to salvage what was left of his troubled relationship, Drew buys her a gift. It's in a small black velvet box.

"I hope it's what I think it is," she says, crunching several Fontina cheese-coated potato chips.

"How can it not be, sweetheart?"

CC opens the box, peeks inside, and frowns.

"What's the matter, don't you like it?"

"But it's a diamond ring."

"Yes. Ten carats."

"Are you completely out of touch? What's the matter with you? Ever since so many diamonds were discovered on the outer planets, the diamond market has tanked. No one wants diamond jewelry anymore. How cheap can you be?" She closes the box and gives it back to Drew. "Thanks, but no thanks."

Drew is stunned.

CC smiles slyly and bats her eyelashes. "Now, a lump of coal," she coos, "that's a rare and beautiful thing."

Bored and disappointed with his life, Drew sees an ad for Congress Drugs, a company that makes the Freedom Plan, low-calorie diet alternatives. Congress Drugs is looking for plus-size sales representatives who will lose weight eating their products. Those selected will have their "before" and "after" pictures featured in ads. However, the company's headquarters is on Mars.

"Mars? *Mars?* A red rock millions of miles from a good restaurant?" shouts CC jumping around like fire ants just nested in her cleavage. "Why would  anyone want to go to Mars? Why would anyone want to eat fake food? Why would anyone want to lose weight? Big is beautiful!" And with that she takes the chocolate cannoli that she was eating and crushes the shell between two fingers. "That's what I think about going to Mars! And don't think I won't tell my father about this, you post-nasal drip!"

Meanwhile I have to learn to cope without Drew. Fighting back tears I make a turkey sandwich. I spread honey mustard over a crunchy seeded roll. I feel a little better knowing that I could never be depressed enough to eat boar's heads, whose signs I saw in my Earth history class hanging in every twenty-first century deli.

Soon I hear that Drew left CC and was headed for Mars to work in some kind of diet food company. I feel like a newly risen popover waiting to be buttered and bitten. I cut and lighten my hair, buy a sexy black skirt with some swing to it, and splurge on a bright yellow spandex blouse that shows off the right places.

I wander into a bookstore and finger the Moon's best seller, *Is It a Food If It Has Less Than 100 Calories?* Then I go to my favorite place: the café.

A young man sits alone tapping a small screen.

"May I join you?" I ask. "My name is Molly Marbles."

He shifts a broad shoulder and looks up. My heart flutters. His deep and sonorous voice says, "Cortland Summers. But only if you will share today's special: a pound of melted garlic butter with a side order of focaccia bread."

"My favorite," I say, wishing he had said chocolate decadence cake.

Cortland's brown hair is twisted with a clip that looks like a G clef. Earrings like little solar systems dangle from his ears. His eyes are as dark and dense as chocolate cherries. He wears black jeans and a black sweatshirt with lightning-gold lettering that says "Cracked Craters."

I lean in, making sure my blouse hints at what lies beneath. "And the Cracked Craters are...?"

"My band," he says thumping his chest. "I write music. Maybe you've heard "Like a Floating Stone"? Third-place runner-up for a Naughty Nebula."

"No, but I'd love to hear it." We add our contact codes to our palm directories, a calling device that looks like a tiny dot in the center of our left palms.

Soon thereafter I receive a chocolate decadence cake with a little cube on top containing a holograph of Cortland and his band in concert. For the next twenty-eight day moon month, a cake with a cube arrives. I'm so overwhelmed I can't tell if I've got a sugar high or I'm in love.

Next, Cortland and the Cracked Craters stand outside my window. He croons the mid-twentieth-century hit "Earth Angel." When I hear him say, "five, six, seven, eight," and the beat rises, I run outside, hair flying, panting to the rhythm. He grabs me from the doorway, spins me like a dreidel, gets down on one knee and pops the question.

"Yes, yes, a thousand times yes," I shout. "A thousand splendid moons!"

Our wedding is held in a domed crater covered with white silk flowers. My dress makes me look like a cream puff bouncing down the aisle. As Cortland and I exchange rings, The Craters play "Clair de Lune." My parents, who pay for the wedding, say that if they knew how much food a plus-size person's reception needed, they would have been less generous. But aside from remarks about tapping into their retirement savings, they are happy for me, especially because I am not marrying Drew Barron, about whom they now admit they had reservations.

I work for the MTA, the Moon Transit Authority, giving out parking tickets.

"You know, Cortland, I'm very overqualified for this job."

"What makes you say that?" he asks, annoyed because I've interrupted him reworking "Moon Rover," his latest composition.

His finger jabs the delete key.

"But it doesn't matter because I'm not going to be working there much longer."

Silence. More deleting.

"I'm pregnant," I say.

Cortland looks up. "Pregnant?"

"Twin girls."

"You're sure?"

"Sure, I'm sure. It's not hard to be sure."

Cortland takes a breath and holds it for a very long time processing the information. I wait until his eyes open wide, meaning: all clear. "Everyone's naming their children after places on Earth. What do you think of *Los Angeles* and *Quebec*?"

"*Los Angeles* as in 'Lois' and 'Becky' for *Quebec*," he muses. "I like it."

"And I'm carrying them internally rather than egg-crating them at 'Free Delivery.' It's more expensive, but I want to do it."

"Expensive?" Cortland sweats.

For years Cortland moonlights as a real estate salesman and is very successful. We live in a polished stone condo that is built into the side of a crater. Its cheerful bright colors offset the stark rugged landscape outside the crater's protective dome. We have lots of interesting friends, take a yearly vacation to a ranch in a canyon called Canyon Ranch, and, as I love to cook, give wonderful dinner parties. But best of all, blond, curly-haired Becky and Lois dance and sing to

Cortland's music like songbirds and win every children's talent contest. By the time they are fifteen, they are tall, willowy, and graceful. As proud parents we think they could become stars. Life is good. I have all I have ever wanted.

But one day while reading the *Larousse Gastronomique*, and trying to decide if I should make puffed-sushi-rice-crusted salmon or duck breast in a coriander fig sauce, Cortland comes up the stairs from his padded basement studio.

"Can I talk to you about something?" he says in a way that makes me death-grip the *Larousse* like a floatable seat cushion before the plane hits water. Unfortunately, I've learned from experience that this innocently worded sentence is usually a prelude to information that leads to sleepless nights filled with overeating everything in sight, including dried bouillon cubes and extra-strength All Bran.

"I've invested all our money in a new shopping center, sweetheart."

"All our money?" My voice rises as I digest the words: *all our money*.

"Well, all that makes a difference."

"A difference: as in for food, clothing, and shelter?"

Cortland stomps around the room. "Things just didn't work out as I planned."

"Meaning?"

"We're broke."

"Broke? As in, all gone?"

"It was such a wonderful opportunity. Near the long prairies, a beautiful spot and so cheap."

"Aren't the long prairies on the side of the Moon that the Earth never sees?"

Cortland sighs. "That's right. I thought it was a minor matter, but as it turns out, no one wants to buy advertising space because Earth can't see the ads."

"What are we going to do?" I stand and walk to a dish of candy and stuff the largest Chocolate Moon into my mouth.

"I've already called my cousin, Billings Montana."

"Billings? Billings lives on Mars!"

"His Little Green Men Pizza chain is expanding, along with hundreds of new communities."

"So?"

"Sooooo," he repeats, dragging out this one-syllable word into as many parts as possible, "if we relocate to Mars, he can guarantee work and in time make me a partner."

Cortland puts his arm around me, but I lean away. "There must be other options," I venture, trying to bolster a losing cause. "How about selling glow-in-the-dark dental fillings?"

He sends a withering look. I reach for more candy and hit the dish at an angle. Chocolate Moons zing toward his forehead.

*Ping!* His head snaps back. "Any more bright ideas?"

When we tell the twins, they do a month-long temper dance. Doors slam, tears flow, threats, screams, hair pulling. They are even more depressed than I am. Calorie, our Maltese parrot, sensing she will be left behind, squawks, "Calorie wants a Prozac!"

The weeklong trip to Mars is stressful. Becky and Lois never stop complaining. Cortland is space-sick. I spend more solars than I should on a weightless massage, during which I float naked while four people knead the knots from my body. But as soon as I'm back in our suite, the tension returns.

"Mind if I watch Mars Media news?" I say.

"Mind if we don't?" the twins singsong like a tragic Greek chorus. They leave.

I click on the news. Barbara Bottled Waters is talking about people getting sick on Mars after eating Tootsie Targets, my second-favorite candy after Chocolate Moons. I adjust the sound. "Craig Cashew, president and CEO of the Culinary Institute of Mars, whose Candy Universe building makes the Tootsie Targets, had all the remaining ones tested. No contamination was found. All stricken consumers recovered. Craig Cashew says there is nothing wrong with Tootsie Targets and it's an unfortunate coincidence."

Unfortunate coincidence? Maybe. Maybe not. A candy mystery is something I can sink my teeth into. If nothing else it's a welcome distraction from thinking about tomorrow's landing.

3

DREW WALKS OUT OF HIS life with CC with the clothes on his back, money for a one-way ticket to Mars, and a half-eaten box of Chocolate Moons.

He arrives at the Mars spaceport and waddles down a long corridor. His 63.9 Moon pounds are now 145.1 Mars pounds. And, although considerably less than the 385 he would have weighed on Earth, it was weight he was not used to carrying. The tall, beautiful Martians, whose citizens win the most solar system beauty contests, walk past in disgust.

"It's cellulite with legs," shouts a man making a nasty hand signal.

Children circle Drew like sharks. "Watch out," yells a handsome blond child. "We're gonna be crushed!" He rolls on the floor laughing.

Jaw clenched, eyes to the floor, legs feeling like balls attached to chains, Drew follows the bright yellow arrows pointing toward Budget Auto Cabs.

When he finally arrives, a tall weary-looking attendant shows him several vehicles.

"That's the selection? They all look too small."

The attendant runs his hand through his red-brown hair. "Hey, buddy, we're not in the moving van business." He points to a cab slightly larger than the others. "That one's fresh from the circus where thirty clowns fit inside. But they need it back in three hours. Want it?"

Drew struggles to fit into the cab. When he yanks the right door, the left pops open. Finally he hears a click. He relaxes and exhales. All doors fly open again.

"Tilt! Tilt!" says the auto cab. "Redistribute weight!"

Drew shifts until his knees are at his chest and the large roll that is his abdomen is covering his mouth.

"Destination?"

"Harrumph!" Drew says.

"I don't compute. Sounded like a curse word. Get out now or I'll take you to Congress Drugs. They're lookin' for guys like you."

After an hour Drew passes through a security checkpoint, drives through acres of farmland, and stops in front of a chrome yellow building shaped like a three-tiered wedding cake. Sandy Andreas, president and CEO of San Andreas Farms and Congress Drugs, has an office on top, management and sales are in the middle, and the Congress Drugs laboratory is on the bottom.

"Please insert three solars," the cab voice says.

"Only have two," Drew manages to mumble.

Congress Drugs photographers, who were watching a national debate about why iced coffee costs more than hot coffee on their palm cams while they waited for Drew, hear the racket and come running.

"Looks like Drew Barron," one says.

"Sounds like Drew Barron," another says.

"Feels like Drew Barron," says a third, poking a finger inside the cab.

Two reach in. One pushes, the other pulls. *Yank! Plop!*

"I'm still owed one solar," barks the cab.

"Get lost," one photographer says throwing a solar into the cab.

"No tip?" beeps the cab pulling away. "I don't get no respect!" Clouds of rear noxious gases engulf everyone.

The photographers hold their noses as they wait for Drew to stop jiggling. He feels even worse than he looks. Then they shoot his "before" holograms. After two hours, a hatchet-faced man wearing a blue-and-gold uniform and a tight peaked hat that says "Congress Drugs Special Services" comes and escorts him toward a building that houses people Congress Drugs uses for its "before" and "after" publicity shots.

"You don't have to walk so fast," Drew puffs, trudging behind.

"Didn't seem fast to me." He stops in front of a white door, hands Drew a key, and leaves.

The room is small, clean, and a color decorators call camel cord rather than beige. There is a bed, media wall, a table and a bare-basics bathroom. Comfortable blue clothes with a gold Congress Freedom logo set in a star-shaped patch over the breast pocket lie on the bed. Drew showers and dresses. A kitchen monitor that is in the center of a wall opposite the bed displays a selection of Freedom Plan foods. Drew scrolls and makes his selections.

After five minutes a monitor blinks. A small window, like one from an old Automat restaurant, opens. He removes a tray that contains an endive salad with candied walnuts, veal parmesan, sautéed mixed vegetables, garlic cheese toast, a glass of merlot, and a generous triple-berry-cream parfait. A card on the side says: "Calorie count 104." The food is better than he thought it would be. But not as good as a high-calorie alternative.

He sees a box of Freedom Plan Chocolate Moons and opens it. They look like the real thing except they are larger like chocolate planets. He puts one in his mouth, bites, gasps, and spits it out.

Nine months later with the help from trainers, tailors, and cosmeticians, the "new" Drew emerges two hundred Earth pounds thinner. His 185-pound, six-foot-two-inch frame has six-pack abs and bulging biceps. The planes of his face, large blue eyes, and cleft in his chin stand out in sharp relief. Drew walks naked to a full-length mirror and blinks. He is better looking than he ever thought possible.

Now, tweaked to the stylish perfection of a newly minted coin, oozing relaxed confidence and sizzling sex appeal, wearing designer clothes and standing in the most flattering light, the "after" holograms are made.

Drew's boss, Sandy Andreas, feared by many, loved by few, is not good-looking. He has blond hair cropped short. His eyes are watery blue. He has an intimidating way of looking monumental as though standing on the narrowest point of an isosceles triangle. Photographers never print full-face shots of him or risk being reassigned without sunblock to the side of Mercury that constantly faces the sun. He is CEO of both San Andreas Farms, a company that dominates the farming industry and sells to every major supermarket, and Congress Drugs, makers of Freedom Plan low-calorie foods.

Fun guy and Sandy are words that never appear in the same sentence. His associates nicknamed him "the velvet hammer" because he frequently seduced his opponents into thinking they got the better deal and when other competition dropped away and they were about to sign, he threatened to pull out at the last minute if his new terms were not met.

Sandy sits in his cavernous wood-paneled office. His shirt is white and crisp; his neck scarf black and blue. Squinting from viewing *Bagels without Borders,* a live-from-behind-the-counter at Zabar's in New York, on one of ten news screens on his desk, he glances at the Mars Media station and jumps. Newscaster Katie Racket is showing footage of Drew Barron, an employee of his, winning this year's top award for his writing of and acting in a commercial, "Congress Drugs: Of the People, By the People, and For the People."

"Get that guy who just won the advertising award now!" he roars to his chief assistant, who sits in a glass alcove adjacent to his office. "He has brains as well as good looks."

This is the moment Drew has been waiting for. In the year he had been with Congress Drugs he had learned everything he could about Sandy Andreas and his companies. He befriended people at the bottom of the mailroom to as near the top of the organization as he could. But he was never able to reach Sandy Andreas. That is, until now.

The "Chariots of Fire" music plays in his head. He checks his mirror, mints his mouth, and enters Sandy's office like a boxer entering a ring.

Sandy walks toward Drew, mouth a straight line. Suddenly he smiles knowing that Drew is a great new face he can use in Freedom Plan commercials. He extends a manicured hand that has either a ring or small communication device on each finger. "That commercial deserves to be rewarded," he says, crushing his hand into Drew's hand. "Where did you come up with that 'Of the people, by the people, for the people' stuff? It's just the kind of thing I was about to think of myself."

Drew does his fake humble but effective *aw shucks, ain't nothin'* look. "Guess I'm just a people person, Mr. Andreas."

"Sandy. Call me Sandy." He shoots Drew a friendly punch. "Now, I'm going out on a limb on this, because I can see you're not one of those yell-and-sell kind of guys. Not only am I going to use you for some new commercials, I'm fast-tracking you to executive vice president in charge of marketing. I'm sure with your imagination and talent; you're not going to have trouble handling a seven-figure income, are you?"

Drew's eyes spin. Every new glow-in-the-dark capped tooth shines.

# 4

"HELP!" I SCREAM, PUTTING ONE foot down on Mars and feeling my 47.6 Moon pounds jump to 108.3. "Help!"

Cortland takes a deep breath, exits, and marches ahead. He pretends not to hear as he waves at his cousin Billings Montana and Billings' wife, Florida. They are hard to miss, standing in front of the green-and-red horizontal-striped Mars flag, with its four white stars, while shaking large round Little Green Men Pizza signs up and down.

Cortland slows, turns his head toward me, and cups his mouth. "She's built like a flamingo," he says.

I groan, "Praying mantis."

Perspiration mats my hair and films my body. I adjust the Cracked Craters sweatshirt I now regret wearing. Flo's jutting lower lip frowns an expression I hadn't seen since I left Earth and makes me feel like a bratwurst. I want to turn and run back to the Moon. I want Cortland to say he made a big mistake. I want to cry.

Florida, like most Martians, is tall by Earth standards. Not unusual for people born and grown in gravities lighter than Earth's. At six-foot-eight and 130 Earth pounds, she towers over the Earth-born fivefoot-seven-inch Billings, who is wearing platform shoes, a company T-shirt, a tomato-red jacket and a black stovepipe hat. Her stylish gray suit has a brown braided belt that circles a waist that could pass through the eye of a needle.

Billings and Cortland hug each other like lost socks in a dryer who find their mate. They pound each other on the back so hard that I am afraid Cortland will hurt for days.

"Where are the twins?" Billings asks. "We can't wait to meet them."

I point to two tall, thin girls in the distance sauntering loopy and lackadaisical through the terminal. Everyone squints.

Billings elbows Cortland and points to the luggage pickup. "Let's get your stuff," he says.

Becky and Lois stroll closer. "What's everyone looking at?" Becky asks.

Each of the twins has colored one side of her body one color and the other side a different color. To confuse everyone as to which twin is which, they used the same colors but in reverse order. Lois runs her green hand through bright pink-and-green hair like breaking cobwebs. She reaches into her bag and pulls out a pair of fluorescent sunglasses and puts them on, making her look indistinguishable from her sister, who donned glasses the minute they left the Moon.

Flo's eyes grow wide. She breathes over my head, "They're lovely. So tall and thin."

"Of course. What did you expect? After all, they were conceived and grown on low-gravity Luna. Bet you were afraid they would look like me, weren't you?"

She raises her chin higher. Her scarf slaps me in the face. "Sorry," she says, ignoring my question.

I wave and boom, "Over here, girls."

We wait. Neither of us tries to fill the silence.

Finally they arrive. Flo and the girls study each other for a moment longer than I think necessary. I make introductions. They give a shy smile.

Cortland and Billings return with the luggage, which floats on a tray next to them.

We trudge toward the parking area. Becky's brow wrinkles as she reads the New English subtitles beneath ads for vacations on Uranus and Pluto written in Uranium and Plutonian. "I can't understand why anyone would ever want to go to Uranus or Pluto. Can you imagine what fashion week is like in such a place?"

Then we hear an announcement. Everyone cocks their heads, cups their ears and strains to understand what is being said. Except me.

Billings slows his pace and turns. "Anyone understand that?" he says.

"It's the official language of public announcements, Garble," I pipe, grateful to show intelligence if not style. "It's an ad for a book, *Pig Latin for Latin Pigs*, by Louie and his associate, Louie."

"Sorry I asked," Billings says. "Some things are better misunderstood."

Everyone plods on. I am so tired. I lag farther behind. Suddenly I hear a familiar voice coming from my left. It sounds like Drew!

I rotate violently, pulling my shoulder. I turn a whiter shade of pale. Drew is standing in the center of a life-size hologram that advertises Freedom Plan foods. He is thin, buff, and gorgeous.

Above him, I read: "This man was once a 385-pound weakling." And below: "Buy Freedom Plan foods. Low-to-no-calorie food alternatives. Available in your local supermarket."

"Oh my God!" I scream forgetting where I am and why I'm there. When I inhale, the Chocolate Moon I needed to eat or I wouldn't get through this day goes down the wrong way. I cry out as loud as I can.

Cortland and the twins turn and run back. Cortland put his arms around me and squeezes. The candy zooms from my mouth and flies through Drew's holographic chest. "It's Drew!" I pant, pointing to the holograph.

"Who's Drew?" Lois drools.

"Yeah, who's the media star?" Becky asks, arching an eyebrow. "Is he wearing a Dolce and Banana Latte?"

"I wouldn't know," I say.

Cortland narrows his eyes and examines the image more closely. "He was your mother's boyfriend before she met me."

"And he didn't look like that. He was fat. He had circles under his eyes. His clothes came from the Gulp."

"No way!" Becky and Lois singsong in chorus.

"Why don't you wear clothes like that, Dad?" Lois asks.

"He doesn't have to," I snarl.

"I never knew what happened to Drew. I guess he left Colorful Copies and then came to Mars."

"Who's Colorful Copies?"

"Nobody."

"Nobody?" they chorus again, realizing that I actually had a life before they were born. "Really?"

Flo approaches, head bobbing like a sunflower on a celery stalk. For the first time, I am happy to see her. "Well," she says, overhearing the end of the conversation. "I'm afraid you're going to see his picture everywhere. He's a celebrity! Everyone eats Congress Drugs' Freedom Plan foods, and everyone wants to know Drew Barron."

"A celebrity?" I feel faint.

Billings shouts, "Are you guys coming or not?" He points. "We're going over here."

Cortland shoves me toward Billings. He stands in front of a floor-to-ceiling wall of water complete with darting fish. A sign next to the wall says "Coming Soon: Hellas Planitia Ocean." I cautiously extend my arm into it and feel nothing but air. Billings grabs my hand before I can pull back. *Yank!* I'm through. The others follow like children behind the Pied Piper.

Billings drives his rover to a clear domed slideway, a transparent covered highway that allows cars to park on it as the road moves. He keys our destination, activates a prepay with his finger, and waits while the rover slides into an empty slot. The motor turns off. He rotates his seat so he faces us.

Lois peers at the petite bracelets that circle Flo's bird-like wrists. "Are you a fashion model?"

"Hardly," smiles Flo, flattered. She adjusts a jade-and-gold earring and straightens her back. "I work for Tasters and Spitters Inc., an independent food-rating company. I take one bite, give it a rating, and then spit it out. I never swallow. I've a doctorate from Lite on the Mayo Clinic."

I turn my head away and stick out my tongue.

"I'm so glad I was able to come to the spaceport today," Flo says. "I tasted a Tootsie Target yesterday and I didn't feel right for hours."

"I heard that story on the transport news before we arrived. I can't imagine how the people who ate them felt," I say.

"Tootsie Targets, Vanilla Craters, Chocolate Moons, they're all the same to me: little bombs of empty calories."

"Ever tempted to swallow?"

"Swallow?" Flo pales, coughs, puts her hand to her throat. "Never." Then she brightens. "You know, those people might have a legal case against the Culinary Institute's Candy Universe."

No one says anything.

Then Lois removes her sunglasses and cranes her neck to get a better look at the sky. "Does the sky have to be pink? The Moon's dome came in every color."

"But it was artificial," Billings says. "Now you're seeing the real sky. Didn't you girls learn any science on the Moon?"

"We're not into atmospheres, are we Becky?"

Becky nods. "You know, atmosphere's not important when you live in a place that doesn't have one."

For a long time, we are all silent as we whiz past miles of pocked, dried red ground with patches of sprouting green moss. Billings watches the road. Flo inserts an earpiece. The twins study a periodic chart of nail polish colors. Cortland falls asleep. My eyes droop. I wonder if Drew and I had stayed together would we have divorced.

Billings directs the rover to an exit that says "New Chicago." Finally he says, "We're here! Biggest city on Mars, right at the base of Olympic Mons Mountain, largest volcanic cone in the solar system." He points to a blue building. "We live over there, on the east side of Baba Ganoush Plaza. Your furnished condo is on the other side. But don't get too comfortable. I have big plans."

# 5

DREW MORTGAGES HIS SOUL AND gets a low subprime mortgage for
a condo in New Chicago's most expensive region, River Area. Hotel
Cap Antibodies is across the street. Its St. Trophy Bar attracts a fast
crowd who likes to buy expensive distractions. It's a favorite of Roderick Packarod, a.k.a. "Rocket," bookie to the stars and pharmaceutical wholesaler known for having a pinky in every pill.

The St. Trophy is dark, noisy and crowded. Drew finds a seat at
the end of the long polished bar next to a man with slicked back hair
wearing a shiny purple jacket, striped pink shirt and black trousers.
He watches him rip a red package that says "Nutrition Plus" and add
it to his drink. The drink fizzes over the rim of the glass leaving an
unpleasant smell.

Drew wriggles his nose. "How can you drink that stuff?"

Rocket looks him in the eye then drains his glass. "It's my special Metamucil Collins." He extends a hand. "Rocket Packarod. First
time here?"

Drew takes Rocket's hand. "Yes, first time. I'm Drew Barron."

"Not Drew Barron of Congress Drugs' Freedom Plan who I see in
all those flashy ads?"

Drew smiles. Rocket raises his arm and catches the bartender's
eye. "A double for me and one for my new friend."

"No thanks, man. Not my style."

Rocket pretends not to hear. He clicks his teeth and thumbs the
bartender, who mixes two drinks and serves. The bartender changes

the holo's channel to the robo-dog races, basically keyboards with legs that run around a track. "Ya know, we're both in the same drug business but at different ends. I'm a wholesale pharmacist." Rocket reaches into his pocket. "Here, take my card."

Drew reads "Roderick Packarod" in large letters. And under it, in smaller letters: "Druggist to the Stars, free delivery from Mercury to Pluto on orders over ten thousand solars." He turns the card over: "I can get it for you wholesale. No questions asked."

"Classy card, isn't it?" Rocket says admiring one before he slips the rest back into his pocket. "Font's in Good Times Roman."

The bartender puts two drinks in front of them. Rocket adds red packs to each drink. Then he puts his hand on Drew's arm and leans closer. "Dare you to finish it. If you finish it, I'll place a hundred-solar bet on Canis Major, the long shot in those robo-dog races. If he wins, I'll give you the money. If he loses, I'll just drink another Metamucil Collins. Whaddaya say? You have nothing to lose!"

Drew takes a deep breath, raises his glass, and gulps it downs. Then their eyes follow the race projected in 3-D around the room.

"And by a nose-key, the winner is Canis Major!" the announcer says.

Rocket reaches into his pocket, hands him a hundred solars, and winks. "How about double or nothing on the next one?"

The drink is more potent than Drew thought and the effects immediate. Two blond girls, dressed in black lace cut down to their navels, overhear the conversation and slither next to him. "Come on. Go for it," says one. She smiles at Rocket, who whistles, looking at her cleavage.

Drew nods yes. He wins again. Rocket slaps the bar. "I knew you could do it," he says. "I wanna stay, but I have a hot date. Let's meet here again tomorrow?"

Bottom line: In time Drew becomes a regular at the St. Trophy and in time owes Rocket lots of money.

Drew meets Kandy Kane, a former Miss Universe, at an art gallery in OhNo, a neighborhood known for trendy art. A nanosecond later she moves into his new condo. She is tall, thin, has blue eyes fringed with long eyelashes, and long, dark, shining hair. Her skin is as smooth as Venusian suede. Although beauty and intelligence can be surgically and genetically enhanced, how far you go depends on the starting point. With the average IQ score now at 160, Kandy's modest 120 doesn't quite cut it. But who cares? Visually, Kandy is the real thing—not, as they say, "a Freedom Plan knockoff"—and a sweetheart in every sense of the word. If Kandy's IQ were one point higher, she would realize how moody and self-absorbed Drew is and pack her bags.

"My friends say I love you for what you aren't, sweetheart. What could they mean?"

"Beats me," Drew says, peering at his reflection in a mirror.

Kandy crosses her long legs, encased in skintight silver leggings, and opens the newspaper.

"Your picture is on Page Six again," she says, referring to River Area's society column.

Drew peeks over her shoulder, breathes in Chanel Number 555, and scans the article.

"That's all for business, baby," he says, in a voice reserved for small children and pets. His hand slides down the back of her pink cashmere sweater. He glances at the opposite page and stiffens.

"Is something wrong?" asks Kandy, sensing tension.

"Someone I knew on Earth's moon is coming to Mars to interview Sandy Andreas. Her father just bought Mars Media and has put his daughter CC in charge of special reports."

"CC?"

"Her name is Colorful Copies. But her friends called her CC. I can't imagine she remembers me."

Kandy frowns.

# 6

THE THREE-BEDROOM CONDO THAT FLO and Billings rented for us is lovely and more comfortable than what I left behind. Cortland and Billings travel extensively scouting future locations for Little Green Men Pizza. Flo rarely calls. She is too busy tasting and spitting, that is when she is not with the twins who bond with her like nuts on honey buns. "Aunt Flo" shops with them at Rodeo Dive's trendy boutiques with their expensive off-planet imports.

Life on Mars is a big adjustment. After years of being an average-sized person on the Moon, I am surrounded by tall, ultrathin, stylish people who give me the same disgusted look Flo gave me when we met; ergo, I have no friends. When I look for a job, the only offer I get is to dress as a Chocolate Moon and stand in front of a candy store. And although it comes with an attractive all-you-can-eat policy, my dignity trumps my appetite, so I decline.

I go into the kitchen and heat a slice of ten-mushroom Green Men Pizza. I sit and pick the mushrooms off the top. There are nine. I can't believe I came all this way so my husband could work for this company.

"NO!" Flo yells at Billings. "I'm not moving to Pharaoh City and live in Arabia Terra. I'm no pioneer."

"But our competition, Red Planet Pizza, has three thriving outlets."

Flo bobs and weaves around him. "It may be up-and-coming, but I'm not up and going. Four generations of my family are in New Chicago, plus all my friends and work. How about your cousin Lawrence? He loves Arabia."

Billings rolls his eyes. Finally he gets up and says, "I've a better idea."

Billings sits in our living room on my favorite floating La-Z-Boy. Bad sign. He is not a sitter. Usually when he visits, he has one foot out the door. I think it has something to do with the pounding music emanating from the twins' bedroom. But I'm wrong.

"All I'm telling you," he says, "is that Pharaoh City is a boomtown. Developers are transforming it so fast environmentalists fear that red Mars is becoming Mars Mall. When you see those new geodesic homes, you'll never want to live in a condo again."

After he leaves I say to Cortland, "If it's so great he and Flo should go." He doesn't answer, but I know we're going.

We all pile into our new Chevy Laid Rover. The rover's license plate carries an ad from the manufacturer that says "Get Laid." I want it removed because I learned in a history class that the phrase was some kind of ancient war cry shouted during the war of the sexes, and I don't want people to get the wrong impression. But Cortland says that was then and this is now. And, I should stop believing everything I read, because he knows for a fact that it is something football players said when they made a touchdown.

Cortland drives to a clear domed slideway, finds a slot, and pushes the red blinking word "Destination" on the dashboard and scrolls to "Pharaoh City." The motor turns off automatically then restarts as we approach our destination. The twins sit in the back, sulking and snapping at each other.

"See what you made me do?" Lois screams, pointing to a chip on her pinky's polish and waving it in front of Becky's face.

"How about a Chocolate Moon?" I ask, desperately shaking a box.

"I would never eat *that*!" hisses Lois. "Don't you have any Freedom Plan snacks? Aunt Flo eats only Freedom Plan snacks."

"Yeah," Becky chimes in. "Aunt Flo eats only Freedom Plan snacks."

Finally we see several exits for Pharaoh and get off at Nefertiti, a suburb known for luxurious housing developments. I try to get the twins to look, but they are too busy checking their mirrors, putting on lipstick, and fluffing their hair.

When we park, a too-cheery real estate agent eyes the girls and points us in the direction of the model homes. The twins announce they hate them before they even see them. My stomach knots.

We enter the first model, a two-story building wrapped around a central courtyard. The kitchen has the latest wave-max appliances, which cook with ninety-degree winds. I touch an electro-spun wall that zings a color change.

Becky rolls her eyes like a martyr in a medieval painting.

Lois twirls her hair and bites her cuticles. Yawns.

I see a large colorful painting in the living room and recognize the style from my art history class at Armstrong University. I pick up a catalog and scan the list. "I knew it," I say. "It's a Hallmark! It's called *Get Well Soon*. I would prefer *Happy Birthday*, but that painting's too expensive."

Becky looks over my shoulder and reads the catalog list. "That one isn't," she says pointing to *My Condolences*.

The girls finally show some interest after they discover that the house temperature can be adjusted around each person, ending the "It's too hot/It's too cold" wars.

Cortland reminds the girls that this year they will be applying to college, and the best music school, King Tut, is in Pharaoh City. He points toward the den and drums his fingers on the wall. "Great music studio!" he says.

The twins say nothing.

Then they wander into the courtyard. They look down at a mosaic of white swans and water lilies in the center of the tiled floor. Large terra-cotta pots hold blooming plants. The twins sink into puffy yellow lounge chairs, put their feet on matching ottomans, tilt their heads, and look up at the sun shining in the pink sky.

Cortland, sensing an opportune moment, says through the doorway, "Guess who's coming here to the Ten Plagues Multiplex?" He walks toward them, reaches into his pocket, pulls out some tickets, and waves them back and forth. "Got these just in case you all said yes." Four blue eyes flash.

"Oooh, Daddy! Elvis Beethoven," Becky squeals. "We studied him in school. He wrote nine polkas. Beethoven's fifth was the theme for the film, *1002*. The conductor was some Swedish guy, Ingmar Bergman."

"Sorry, I'm sure it was Ingrid Bergman?" Lois corrects.

"Whatever," Becky says. "I only remember that he ate wild strawberries and wore a watch that had no hands. He must be a psychic."

Flo, having no children of her own, has second thoughts about the girls moving to Pharaoh. She eats half a rice cracker and downs three vitamins Cs. But Billings is overjoyed. Having taken no chance that I would not leave New Chicago, and not realizing I would do almost anything to get out of there, he taps all his contacts at the Culinary Institute whose headquarters are in Pharaoh and lands me a job as a security guard. It comes with a free lunch at its Quantum Corner Café famous for the Olympic Mons soufflé.

My mouth waters: I can't wait.

I overhear Becky say, "Can you believe she'll be a security guard at the Culinary Institute? It's like putting a fox in a hen house. I'm so depressed I could eat mascara."

"Mascara topped with lipstick," Lois groans.

I go into the bathroom and step on my old scale that still registers my weight in Moon pounds. Without dieting I have lost twenty pounds living in heavier gravity, but my metabolism is slowly adjusting.

7

KANDY CHECKS HER MAKEUP in a hand held mirror and smiles. The thought of CC coming to Mars flits through her mind like a brief sun shower. She knows that CC is no competition for Drew's attention. Numero uno is collecting fine art.

Ever since Drew attended his first auction and acquired a lock of bacon from the head of Francis of Bacon that he keeps under glass with an egg, he's been a passionate collector. Now a rare twentieth-century sculpture by the Swiss artist Alberto Giacometti is being auctioned at Park Bengay, and it's all he talks about.

The Giacometti is such a news breaker that art historians interrupt their debate on what came first, the gift shop or the museum, and examine theories about Giacometti's vision. Many think his thin emaciated-looking sculptures are precognitive of what people would look like in the future. But there are serious rumors that the sculpture is a fake, a media ploy by Park Bengay to draw people to its new dance club below its auction house where socialites get heady doing the sweaty Giacometti.

Drew and Kandy exit a chauffeured white limo and pass through the golden arches of the auction house. No one suspects that with his high life and beautiful girlfriend Drew has big stock market losses and large gambling debts with Rocket Packarod. No, no one suspects.

Kandy sits up front next to Drew, her beautiful head perched on a long neck encased in a crisp white blouse. Drew drums his fingers and taps his foot. Kandy puts her hand on his arm.

He pulls away.

Then the room quiets and the bidding begins.

Drew stands, gyrates, raises his paddle high over his head again, again, again—until the auctioneer shouts, "Sold to Drew Barron!"

He runs to the podium, grabs the scrawny twig-limbed sculpture, waves it over his head, and bows.

Kandy blushes, not knowing if she should be embarrassed or proud.

Acquiring the Giacometti puts Drew in a class with Mars' top collectors like Craig Cashew, the Culinary Institute's CEO, whose love of art rivals his love of food. At the last auction, Craig acquired the coveted brown-on-brown sculpture *Jasper's John* and a rare etching of the great English chef from the Falklands, Margaret Thatcher, standing in front of Folsom Prison holding a rolling pin over the head of finance minister Johnny Cash.

Craig Cashew built the Culinary Institute. He took a small gourmet take-out shop and turned it into a complex of restaurants, shops, schools, the Flying Saucer Supermarket, botanical gardens, and farms that consistently rank in the solar system's top ten tourist attractions. His work on discovering how many sushi make a sashimi is summarized in two ancient, unique and rarely used descriptive words: awesome and amazing.

But most consider Craig an enigma wrapped in a riddle covered in a menu. He's one of the few Mars natives not bone thin. He resembles a double-door subzero refrigerator held together with suspenders and a bow tie.

"You said getting the Giacometti was a sure thing," Craig growls to Park Bengay's director, Ozymandias Glitzstein, in a voice that sounds like the dredging of a chocolate malted through a thick straw.

"We didn't think Mr. Barron would be interested in the classics," Ozymandias says, wiping his brow.

"Well, you were wrong!"

"May I offer you a reduced price on an etching by Giacometti Jr.? Or the Venus de Milo's arms? We just had them tattooed."

Craig glares.

"How about X-rays of Picasso's hands with woodcuts of his feet?"

Craig turns and marches away. Ozymandias runs after him. "Please! We just received a very rare painting of the last burger by McDonald."

"Sell it to Drew Barron," Craig snarls over his shoulder. "He can afford it!"

Drew is home alone. His palm signals a call. Loud music and clinking glasses almost drown out Rocket's voice. "Must be your lucky day. I'm right across the street having a Trophytini at the St. Trophy. Heard you were the highest bidder for the Giacometti sculpture. Mind if I stop by and take a look?"

8

DREW OPENS THE DOOR WEARING casual beige clothes that complement the room's large, white, open space, sand-colored floor and carefully arranged furniture. He runs his eye over Rocket's bright ultramarine blue jacket and thinks the only way it would look good is framed and hung on a wall as a piece of period kitsch.

"I can't believe you want to see my Giacometti, Rocket. I could have hologrammed an image. You must have another agenda."

"Whaddaya mean? I love art. I won a kid's art contest by cutting an ear off my Mickey Mouse doll. My teacher said it was very avant-go and renamed it Vincent Mouse."

Drew says nothing. His jaw clenches. They walk across the room toward the sculpture.

Drew points. "Well, that's what you've come to see. Don't you think it's beautiful?"

Rocket peers at the Giacometti. His hand slides over the veined gray marble table it stands on. "Guess everyone's sense of beauty is different. I would never bother with this stuff if I had Kandy. She's what I call a work of art. Of course, you can't sell her at auction. But I bet you would for a million solars?" His thin crescent eyebrows rise.

Drew is not amused. He walks toward two pale sofas placed diagonally next to a wide picture window. Rocket eyes an expensive antique chess set. He fingers translucent silver mesh curtains that filter the light from River Area below.

Drew sits on the right sofa. Rocket sits on the left.

Rocket says, "Nice view. What's with all the gray and beige? You should brighten the place up a bit." He takes off his purple polka-dot neck scarf and drapes it over the back of the sofa. "There you go. Nothing like the color purple to give things a boost. Gonna offer me a drink?"

Drew sighs. "What would you like, Rocket?"

"A scotch sour would be nice, but only if you have Johnny's Walker. But of course you must. You're a first-class kind of guy, aren't you?"

Drew studies the keypad on the sofa and codes scotch sour. He adds a mineral water for himself. Almost instantly a shiny service-bot wheels out the drinks. Rocket takes his scotch off the tray. "That service-bot must have cost plenty. Mine only vacuums and scratches my back."

Rocket reaches into his right pocket and takes out several pills. Then he reaches into his left pocket and takes out several more.

"What are those?" Drew asks.

"Liver protonics and multiminerals from Mercury. Very expensive."

Drew shakes his head. "You take too much of that stuff. One day you'll make yourself sick."

Rocket frowns. "Since when are you an authority? You live on Freedom Plan foods. This is good stuff; it's health food, strictly natural." He pops them into his mouth and swallows. He leans toward Drew. "How's the testing on the anti-flavonoid going at Congress Drugs? Sandy Andreas must be getting a little tired of waiting for Congress Drugs to finish the testing on his latest miracle medicine."

"How do you know about that? It's top secret! We just tested it on a few animals."

Rocket's mouth opens like a viper. "I have my sources."

"Well, it's stalled. We can't get approval to test it on human subjects because the animals fell into comas."

"Did the animals die?"

"No, but they don't know how to get them out of the comas."

"Didn't die! Then it's no problem!"

Drew unbuttons his shirt collar and frowns. "What's no problem?"

"Everyone's overreacting." Rocket takes a Bourbon Berry from a silver dish on the kidney-shaped coffee table in front of him. He pops it into his mouth. Then he gets up and walks toward the Giacometti, patting it on the head. "How much did you say you paid for this thing?"

Drew doesn't answer. Rocket circles silently back to the sofa and sits.

"I want to do a favor for some of my friends," Rocket says quietly. He takes another berry. Sucks out the liquor with a *whoosh*. Before Drew can react, Rocket reaches for another and slurps it in. "Interested?"

"It depends."

Rocket's voice rises. "*It depends* is not the correct answer. You owe me a lot of money."

Drew says nothing.

"Congress Drugs' stock has been hitting the Milky Way ever since people heard rumors that it developed a new anti-flavonoid that lowers cholesterol and blood pressure even if you eat your weight in mascarpone cheese. What do you think would happen to the stock if the public discovered there might be questionable side effects to the anti-flavonoid? What do you think would happen if the Food and Drug Administration doesn't approve it?"

"But it may not affect people, only animals. I just told you we haven't done any tests on human subjects. There's always some delay."

"I'll tell you what this overpriced, begging-for-a-correction stock would do. It would drop into a gravity vortex. Such information could help some of my friends know the right time to sell a few fat companies short."

Drew gets up, crosses the room, and increases the airflow. The light on the front door blinks red. Then green. It opens. An auto voice says, "Kandy Kane entering." Kandy steps through the doorway carrying bags and boxes. She drops one, picks it up, and puts it on a table near the door. "I didn't know you were coming, Rocket. Sorry, I can't stay." She flips her long brown hair, blows two kisses, and leaves.

"Expensive girlfriend. Expensive lifestyle. Be a shame to lose it. Wouldn't take Kandy long to find someone else." Rocket cracks a knuckle. Drew winces. Rocket smiles and says, "I think I have a way to test these anti-flavonoids on humans. Got the idea when I heard the news about people getting sick from eating Tootsie Targets made at Candy Universe."

"Were you responsible for that, Rocket?"

Rocket holds up his hands. "Hey, no way. I love Tootsie Targets. Ya know, I'm not responsible for every piece of bad news. But when I heard about the trouble with Tootsie Targets, it gave me the idea about testing the anti-flavonoids using Chocolate Moons."

Drew crosses his arms. "What do you mean?"

"You don't need to know details. Just get me a small amount of the anti-flavonoid and I'll take care of the rest. If the stocks take the kind of hit I just explained, I'll erase your debt plus give you 10 percent of what I make selling short. It's the opportunity of a lifetime! What have you got to lose? You're already taking a long walk with a short air hose in a vacuum tunnel."

Drew's eyes widen.

"Otherwise," Rocket says in a soft lethal tone, "I can call some of my associates in the collection business and you can donate a body part to a sick person. But wouldn't it be better to pay off your gambling debts and have some extra money to buy another ugly skinny sculpture?"

Drew's expression is blank, but he knows he's trapped.

"By the way, if you ever want to store any of your art, I know a cool chick named Scheherazade who runs the ABC."

"The ABC?"

"Ali Baba Caves. Best storage facility in the solar system and its right here, halfway between New Chicago and Pharaoh City."

"Never heard of it."

"She doesn't advertise; besides it's underground. She also has an art factory that makes repairs on fine art, creates duplicates, that sort of thing. Seeing her day after tomorrow."

"I don't trade in duplicates, Rocket. Frankly, I'm insulted."

"Really? Well, you might like to know that some of her stuff is worth more than the originals. Even the experts at Park Bengay can be fooled." Rocket walks toward the Giacometti and curls his fingers around it. "Why don't I take this as a down payment and lock it up at the ABC? I can always have Scheherazade make you a copy."

Drew yanks the Giacometti from his grip. "I'm not letting any of my art out of my sight."

"Okay. But make it fast. Patience isn't one of my virtues."

## 9

PLUTO PASTRAMI IS A CONTRACTOR, as with a gun not a hammer, for several postmodern mafia families. He has an average build, medium-length brown hair, and brown eyes. He looks like a neighbor you'd have no interest in getting to know. It took him a long time to perfect "average." It is one of his most intricate and expensive disguises.

Pluto's talent to disappear in plain sight is so good, even his rich cousin, Solaria Pastrami Andreas, who is also CEO Sandy Andreas' wife, can't recognize him when he's "in costume." That is, unless he forgets to use his vocal adaptor. Then, his distinct nasal tone seems to float up from deep underwater and becomes a giveaway.

Pluto lives with saucer-eyed, perky-looking, former stewardess Breezy Point in New Chicago. They met on a space bus that did the Jupiter and Beyond run.

"You look so perky," he said the first time they met.

"Don't you mean *pretty?*" she asked, as she always did when people said *perky*. "*Perky* is so superficial." Then she shook her hoop-shaped earrings dangling from her pink shell ears and blew him a kiss from her bow-shaped mouth.

Breezy is complex. She craves thrills, adventure, and interplanetary travel, albeit with health insurance, a pension, and a thousand-year contract for cryogenic freezing upon death. She never even batted an eye when Pluto said, "That combination is oxymoronic. If you want safety, you can't take risks."

"Says who? Since when are you an expert? I do oxycodone all the time."

When Pluto first asked her to assist him in a job, she tilted her heart-shaped face and chirped, "You're kidding, right?"

"But sweetheart, it's an emergency. Besides you're the only one I can trust."

"Really?" She batted her eyelashes and immediately reached for a tube of her brightest red lipstick, a well proven line of defense in all emergencies.

"And they're going to pay me a lot of money."

"Well, why didn't you say that in the first place?" said Breezy applying the lipstick and placing the tube in her cleavage. "Ready when you are."

Pluto and Breezy tracked their suspect then circled around until he was cornered. Then Breezy, wearing one of Pluto's superhero costumes and feeling the wrath that hath no fury, squared her jaw, raised her arm, and gave him a wallop. There was a loud *ding!* followed by a louder *dong!* from two metal plates inside his head. And although not a music lover as such, Breezy thought it was the music of the spheres.

*I must be experiencing a spiritual climax like satori*, thought Breezy, whose only basis for comparison was the very spirited feeling she got after drinking a triple apple mojito with a rim of powdered cinnamon at the Zen Bar. Dizzy with the sensation and feeling like she had yanked a tablecloth from a table without upsetting the china, and not wanting to overlook anything related to having a climax, instantly decided to pack her bags and move in with Pluto.

Pluto returns from a job exhausted. He runs the shower and feels the water. Too hot. He adjusts it and steps inside. He washes the blond rinse out of his hair, lets his temporary green contact lenses float away, and watches an expensive blue airbrushed tan that was popular on Titan, the last place he had a job, circle the drain. He lets the warm breezes blow over his body in the dry cycle while he is sprayed with grass scented moisturizers and powders. Just when he closes his eyes and relaxes, the holo rings in the next room. He jerks to attention, shifting his head so quickly he almost pokes himself in the eye.

"It's for you," Breezy calls into the bathroom, noting the private-caller code. She kicks off her gold genie shoes with the curled-up toes and pushes them under the bed. Then she crosses the room and picks up a brush from a table and runs it through her long blond hair. She reaches for a bottle of Menthe, an expensive scent that causes heightened sexual pleasure named after Menthe, the young nymph with whom Pluto the Greek god of the underworld had had a passionate fling.

Pluto comes out with a towel draped around him and sits on the edge of the bed. Breezy hands him the holo and plops down next to him so she can hear.

Pluto says, "You have a job for me?" Pause. "Where?" Pause. "You're kidding." He throws his head back and laughs. "Breezy has been after me to take her there forever. At last, business and pleasure."

Breezy leans in closer but can't hear.

"When do you want us to leave?" Pause. "Done deal." He lies down on the bed, smiles, and breathes in the Menthe.

Breezy gets off the bed and holds up a black lacy gown. "Bet it was Rocket, right?"

"Right."

Breezy turns her back and pretends to stick her finger down her throat. "You know, my father and Rocket go way back. They used to be partners. But Rocket cheated him out of the patent for his orange-blossom spray in Las Venus, and they had a bitter falling-out. Did I tell you this?"

"Yeah, like every time Rocket's name comes up. Enough, okay? Your father got rich from that spray. Who would have thought that human flatulence contained vitamin C? And who would have guessed it could be converted into a spray with an orange-blossom smell? Your dad still holds all the patents, right?"

Breezy walks over to a night table. She opens a drawer, takes out a pink can that says "Decibel Point's One and Only Orange Blossom," and squirts Pluto. "Need I say more?"

"How is Daddy Decibel Point? Has he lost any weight? Or does he still stand out like a zero in a room full of ones?"

Breezy thinks and then based on past conversations decides to say nothing.

"Well, he's a brilliant chemist," Pluto continues. "Four-flame winner of the Bunsen Burner prize, but I'm not surprised that Congress Drugs keeps him under wraps and behind the scenes. People

would go nuts if they learned that a fatty invented Congress Drugs'
Freedom Plan foods, which he never ate himself. And his new anti-
flavonoid project at Congress Drugs? The one he told us about at the
Milky Way Bar last week? What's that all about?"

"Beats me," Breezy sighs.

Breezy picks up a nail file and begins to move it back and forth
against her thumb. Pluto grabs it from her hand.

Breezy yanks the nail file back. "Could we talk about something
else, Pluto?"

He rubs her back and spots her latest tattoo, a rose with wings.
"I like the new tattoo. Matches the rose one on your pinky." He takes
her hand and puts her pinky in his mouth, runs his tongue around it.
Sucks and sucks.

Breezy pulls her hand away.

"Look, Rocket has a job for us at the Culinary Institute in Pharaoh
City. It will be nice to get out of New Chicago for a weekend. Besides,
this is too easy and too good to pass up."

Breezy's eyes widen. Her lips purse. "Really, the Culinary? What
does he want us to do?"

"Rocket just wants us to have a good time. Is that so hard to
believe?"

"Well, as a matter of fact..."

"We can eat at the Quantum Corner Café and shop at the Flying
Saucer Supermarket. What could be better?"

"Yeah, right. And what else?"

"You're always putting Rocket down. I'm telling you, he wants us
to enjoy ourselves. Have a little vacation. All expenses paid."

"So far 'all expenses paid' is the only interesting part."

"We'll say we're on our honeymoon, stay in the honeymoon suite,
and take the tour of the Candy Universe. Consider it honeymoon
practice."

"That's a new one. What do you think we've been doing, Pluto?"

"Look, what Rocket wants takes one brain cell and one moment."

Pluto lets the idea marinate. He draws her close and smells her
neck.

"Breezy, sweetheart, it's a piece of cake."

"Yeah, but with how many calories?"

# 10

I LOVE MY JOB AS a security guard at the Culinary Institute. My partner who was assigned to me is a woman named Jersey. She is also my best friend. Like Flo and practically everyone else on Mars, Jersey is much taller and thinner than I am. We're nicknamed "Mutt and Jeff" after an ancient cartoon strip where one character was short and fat and the other tall and thin.

When Jersey was a child, she was in a bad accident. The only detail she will reveal is: "I lived." Doctors implanted transparent liquid crystals into her eyes. Now she can see from microscopic to telescopic and from ultraviolet to infrared. They look like two sharp targets. She wears pink-tinted glasses to soften them. Her indifference to food is so great that I always wonder why she works at the Culinary Institute, a place where open kitchens send irresistible aromas of fresh bread, grilled meats and melted chocolate wafting through the halls.

The Culinary Institute is beautiful. Major food companies and wealthy individuals donate millions to have their names put on its jeweled glass walls. There are eight public restaurants, linked to the main building by Tuscan-like bridges. Glittering chandeliers imported from Venice on Venus, make every building sparkle including the Flying Saucer supermarket famous for produce like the poton, a hybrid of a potato and an onion that grow in long ovals because of Mars' lower gravity than Earth.

The Candy Universe is the Culinary Institute's most popular building. It's where Chocolate Moons are made. The inside combines the design of a Las Venus casino with Sephora, an ancient store on Earth that sold makeup. Clients entering Sephora were lured to the right by indecision and lured to the left by insecurity contributing to the sales of the most esoteric brands, most of which now reside in Mars's Makeup Hall of Fame. It took me over a month to learn how to walk from front to back without swaying or straying. Jersey insists I still haven't mastered the chocolate area.

As soon as school groups roll through the triple arches of the Culinary, few look at the fields of golden wheat, orange groves, apple orchards and rose gardens that produce seven-inch blooms. Nor do they think about the bioengineering that created a paradise of greenery on a planet of dry rock and sand. All anyone is thinking of is being the first to spot the red-and-white-striped stack that spews holographs of swirling candy and start chanting, "Candy! Candy! Chocolate Moons!"

Victor and Hugo are among thirty children, age ten, who are in excellent health when they go on their class trip that starts at Mars Disney and ends at the Candy Universe. No one fidgets and no one punches his neighbor as they pile off the bus and make two straight lines. They march erect and silent into the lobby of the Candy Universe, take one deep chocolate-scented breath, and swoon as they wait for the large bronze door in front of them to open.

Then a trumpet fanfares. A blinding white light makes eyes snap shut. And when the doors open, more shapes and colors than anyone has ever seen ripple and reflect into infinity.

A giant wheel of fortune made of jelly beans plays carnival music. Chandeliers sway beneath pink clouds of cotton candy, swings twist on taffy ropes, a chocolate malted river circles the room and ends in a bubbling waterfall, and everywhere transparent cases overflow with mouthwatering, tooth-cracking, jaw-breaking, calorie-and choles-terol-loaded pleasures.

I watch some tilt their heads, mouths open, tongues extended—trying to catch freeze-dried ice cream flakes falling from the ceiling. But, just as I begin to salivate when hands are loaded with lychee-ginger jam, raspberry-apple, cinnamon caramel, butter cream, and for the brave, habanera pepper chocolates, Jersey says, "The head of the security office wants one of us outside to monitor broccoli. I mon-itored sugars and spices last week, so it's your turn."

I exit the building vexed that Jersey, who doesn't appreciate the subtleties between sugars, spices, and everything nice and, say liver, has that job while I get broccoli.

When I finish and go back inside, I see students and teachers in an opiate state blind to anything but the taste of candy. Then I see Victor and Hugo wander behind the Chocolate Moons counter, reach in, take a handful and down them. A moment later they sway forward, fall to the ground, and shake in a convulsive seizure unconscious in the fetal position, their backs swollen like hunchbacks.

The boys are flown to Pharaoh Medical Center, a place that has very tight security and holds no fond memories for me. Before I was let up to see a sick friend, I had to register. A stone faced woman asked so many questions I was so stressed that I ate all the chips and dips reserved for dying patients' last meals out of the vending machines.

Five minutes later Flo calls from Tasters and Spitters Inc. and screams, "You never should have taken that job as a security guard! Remember when I told you I felt sick after sampling their Tootsie Targets? And I didn't even swallow!"

"How did you get the news so fast?"

"Everything has been ringing off the hook. Believe me, the tongue knows."

"What that's supposed to mean?"

"Gotta run. Bye." *Click.*

Jersey grabs my arm and yanks me toward the other security guards, who buzz with theories but don't have a clue. I need some quiet so I find a seat away from them. Then I remove my i-Chip from my side pocket, and type *therapies tried on comatose patients. Sensory Dynamics* pops up. I read the article and wave Jersey over. "I think I found something."

"Sweet or savory?"

"This isn't about food. Not everything I find interesting is about food."

Jersey tilts her head, gives me one of her looks, and then begins straightening the buttons on her jacket.

"Ever hear of Sensory Dynamics, new offbeat therapies that have been tried on comatose patients?"

"No. So, what happens?" Jersey stops fiddling with her buttons and puts a hand on a hip, signaling *sounds like a blind alley to me, so make it short.*

"Patients are bombarded with cultural stimuli. The most successful have been those who use French culture. The patient's room is filled with French perfume while Edith Piaf's voice wafts over linguists arguing about the pronunciation of French vowels. The cancan song plays when bedpans are emptied."

"You're kidding. I love the cancan."

"No one understands why this works faster than the smell of chicken soup and the sounds of Jewish mothers wailing guilt-loaded philosophical questions like *Have a nice day? Who am I to have a nice day?* And *Why will it be any different than any other day?*

"All that is known is that upon awakening, 49 percent of the patients' first words are *I'll have a glass of white wine,* another 49 percent ask for red, and 2 percent said they should of had a V16."

"I wonder what they'll say when the V32 hits the stores."

"Stay focused, Jersey."

"When they tried the paradigm of an Irish pub, three people who regained consciousness immediately asked for a beer."

"What kind of beer? Light beer is healthier."

I ignore the question. "All the products that they used had a very short expiration date, which made testing difficult. I wonder if they were organic. Organic products have no preservatives therefore a shorter shelf life. That could be significant."

"I love preservatives, because I can't throw anything out."

"Well, I can't go further without a scientist's advice. Your husband, Trenton, is a brilliant scientist and he works with the Mars Yard forensics. Mind if I ask him?"

"Just give a call."

I check the time. "We better collect the security cubes and start our scans. Detective Lamont Blackberry and his partner, Sid Seedless, are on their way."

# 11

LAMONT AND SID ARE HALF-BROTHERS, related to the wealthy Melon family. They are descended from the branch whose mothers belonged to the Flying Cantaloupes, a circus group known for girls who had "big ones."

Lamont Blackberry has a first-class mind in a second-class body. Sid Seedless has the opposite. Lamont's face looks like garlic pushed through a press. He considered getting a makeover, but in his line of work it is an asset to have an appearance that doubles as a weapon.

They both wear dark brown fedoras, black turtlenecks, khaki trousers, and loose gray coats with lots of zippered flaps containing handcuffs, kits with various chemicals, magnifying glasses, mini vacuums, a spectroscope, recording devices, gas masks and gloves. On the back of Lamont's coat, in large red letters, are the words "Chief Detective." Large red letters on the back of Sid's coat say "See Other Side," where tiny red letters say "Call 1-1-9."

Lamont grabs the rim of his fedora and slides it down over his eyes. Sid reaches up and tips his hat over his eyes. Lamont hunches his shoulders and raises his collar. Sid does the same.

"You know, Sid, you don't have to shadow my every move," Lamont says.

"Maybe I'm doing these things first and you're copying me?"

"Ridiculous. You're in back of me."

"Well, then, you should be flattered by my sincerest imitation."

Lamont pushes the door to the Candy Universe open. As soon as Sid smells the intoxicating aroma of melted chocolate, he clutches the wall. Lamont gives Sid a shove. "It's Showtime!" he says. Then he points to the other side of the room. "Use your magnetic-resonance-residue spectroscope to detect any discrepancies in the chemical compositions of the remaining candy."

He turns his back to Sid, looks right and left, dips his hand into a bin of licorice, then, like a child who knows he has a mouthful of cavities and sees the dentist's drill come closer, covers his mouth with his hands.

"I saw that. I saw that. You just took some licorices from that container and ate it," Sid says. "Can I have some?"

"For your information this procedure is called evidence testing." He scoops a handful of jumping jelly beans and puts them in his pocket, but most leap out and dance on the ground. "Now see what you made me do?"

"Looks more like *tampering* with the evidence," Sid says, reaching beyond the jelly beans for a cherry chew.

Jersey and I walk closer. When we step on the jelly beans, we grab each other's hand to steady ourselves as we slide toward Lamont and Sid.

Jersey hands Sid the original image cubes, installed to deter the theft of the candy that we made before they arrived. I keep duplicates for the Culinary's files.

Sid slides a honey asteroid into his mouth.

"I saw that," Jersey glares. "You're not supposed to eat that."

"It's part of our research."

"Yeah, right." Jersey says, closing in on him.

Sid, not paying attention to how close he is standing to the chocolate malted river, takes a step back to avoid Jersey's index finger jabbing his chest. He slips and splashes into the chocolate malted river. Head bobbing, arms flailing, he grabs at a taffy swing that lifts him up and quickly hurls him toward the jelly bean wheel of fortune. He whirls around then tumbles back into the chocolate river. When he comes around the next turn, his speed accelerates. He grabs my leg. I stagger, then *plop!*

Everyone gawks as we're swept away.

Two little girls jump and shout, "They're headed toward the waterfall!"

I hold my breath and close my eyes. Sid and a Niagara of melted chocolate pound over me. As soon as we're yanked out, the freeze-dried ice cream flakes that drop from the ceiling make us look tarred and feathered. Children clap thinking it was an act. We stagger to the employees' locker room and clean ourselves up.

By now Lamont has collected information using his magnetic-resonance-residue spectroscope and has forwarded the information to computers at Mars Yard. He is sweating and pacing, waiting for results.

Everyone in the room wants to go home. Lamont gets looks that could kill a yogurt's lactobacillus. Suddenly his palm registers an incoming call. "Attention, everyone," he says with the voice of authority. "Mars Yard has just confirmed that twenty-three other cases of poisoned candy are being reported."

"Oh no!" the crowd choruses.

"The problem is more widespread than we first thought," Sid says, spitting out the honey asteroid.

"This also means that the candy was probably poisoned before today. It takes at least one day after the candy has been packaged for it to arrive in shops," I say.

Lamont looks at me and frowns. "And since when have you become a detective?"

"This case is important to me. I have a personal interest. I practically live on Chocolate Moons."

"That's true. She does," Jersey says, rolling her eyes at Lamont.

"Well, none of this is our fault. We want to go home," yells a thin young man with a head of popcorn-looking curls.

Everyone chants, "Home now! Home now!"

Lamont waves his arms in the air. "Another message!" The crowd quiets. "Mars Yard's analysis finds that none of the candy remaining in this room is contaminated. You can all go home."

The crowd stampedes toward the exit.

"At least we have everyone's contact information," I say. "With a hundred eyewitnesses and a hundred different stories of what happened today, I'm sure there will be more questions."

Lamont glares at me. "For all I know, you and your skinny friend may have been in cahoots and poisoned the chocolate yourselves. You certainly had easy access."

"Easy access but no motive. I consider Godiva and Hershey saints and chocolate to be the food of the gods. As far as I'm concerned, a person who would stoop to poison Chocolate Moons is a person who could poison Communion wafers."

Lamont looks at Jersey. "But I bet Chocolate Moons are not your favorite. You look like you never eat candy and might welcome a transfer."

Jersey blushes and freezes, her mouth open. She knows it's true. She never eats candy. And just the other day she thought of transferring to the executive wing.

"You're only saying this so we won't say we saw you and Sid eat some of the evidence," I point out.

Lamont squares his shoulders.

"I think you may have overlooked something," I add.

"And what is that?"

"The paper in the display case that had the poisoned Moons has one area with a strange stain."

We walk to the display case. I point to a small dark purple stain. "I would analyze that if I were you."

"Your job, Sid," Lamont says.

Sid dons a pair of protective gloves and puts the display paper into a police bag.

"I'm going to recommend that the Culinary remove all the candy and send it into space."

"Isn't that a little extreme?"

"Can't be too careful," Lamont replies, looking at his watch.

My hair knots and my dental fillings vibrate. I close in on Lamont like an avalanche of soft butter, stopping just short of pinning him to the wall. "How can you say that? Mars Yard's analysis shows that there is nothing wrong with any of it. You can't actually mean all the Gum Craters, Malted Meteors, Toffee Planets, Rum Rockets, Vanilla Comets, the…the…oh my God, not the rest of the Chocolate Moons?"

Lamont and Sid walk away. Lamont turns, puts his hand to his throat, and makes an off-with-your-head motion. "Too late. While you were having your little tantrum, my palm registered a message from the Culinary's top security office. They thought putting the candy into a rocket quarantine pod and sending it into space was such a good idea that, as we speak, a truck is collecting it now."

When Jersey and I lock up, I say, "Let's go back to the Chocolate Moons case and see if we can scrape another sample so Trenton can do an independent analysis."

"But Lamont will send his sample to Mars Yard forensics. Trenton can read their report. Isn't that good enough?"

"Something makes me think that Lamont doesn't believe that 'The Case of the Chocolate Moons' has the gravitas of cases like 'The Hasidim of Baskerville.' I'm tired of candy being considered a second-class food. I've got to get to the bottom of this!"

I shake so hard that a box of Chocolate Moons falls from my pocket to the floor.

"You're not going to eat those," Jersey says, watching me pick them up.

"Probably not," I say.

"Probably? You have a thing about living dangerously?"

CEO Craig Cashew is very upset. When it is dark and everyone has left the Candy Universe building, he taps a code into the lock and enters. He runs his hand over the empty display cases and sighs. He crisscrosses the room several times. His foot taps something not far from one of the chocolate vats. He picks it up and sees that it is small, smooth, and rectangular with a button in the middle of one side. He slides it into his pocket and leaves.

## 12

I LEAVE THE CULINARY INSTITUTE emotionally shredded and sizzling like a bubbling caramel. I head for my silver Flexcar and inflate it. I ease myself inside. My home is on the east side of Pharaoh City; the Culinary Institute is on the west side. After a twenty-minute drive, I pull into the garage. Lois and Becky, who now call themselves the Lunar Tunes, are rehearsing. The vibrations coming from their thumping music are loud enough to crack an airlock.

Cortland couldn't make a go of his band, Cracked Craters. For months he was more depressed than a B-flat. When he heard the twins sing in harmony and clap syncopated rhythms, he arranged all their music. Now he thinks he'll be the next Gordy Blueberry managing the Subprimes.

Becky and Lois are nervous wrecks because they have made the finals in a talent contest sponsored by the Mars Malt Beer Company by singing "You Light Up My iPad," a song Cortland wrote for me when we were courting. They are unnerved because their competition, Max and the Plancks and Neils and the Bohrs, are both past winners of the Venus Biennale.

Sandy Andreas and his wife, Solaria Pastrami Andreas—whose family owns the Mars Malt Beer Company—will host and judge the event at their forty-thousand-square-foot French-exterior hyper mansion in Redwich, a luxury gated suburb of New Chicago.

I enter a small room near the laundry and peel off my bodysuit. A hook pops followed by a rip that feels like marching insects with very sharp teeth. This depresses me more because now they only sell the lighter, tighter type, which is more flexible and, which I am told, feels like a second skin. But I have enough skin and have no desire to show more.

I thrust my arms into my pink terry-cloth robe, slide on a pair of worn velveteen slippers, and paddle into the bedroom. Cortland is on the floor, stretching on his exercise mat. He rolls over and pushes himself up. "You had quite a day," he says.

I groan and charge into the bathroom. I key *Hot Aqua Shower: Double Massage.* I would have stayed in longer, but Cortland calls and says that the evening news is starting, so I leap out, drape my robe around me, and go back into the bedroom.

When I lie on the bed, Cortland puts down his Mars Malt and hands me his special pomegranate margarita. He's circled the rim with colored vitamins to cheer me up. "Nothing like a glass of anti-oxidants to change a gloomy mood," he says.

I take a sip and know why I married him.

Cortland grabs the remote and switches channels.

"Stop!" I say. "You just passed the Mars Media station! Look, it now says it is owned and operated by Carbon Copies Media. CC will be interviewed by Nova Scotia on her program, *Getting Creamed with Nova.*"

"So what? I want the super solar broadcast from Earth." His thumb plays with the remote. "Who's CC?"

"CC, Colorful Copies—the girl I told you about, the one who stole Drew from me. Her father owns Carbon Copies Media and Mars Media. I read that she's become an investigative reporter. She visited San Andreas Farms and Congress Drugs and got an exclusive interview with Sandy Andreas."

"Oh, *that* CC. The girl with the rainbow-colored eyebrows." Cortland touches his own straggly brows.

"My friends back on the Moon told me that when Drew left she was bitter and vowed revenge. I wonder if she still holds a grudge." I punch up my pillow and sip my margarita. "Do you think she saw Drew when she was at Congress Drugs?"

"Yeah, yeah, thin, handsome Drew Barron." Cortland sharpens the holographic image of CC that appears in the center of our bedroom.

If I didn't recognize CC's voice and rainbow colored eyebrows, I wouldn't know it was her, because everything science, medicine, makeup, and wardrobe can do CC had done. And done very well! Her mousy brown hair is sleek, long, and blond. She wears a pink-and-gray jacket in a floral design, a gray skirt, and a tight silver tank top. Gold charms of antique computers dangle from a bracelet on her wrist.

"Thank you for coming on such short notice, Colorful Copies," says Nova Scotia, whose salmon-colored hair is in a high beehive style.

"Please call me CC. All my friends do."

Nova smiles. "What a lovely bracelet, CC."

"Oh, that." CC flicks her wrist and beams into the camera. "Well, Daddy gives me a charm every time he promotes me. So far I have eight." She holds her arm to the camera and counts. "Oh, no!" she stammers. "Seven! I have seven. I must have lost one." She lowers her arm and rubs her wrist.

"I'm sure you'll find it," Nova Scotia says, leaning toward CC and giving her a knowing wink. "You spent two weeks at San Andreas Farms and Congress Drugs. What was your impression of Mr. Andreas?"

"Sandy's such a sweetie-pie! All my time was spent with him except for an hour at Congress Drugs, when he was called away and I was on my own with a room full of robots and one very fat scientist. He was working on making cheese from an ancient dairy product popular on Earth called milk of magnesia. He said it's a dangerous explosive. When he learned I was with Carbon Copies Media, he said that Congress Drugs should upgrade its testing procedures, because it was cutting corners to get new products to market faster."

"Did you get his name?"

"Something with a *Point* in it: Needle Point, Pencil Point."

"How about *Decibel* Point?"

"Bingo!"

"It is unfortunate that the troubles at the Culinary Institute's Candy Universe have come during your visit to Mars. Will you interview the Culinary Institute's CEO, Craig Cashew, when you're there?"

"I've been trying to set a date, but our meeting has been delayed because the police are investigating the incidents at the Candy Universe. Mr. Cashew assures me that I won't have to wait much longer."

"We would love for you to come back and tell us all about—"

Cortland clicks to Earth's channel. "Seen and heard enough? I never cared for either Mars Media or Carbon Copies Media. I still want to watch Earth's version of the news."

I drain my pomegranate margarita. All gone.

The holograph shifts. A voice over music says, "Welcome to evening news. Live from the only city Earthlings could agree on for their capital because it sits on the equator—Quito, Ecuador. Reporting tonight is our very own sanitized, purified, and distilled Lourdes Bottled Waters."

Lourdes announces, "Tonight's story is about two children poisoned after eating Chocolate Moons at the Culinary Institute on Mars. Live from Pharaoh Specific Hospital in Pharaoh City, Mars is Katy Catty."

Katy Catty says, "Two children are upstairs in comas, Lourdes. This happened immediately after the two ate Chocolate Moons at the Culinary Institute. Laboratory analysis reveals that blood samples taken from the children contain a strange substance that in larger doses would have caused death. More tests are needed. There are now twenty-three similar cases around the planet of people falling into comas.

"The mystery remains: although each person ate one Chocolate Moon, all the remaining Moons in the packages tested negative for additives or poison. I learned that all the candy was made at the same time and reached consumers in other cities the same day the candy was placed in the cases at the Candy Universe. This was done so there would be a consistency in the shelf life of every piece. Maybe random candies absorbed the poison, leaving the rest—either in the boxes or in Candy Universe display cases—harmless. Back to you, Lourdes."

I say to Cortland, "I'll ask Jersey if she knows how they distribute Chocolate Moons."

"Shh," he says. "Want to hear this."

"Now for our financial report, brought to you by *Money in Space*. Reporting from the floor of our space station is Barter Roma."

"Correction, correction, Lourdes. I'm not on the floor. I am standing on what might be considered the ceiling, wearing magnetic shoes. The market looks a lot different from this vantage point. Everyone knows that financial markets are too important to be restricted by gravity, and that was the main reason those who meet and eat at the Warren Buffet decided to relocate the financial markets to space, the final financial frontier."

She takes two clunky steps toward the camera and pushes away the hair that fell toward her eyes. "And just to remind viewers, we reporters report. We don't judge. We graph the charts and chart the graphs. We make bar codes and codes for bars. Ah, the medium, the message, the perception, the reality. So, stop asking me to give you any tips!" Barter Roma points a finger toward the camera and trills, "But I love you guys anyway."

"Hmm," Lourdes says, sensing that Barter Roma is getting carried away. "This has been quite a day, hasn't it, Barter?"

"Yes, it has. Especially for the Culinary Institute's Candy Universe, that makes Chocolate Moons, and San Andreas Farms, which grows and supplies all the chocolate. Their stocks tumbled and tumbled. And then they really tumbled. By the way, Lourdes, do you see Coconut Comets floating outside? My kids would love those."

Barter Roma winks and waves at the camera. "Hi, Ritalin. Hi, Risperdal."

"I love this show!" Cortland says. "Teaches you how to be rich and poor at the same time."

Lourdes Bottled Waters says, "No matter what the perception, we have just confirmed from Craig Cashew, CEO of the Culinary Institute, which houses the Candy Universe, that all Chocolate Moons have been pulled from the market. Government Health Commissioner Pliny the Elder recommends that Chocolate Moons be replaced with Lemon Suns." Pause and music. "Coming up next and live from Mars, *What a Racket* with Katie Racket. Tonight, Katie's guest is Drew Barron, executive vice president in charge of marketing at Congress Drugs."

I freeze. A pink flush spreads over my face. I grab a tissue and ball it into my fist.

"Drew Barron?" Lois shouts from the next room, interrupting her study of hair colors for square roots. "Your old boyfriend, Mom!" The twins flutter to my side. They plop on the end of our bed and, for a rare and brief moment, are silent, watching the screen.

Drew waits in the studio. And although he knows that Katie Racket is called "Katie Attack It," adrenalin pumps confidence. He adjusts his blue paisley tie.

"Don't forget to sit on the bottom of your jacket, Mr. Barron," the makeup artist says, applying a light dusting of face powder to Drew's forehead. "That keeps it from riding up around your shoulders."

While Katie Racket's intro music plays, she touches her sleek chignon, narrows her feline green eyes, straightens her back to show off her smooth tanned body and eighteen-inch waist, and clicks her purple pumps together. She peers with wide-eyed, loving innocence into the camera and in a throaty voice says, "Welcome to our show, Drew. You don't mind if I call you Drew?"

Drew smiles a dental-convention smile. "Glad to be here, Katie. Thanks for having me."

Katie Racket leans in with a fastball. "So, do you think there is a connection between the problems with the chocolate the Candy Universe received from San Andreas Farms and the manufacturing of Chocolate Moons?"

Drew looks at Katie then looks innocently at the camera. "I have no idea. Your guess is as good as mine. All I know is that all our products are the best and the finest. We even export to Earth."

"But that didn't stop San Andreas Farms, Congress Drugs and the Culinary Institute's stocks from crashing as soon as the news of people getting sick was announced. Who knows when and where the poison was inserted into the chocolate. Could have been contaminated on a San Andreas farm or during shipping."

"That's true, Katie. There are several points along the way to the Culinary Institute's Candy Universe where the chocolate could have been contaminated. But I think you are overreacting."

Katie frowns.

"*Crashing* is a harsh term," Drew cautions. "Perhaps San Andreas Farms, Congress Drugs and the Culinary Institute's stocks were high and needed correcting. These bursts happen all the time. It was a coincidence unrelated to our product. Lots of other stocks took a tumble."

"Any likelihood that some people were privy to insider information, and when stocks dropped in value, insiders sold short making a bundle?" Their eyes lock. "Care to comment about the people who ate Chocolate Moons and are in comas in the hospital? What are the chances they will not recover and will die?"

"Like everyone, Katie, I feel terrible but as I said, I have no more information than you." Drew's hands rise for effect.

"And what about Congress Drugs' practice of giving educational grants to doctors and groups who advance drugs before they have completely cleared the testing process?"

"One question at a time, Katy. Mr. Andreas does have a scholarship fund that brings its recipients to Mars to study. Are you accusing us of unethical practices?"

Katie ignores the question and strikes. "What about Congress Drugs keeping negative findings on their products' secret and publishing only positive results?"

"That's ridiculous."

"To me, the term *investigational drugs* are incomplete or vague and smacks of a smokescreen."

Drew leans forward and is about to answer, but Katie raises her hand. "We'll be back with more questions for Drew Barron, executive vice president of Congress Drugs. Stay tuned."

The twins look at their father, slumped in his faded gray Cracked Craters sweatshirt, the one he refuses to throw out. "Drew looks so much younger than you, Dad," Lois whines. "Are you sure you're the same age?"

I give the girls a serious look. "I told you at the spaceport when we arrived and you saw Drew in the Freedom Plan ad that he didn't look like that when I knew him. He was fat. He had circles under his eyes. His socks had holes. His hair was blue. Our friends called him Lord of the Onion Rings. He looks like that now because he takes all those fake food supplements and professional stylists groom him and pick his clothes."

"Well…" Becky and Lois singsong.

"Well what?"

The girls roll their eyes. Compared to Drew, Cortland is flabby, old, and overweight.

I put my arms around Cortland and squeeze. "Fake food from a fake guy. This is what the real thing looks like, girls."

Becky and Lois look at each other, shake their heads, and sigh. "In that case we're never getting married," Lois says.

# 13

ROCKET KEEPS A SMALL APARTMENT on Titan, one of Saturn's moons, a place of fancy boutiques, trendy restaurants, vague laws, and obscure regulations, and whose "religious freedoms" allow its citizens to worship the law in spirit rather than in practice.

Rocket arrived yesterday. The trip on the Mars–Titan transport offered a rare break from the tensions and unwanted surprises that usually fill his life and the best place to buy duty-free unregulated products at the transport's popular Hogwarts Health Foods.

Rocket adds a packet of rare Uranium minerals to a pot of fenugreek tea. He sniffs and stirs until it turns blue. Then he pours a cup, sits, slurps, and admires his copy of Andy Warhol's *Dollar Sign*, which he bought on his last visit to the ABC (Ali Baba Caves) from Scheherazade that hangs on one wall. This makes him think about the auction at Park Bengay that made headlines when Drew Barron outbid Craig Cashew for the expensive Giacometti sculpture. He swallows a vitamin C covered in a vitamin B and lets a few ideas concerning Craig Cashew and Drew Barron percolate.

Rocket remembers a time twenty years ago when his path crossed with budding gourmet Craig Cashew, when both were students at Why U. He still laughs thinking how Craig gasped watching him put flaxseed oil on chocolate cake.

"Don't knock it till you've tried it," Rocket said. "Marketed correctly, chocolate flaxseed oil could be the next big thing."

Craig, who didn't know what to make of Rocket, was taken aback but intrigued. He knew that food fashion, like all fashion, is fickle. Rocket could be right.

Soon thereafter, Rocket lured Craig into an illegal game that used hallucinogenic drugs called glass beads, run by a former classmate whose real name was Sondra Audrey Goldwyn but changed to Scheherazade to annoy and end-run her parents, who wanted her to marry a proctologist. Scheherazade had been kicked out of school for selling what she insisted were strands from a shroud from Titan but were really cut-up sweaty towels stolen from the girls' locker room. The game was held in the back of the home economics lab, where the hypnotic smell of freshly baked garlic bread and one too many gin-soaked matzo balls gave Craig Cashew misplaced confidence.

Craig took a big hit. To erase his debt, he agreed to help Rocket and Scheherazade transport a shipment of glass beads off-planet. Craig overheard Rocket say to Scheherazade, "Don't worry; I took my own 'insurance policy' out on Craig Cashew," meaning Rocket kept proof of this transaction and could use it in the future to blackmail him.

When Scheherazade made enough money from the bead game, she reinvented herself as a high-class art dealer selling to many of her former glass bead clients. She bought land between New Chicago and Pharaoh City, where she built the Ali Baba Caves, a vast underground complex that housed her apartment, offices, art factory, and a storage facility promptly filled with acquisitions from a disproportionate number of people named Anonymous.

Scheherazade sits on a rose-and-cream-striped Viennese Biedermeier sofa in her large living area that was copied from a design Brunelleschi used for the Pazzi Chapel in Florence. She extends her pinky as she raises a Wedgwood blue cup of mint tea to her red lips. Her eyes wander over the mosaics that rival those in Ravenna, Italy, that cover the floor. Then she admires a large copy of Giovanni Bellini's *St. Francis in Ecstasy* that hangs from one wall and a copy of Botticelli's *Birth of Venus* that hangs from another.

Her craftsmen have placed six copies of Rodin's sculpture of Balzac recently made in her art factory to the side of the room. Three are larger than the original and come in fluorescent red, yellow, or blue; and three are smaller in Scottish plaids—all best sellers to those living in McMansions on McSatellites.

No sooner does she put her tea down than her palm signals a call from Rocket.

"What can I do for you, Rocket? Want another Andy Warhol?"

"I want a copy of the Giacometti that Drew Barron got at Park Bengay."

"Giacometti. No problem. Can I interest you in a pair? Two for the price of one, this week only. I also have three *Davids* by Michael and Angelo in tall, grande, and vente. You might want to know that Park Bengay just reserved the grande."

"Hmmm," Rocket says to show that he is listening.

"Or a sculpture of Mozart the Fortieth, a brave man of La Mancha, standing near a gang of wolves. Lenny Bernstein's barbershop quartet just confirmed that the flute that he is holding is magic."

"No thanks. I bought a Mozart last year when it was rated A-sharp and I ended up selling it in D-flat. No need for another Mozart's requiem. Just make it one Giacometti."


Rocket calls Drew.

The moment Drew answers, two women Rocket previously made an appointment with arrive earlier than expected. He clicks off the visual, because they are putting him in a compromising position. Then he hears Drew say, "You must want something important, Rocket, or you wouldn't be calling."

"I'll be at the St. Trophy Bar next week. I want to stop up and see that Giacometti sculpture again."

Drew is suspicious. "Again? Why do you want to see it again?"

Rocket doesn't answer. Drew hears several soft *oohs* followed by several louder *ahhs*. "Rocket, are you all right?"

Drew hears him clear his throat. "Just having my windows washed. They're using new equipment that does a lot of deep, heavy blowing. What's a good time?"

"Okay, Tuesday noon solar time."


Drew opens the door. A gray antigravity case floats next to Rocket. Drew points to the case. "What's that?"

"A little surprise. But first I wanna tell you how brilliant you were on the Katy Racket show. Also, I got you and Kandy a reservation for the Nirgal Palace next weekend. It's that new luxury hotel that circles Mars on its own space station.

"That's very nice of you. Every time I call, they say they only have a small inner ring room or they're booked."

"You gotta know someone. And lucky for you, you know me. I'll be there for business, but I'll make time for a drink. Love to be seen with Kandy."

They walk over to the sofa next to the picture window. Rocket sits, takes off his electric-blue-striped jacket, and places it next to him.

"Beautiful view, Drew. Gotta hand it to you. You really know how to live. But I've told you that before, haven't I? Hope you haven't spent all the money I gave you after the market did its little dance. It's nice to be even so we can start all over. It's not too late to place a bet on a weightless pie-eating contest on Uranus."

"Not interested, Rocket."

"Not classy enough for your tastes? Doesn't have the cache of the races at Epsom Salts?"

This is true, but Drew says nothing.

Rocket takes out a piece of gum that has the letters *VV* on it, pops it into his mouth, and starts to chew. He holds out the box and offers Drew a piece.

"What does the *VV* mean?"

"Very vitamin," Rocket answers.

Drew shakes his head. "Still taking all that stuff?"

Rocket frowns. "It's good for ya. It's a health food. Better than most of those Congress Drug food supplements that you take. It's amazing how much people will pay to eat nothing."

"You've mentioned that. So, why are you here?"

"I want another sample of that stuff you got me from Congress Drugs."

"No can do. After the poisoning of the Chocolate Moons, Congress Drugs as well as every other drug Company, is super careful and weighs every gram of its products daily. Everyone is making sure that nothing is out of order. These investigations are making everyone in the drug business edgy. Until they find out what made the Chocolate Moons poisonous, everyone's under suspicion."

"Which means no one is under suspicion. Look, why don't you just replace the missing grams with something else? You're a clever guy. Plenty of things look like an innocent white powder and weigh the same." Rocket cracks his knuckles.

Drew stands and looks down at him. "Do you have to do that? I hate that sound."

Rocket takes out a large white handkerchief with the initials *RP* and blows his nose. He reaches out and puts his arm on Drew, who yanks away.

"Now, ready to hear my punch line?" Rocket returns the handkerchief to his pocket.

Drew sighs. "Didn't I just hear it?"

"It's about an opportunity to get in on the ground floor of a big one."

"A big one?"

"Titan Labs is a new freelance drug company not far from my apartment on Titan." Rocket points his thumb at himself and says, "Yours truly has just bought it. I want to develop my own generic brand of the anti-flavonoid and my own product to compete with Freedom Plan foods. That's why I'm asking you to get me another sample. I promise Titan Labs won't produce any of the anti-flavonoid for two years. That way people will think everything was developed independently. No one would be able to link you to this, except me, of course."

Rocket takes out his handkerchief and blows his nose again. He looks up. "What are those little colored dots on the ceiling? Some kind of new artwork?"

Drew looks. "What little dots?" He squints for better focus. "I can hardly see them, Rocket. I can assure you, it's nothing."

"I hope they're not some kind of listening device. You better be right, because you don't live long in my business if you're wrong." Rocket narrows his eyes. "Look, we could use an experienced CEO like you at Titan Drugs. I'll double your current salary. You'll only be young for another fifty or sixty years. Think of your future."

Rocket stands. He raises his hand, and the antigravity case rises too. He heads toward the table where the Giacometti sits. Drew is close behind. Then he slides the case on the table next to the Giacometti and pops the lid. Drew looks and gasps. Another Giacometti, identical to his, is inside. Rocket reaches in and places it next to Drew's. Then he puts a hand on each one, and, like a professional three-card Monte player who always wins, rapidly crosses them several times.

"Stop!" Drew shrieks, waving his arms. "Stop!"

Rocket grabs one of the statues and tosses it into the case. A DNA-coded bolt sounds, and Drew knows that only Rocket can open it.

"How do I know which one is mine?"

"You don't. That's the point. But I'm not going anywhere soon, and you know where to find me." Rocket puts out his hand, and the case rises next to him. He walks to the door then turns back to Drew. "Did I mention that the four-flame Bunsen Burner prize-winning scientist Decibel Point, who invented the formula used in Freedom Plan foods, and I used to be partners? We had a falling-out many years ago, but if I give him his own lab at Titan Drugs, maybe he'll join my team."

"Decibel Point? I see him all the time at Congress Drugs. He's easy to spot because he's so fat. Didn't know he invented the Freedom Plan foods!"

"Sandy Andreas does everything he can to hide that information. Business could suffer if people knew that a fat guy who never eats any Freedom Plan foods himself invented the stuff."

The next morning Drew takes the Giacometti that Rocket switched to Smart Art Appraisers.

"You are wise to have this independently appraised, Mr. Barron. Theft and counterfeiting is big business." The appraiser inserts a small needle into the statue's foot and extracts some material. He squeezes a liquid on it and inserts it into a microscope. Drew taps his fingers on the counter and waits. When the appraiser finally looks up, he says, "Sorry, Mr. Barron, feet of clay."

## 14

Lunch time. My favorite time. Jersey and I walk through a long, high hall that leads to the Quantum Corner Café. Fragrant spices hang from twisted vines that dangle from ceiling to floor. And although Jersey's implants give her extraordinary vision, she has a poor sense of smell. Every day she watches me inhale the delicious aromas that waft through the halls, and every day she is amazed.

Wine racks designed by Beowulf and Grendel Associates hang in grids. We know, as insiders, that the Dewey Decimal System and the Code of Hammurabi have been woven into an intricate, unique pricing system that only the top brass can understand so they can justify charging astronomical prices.

The flower of the week, the fuchsia, heart-shaped Rosa-Parks, stands in a large green-and-yellow paisley vase in the front of the the room, while smaller matching vases sit on tables. I pass three glass cases that hold rows of pastries and crusty breads that I can practically taste just by looking at them. I smile at the clerk behind the counter. She waves and returns my smile.

Jersey looks neither right nor left and marches straight to our table, where she begins her table ritual. First she taps each corner of the table twice to make sure it is steady. Then she realigns every knife with the glasses and measures the distance between the forks and the spoons before straightening the rest.

"There is no problem with the table," I say. You find something wrong with the setting every time we're about to sit down. Stop it. I can't relax."

"Well, I can't relax and eat when it is so unbalanced."

"Just sit. You're embarrassing me."

Jersey sits. A waiter carefully places a roll on her plate. She picks it up and crumbles a piece. I know she does it to look like she is eating, but the food never goes near her mouth. It is something I've seen Flo and her friends do whenever anything with more than ten calories gets near them. Jersey orders a raspberry quince iced tea that I know she could make last all day and a leafy green salad with no oil and balsamic vinegar on the side.

I butter my roll and pop it into my mouth. I order a double cheeseburger with fries. The fries are made from potatoes that are long and thin like bananas because Mars's lower gravity makes all produce elongate. The twins won't eat any round foods from Earth because they say those foods must have more calories. Jersey says the hypothesis is reasonable.

"Whoever put something in the chocolate vat did it during the day, right under our noses," Jersey says, sipping her tea. Unusual things happen in plain sight all the time. Besides, people on tours are like a flock of sheep. The Culinary, and especially Candy Universe, is filled with people being told where to walk and what to look at. They are listening to the guide, not listening for strange sounds."

A waiter brings our orders. "And the salad is for...ah, let me guess."

My eyes narrow. "We're not leaving this one a big tip," I whisper. I take a bite of my burger and swallow. I look at Jersey's roll. "Are you going to finish your roll, Jersey?"

"No, I'm not. I didn't like its shape." She is happy to push it closer to me. And before you can say *carbohydrates*, I move her roll to my plate.

"One doesn't eat a roll for its shape," I say.

"But the right side is higher than the left side."

I take a small bite and hold it up. "Not anymore." After a larger bite, I say, "Tell me, how do Chocolate Moons get made?"

Jersey sits straight up and brushes crumbs on the table into a tissue and hands it to a passing waiter. She slowly presses her napkin flat with the palms of her hands and folds it into equal quarters.

"San Andreas Farms roasts and shells the beans at a factory on its farm. The company only sends the nibs, the part of the bean that makes the chocolate. I think one guy with a computer can do the whole process, except for the picking."

"What happens after the Culinary gets it?"

"The beans are ground into liquid called chocolate liqueur but there is no liqueur in it."

"Mmm, too bad."

"Then they add other ingredients and it all gets heated and mixed. The art of chocolate making is in the mixing. That's the part that the tourists see. Everyone tells me it smells so good, but as you know I have a poor sense of smell."

"You mean like the smell of those brownies the waiter is carrying? I never realized your condition was so serious." I breathe in their aroma and signal the waiter to bring me an order.

"We just finished lunch. We haven't even left the café, and you had an extra roll. Now you're ordering brownies."

"Maybe I'll take the order out and save them for later."

"Ha, with you and chocolate, there is no 'later'!"

"You never know."

"I know."

"So where does the chocolate go after it is mixed in the vat?"

"It's sent to different areas and poured into individual molds, one of which creates Chocolate Moons. When they have hardened, they are sent to three different tasters. If they approve, they are sent on to packaging."

"I know a professional taster. She's married to Cortland's cousin. Her name is Florida. I never see her eat a thing."

"Bet she has beautiful clothes."

"Stay focused, Jersey. What happens to the chocolate next?"

"Twenty-five pieces are put into each box. Then the boxes are sealed and wrapped."

"Who puts the pieces in the boxes? Sounds like a good job."

"Robots put the chocolate in the boxes. Can't worry that someone like you would slip through the screening process and eat the goodies. And, after they are packed they are sent to local middlemen at various distribution centers, who deliver them to neighborhood shops."

"So, since Chocolate Moons are the most popular product, most tourists want to see how they are made. Right?"

"The only time the vat is exposed is when the melted chocolate is being mixed, which is done right in front of the tourists so they can get the maximum smell, which of course increases sales. Every tourist wears a sterile gown, hat, and gloves so there is no contamination."

I close my eyes, imagining the scene and the smell of melted chocolate.

"Are you with me or not on this, Molly? You look like you're in a trance."

I open my eyes.

Jersey continues, "After the melted chocolate is poured from the mixing vat into molds, the tourists are led to the gift shop. No one leaves the Candy Universe without buying something, even if it's just a candy statue of Saint Hershey, OBM."

"OBM?"

"Of Blessed Memory."

I raise my eyes. "Amen! Unless the tourists are like you and can't smell at all." I peer at Jersey. "But you're an exception that way. Aren't you?"

"Yes. Martians can smell as well as you."

"At least my sense of smell is something I have in common with you natives. Because when it comes to food, it sure looks like native Martians don't love it the way I do."

"Oh, we love food, but we usually don't eat much of it."

"Yeah, like you eat but don't swallow."

Jersey says nothing.

"Let's backtrack. The chocolate vat is exposed in front of the tourists. What if a foreign substance were put into the vat? Would it be possible for nanosized amounts to mix with the chocolate then randomly scatter down the line before it is poured into the molds? And then when it is packed, one piece could be infected and the rest not?"

"Yes, I suppose it could happen."

"Hmm, mixed but not dissolved." I finish the brownies.

Jersey frowns. "I knew there was no chance you would save those for later. Let's check and see if any of the lab reports and security holographs are ready. Unless of course you want to start lunch all over again."

"Not funny, Jersey." I sigh. "I still want to come over to talk to Trenton about my hunch. The last time I was at your home, he showed me his new laboratory equipment."

"He's a forensic freelancer for Mars Yard now, so he has even more stuff. Come any time. Ever since his race car accident, he's had so many body parts replaced he needs tune-ups rather than check-ups. The media called him a human-android. Not everyone is comfortable being with him.

"Too bad he didn't win the four-flame Bunsen Burner prize and only got the three-flame for finding out how many filberts were in a filibuster."

Jersey leans back and takes a last sip of her raspberry quince iced tea. "Although that was brilliant it couldn't match Decibel Point's discovery of what came first—the gin or the tonic."

We stand. Jersey pushes our chairs carefully under the table. A waiter approaches holding a tray. "Won't you try a free sample of our new Freedom Plan coconut cream candy before you leave?"

We each put one in our mouth. Jersey swallows.

"Not bad," I say. "Reminds me of pureed okra." When the waiter's back is turned, I spit mine into a napkin then reach for some regular spearmint taffies that sit next to the pay-scan.

"Not going to get me to eat that Freedom Plan junk," I say.

Jersey represses a giggle. "I thought it was good but not as good as pureed okra."

We exit the Quantum Corner and walk down a hall lined with large picture windows that show off the tiled open kitchens with hanging copper pots. I watch a chef pipe snowy whipped cream around the tiers of a wedding cake.

"I love working here. Even with all the recent troubles, what could be better?"

Jersey marches, arms at her sides, head high, eyes straight ahead. "Maybe a bank," she says.

I gaze at Jersey and think, *Ah the smell of money. How sweet it is.*

Breezy lies curled up on their four-poster bed. She wears a t-shirt with a picture of a man with three eyes that says property of MOMA (Museum of Martian Art). Her hands cover her ears. Pluto is screaming. "What do you mean you can't find the remote control I gave you when we were at the Culinary?"

Breezy lowers her hands and sighs.

"After they examine the security cubes and check the time everyone was distracted by the alarm sound, they'll find that it was the same time everyone looked away from the chocolate vat."

Breezy pouts. "They could think it was a coincidence?"

"Not if they discover that the remote can trigger an alarm. What's more, it's possible that the holo cube recorded my hand raised near the chocolate vat at the same time all that was happening."

"I must have dropped it when you were rushing me. You're always rushing me, Pluto."

"Oh, now it's my fault you lost it."

"I didn't say that. I just said you rushed me."

"Think back. When was the last time you remember having it?"

"I think it was in the Chocolate Moons room at the Culinary. I thought I dropped it into my purse, but it must have fallen on the floor. Then with all the confusion, I didn't realize it was gone. It was hard to do two things at the same time."

"Yeah, like walk and chew gum."

Breezy starts to cry. "You don't have to be so sarcastic, Pluto," she sobs. "I'm sorry."

Pluto puts his arm around her. She reaches for a tissue and blows her nose. "The robotic crew that collects garbage might have chewed it up and tossed it into the recycle. I guess we're going to have to wait it out and see what turns up. To do anything else looks suspicious."

Breezy gets up from the bed and goes to the bathroom to wash her face. When she comes out, she is more composed. "My father wants to have dinner with me. On top of his regular work at Congress Drugs, he consults for several off-planet unregulated labs on the outer moons."

"Three cheers for Daddy Decibel Point! It's about time Sandy Andreas and his Congress Drug company gets some serious competition."

"He is also having problems with Rocket. Rocket says he found a loophole in an old contract that says if Dad develops any new products, they are his to market. But he's willing to drop it if he helps him in his new laboratory on Titan that will make generic drugs."

Pluto interrupts. "I don't care if your father and Rocket are in business together or not, just as long as your father doesn't ask me for any money."

"Who said anything about money, Pluto? You're always thinking about money."

Pluto smiles. He puts his hand on Breezy's breast. "Not always," he says.

# 15

CRAIG CASHEW SITS AT HIS desk in his office at the Culinary Institute and stares at the stack of mail labeled "hate mail: Chocolate Moons." Opposite is a small gold bag marked "Eyes Only." He reaches for it and rips its seal. Three large chocolate fortune cookies containing new recipes from Al Lacart, his head chef, tumble out. He cracks one, nibbles, and frowns. This is not a good time to try anything new. Or, for that matter do anything new like build Culinary satellites in other cities, a project he hoped would deflect the constructing of a convention center that some board members were touting, because it would destroy beautiful natural areas.

Craig opens a desk drawer and pulls out the device he found on the floor of the Candy Universe the day the Chocolate Moons were poisoned. He suspects that the device might be connected to the unfortunate event. He examines both sides, slides it back into the drawer, and turns the lock.

He steeples his fingers and folds them into fists, shifts in his chair, pushes his hand through his silver hair, and thinks about the Giacometti sculpture he lost to Drew Barron at the last Park Bengay auction. His stomach tightens. Although another work by Giacometti called *The Palace at 4 a.m.* is up for auction next month, Craig already owns *The Palace at 9 a.m.* and thinks it unwise to downgrade, because he reasons a nine must be worth more than a four.

Craig sighs. He knows he must call a board meeting immediately to discuss what happened at the Candy Universe and how to restore confidence.

Board member Sandy Andreas, CEO of the major supplier of produce to the Culinary, is the first to arrive. As a young man, he worked for several farming communities and put all his money into an emerging spice market. He bought a small piece of land near Aram Chaos, an area close to the equator, and grew exotic blends that he sold to the first luxury upscale restaurants. It's never been clear where he got the money to expand his products that gave him his mega-bucks.

The San Andreas Farms company runs the farms that surround the Culinary. Sandy calls these farms his "trophy farms" because young seeds are planted next to rich old plants. Now, thanks to Drew Barron, who insisted he change the words *artificially bioengineered* to *new organic*, sales here and on all his farms have tripled.

One by one, the Culinary Institute's other board members file into the long rectangular room and take seats around a large brown oval table that sits under a ceiling fresco of the first Mars landing depicting Captain Colombo on the deck of the *Margarita* with his arms around Nina and Pinta drinking a tall one.

No one smiles, not even when lunch arrives from the Quantum Corner Café: blackberry-pear soup followed by Coquille St. Jacques with Freedom Plan heavy cream accompanied by white and blue asparagus topped with truffle shavings. Everyone drinks watermelon iced tea.

A rum-raisin almond tart is dessert. The tension is so great that several board members almost come to blows arguing over how much rum is in a rum raisin. Still others argue about how long it takes to make a raisin in the sun, and whether it's fair that the people on Mercury, who get so much sun, have an advantage over the people on Pluto, who get so little—and should the same arguments apply to sun-dried tomatoes?

Finally Craig Cashew clinks his glass with a spoon and, in his deep sonorous voice, quotes Rosetta Stone, a Martian philosopher, who said that rocks always look redder on the other side of the crater, and will everyone just cool it? But since no one stops arguing, he resorts to the Khrushchev technique: pounding the table with his shoe.

The table quiets. Craig clears his throat. "Can we now discuss what we have all come here to discuss?" he says.

This time, they stop midsentence and turn to Craig. "We have to do something to restore confidence in the Culinary. And we have to do it right here and now."

Heads nod.

"Everyone's sales are off. Attendance is down."

"We could restructure the company and rename our products and services," one board member says.

"But everyone knows those are things done when no one has any real answers," says Craig, who just realized he left his shoe on the table and watches in silent horror as a busboy removes it and fills it with leftover rum raisins.

Then Sandy Andreas peers over his glass and says, "I have a plan to restore confidence." He lowers his voice so everyone will have to lean in closer to hear him reveal what feels like a secret. "If an exclusive enclosed garden that grows rare herbs and flowers was built at the far end of the property—a garden that required a key to enter—and we added a private club with a private restaurant that was attached to the executive wing of our new convention center, it would show that not only is the Culinary growing, but it is thriving. We could levy a hefty surcharge for membership that would increase our revenues. And we could be very picky about whom we let join."

A board member who never says anything except *Can I have a take-out order of this lunch?* pipes up, "Like, for example, Rocket Packarod, and Scheherazade, who runs Ali Baba Caves. She makes it easy to put things into storage but makes it almost impossible to get them out. Some people have disappeared trying to claim their properties."

Everyone shoots him a *How do you know that?* look.

Then Sandy adds, "We can throw in some free memberships to media stars." The board members frown. "Of course this is for a limited period of time." The board members smile. "And when the public sees all of them and business tycoons having dinner at the new restaurant, everyone will want to come and join."

Craig listens with a no-expression look, pressing his palms down on the table. He breathes in, but no one sees him breathe out. But everyone knows, especially Sandy Andreas, who doesn't always know what to make of Craig Cashew, that his circling rim shot just fell through the basket.

# 16

BECKY AND LOIS ARE NERVOUS wrecks. In addition to rehearsing for the Mars Malt contest, they're studying for their final exams at the King Tut School of Music. The exams are designed by the Bored in Colleges, an independent study group, which delights in designing tests its own members can't pass.

Cortland paces, quizzing them. "This is bound to be on the test. What country on Earth did Ludwig Beethoven come from?"

Becky gulps and ventures a guess. "New Orleans?"

Cortland rolls his eyes. "Well," he says, "I see you girls are struggling. Ludwig Beethoven was born in a country that produced many brilliant musicians and scientists. It also had a lot of germs, which was why it was called *Germany,* meaning land of many germs."

Lois pops a piece of gum into her mouth and hands one to Becky. "Wow! Less than six degrees of separation between germs and music?"

Cortland smiles. "Back then people were afraid of Germany because they knew that germs led to world wars."

"Ooh, world wars. Is that like the war of the worlds?" Becky asks.

"That's a stupid question," says Lois giving her sister the elbow. "How different can they be?"

"You girls need to take a break. Let's talk about the Mars Malt contest."

Becky and Lois sigh in relief.

"I went through some music archives and ancient newspapers like the *New York Times*."

"The New York what?" says Becky. "Daddy, are you sure it was an important paper? I've never heard of it."

"You mean more important than *The Globe* and *The Enquirer?* I can't believe it!" Lois rolls her heavy black-kohl-lined Egyptian-looking eyes. "We studied about Earth and we saw pictures of old supermarkets. No *New York Times* up front near any of the cash registers that I could see."

"Well, reliable source or not, I found a few concert reviews that described a way to pick up a tempo without destroying the line of the music, and I want to try it. I also found these ancient clips from the late twentieth century about some guy named Mick Jagger. Watch how he walks and points at the audience. I think we could adapt some of that." Cortland clicks the holo screen and enlarges the image.

"What's that stuff on his face? Those lines?" Becky asks squinting through gold-colored eyelids.

"Must have been a popular style," Cortland says. "Most of the people in those days wore them but they look like they hurt."

Lois fine-tunes the optic fibers on her harmostring guitar and looks up. "Didn't he live in a country called the United States?"

"I know about the United States," Becky chimes in. "It was important because it was near the Virgin Islands, where all the virgins lived. I learned that they used paper money with pictures of dead presidents and coins that people dropped into baskets at the end of a religious service called bingo."

Cortland snaps open a flat black box. "Focus, girls. Look at these pictures of masks from Earth's Africa."

"Ooh, we love them," Becky says, admiring the pictures. "Don't we Lois?"

"I'm thinking of having you wear masks like this one for the opening." He points to a picture of five women. "This is a rock group called Les Demoiselles d'Avignon. A guy named Picasso was their manager."

"Oh, Daddy, you're so smart. I was afraid you wanted us to wear scratchy-looking lines like those on Jagged Jagger's face."

"Mick Jagger," Cortland corrects. "He was very famous."

"Really?" Becky says flipping her hair. "Not my type."

Flo calls. I grit my teeth. I know what she wants.

"Who's that?" Cortland asks, sensing trouble.

I put my hand over my palm so Flo can't hear. "She wants the girls to take the shuttle from Pharaoh City to New Chicago to shop for something spectacular to wear for their concert. We never asked her to do this. And I don't want them shopping with her before I've had a chance to go with them."

I reach into my pocket and pop two stale Chocolate Moons into my mouth, which I had hoarded in case of an emergency.

"Thanks, but no thanks, Flo. I'll shop with the twins myself."

The girls, who have been listening, rush to my side and whirl like dervishes around me. I look at them and say, "Yeeees? Whaaat?"

Lois's whine feels like nails scratching a chalkboard. "Please, please, on a comet's tail, let us go to New Chicago and shop with Aunt Flo. Don't you want us to look our best and win?"

I wonder: *What could I have done to deserve this?*

The next day I take the recently reopened Carpal Tunnel to the Canal Mall. The new construction cut out the syndromes that made traffic crawl. The twins, wearing the darkest sunglasses that they could find, don't say a word and crack Freedom Plan gum as close to my ear as possible. If I hadn't automatically programmed the rover to get us to the mall I don't think I could have made it.

Once inside, the twins march quickly past several store windows. They are neither tempted nor impressed. Finally I spot a sheer multicolored dress in a Mars Marcus outlet window. "Stop girls," I say in a cheerfully forced voice. "Look, how about that?"

The twins peer with faint interest over their glasses. "That's almost something Aunt Flo might choose but, no, not enough energy density. Too yesterday," Lois says. "We could go naked and paint our bodies in neon stripes. Think of the money you'll save, Mom."

"Or we could just wear a thong and a bra," Becky taunts. "There's nothing here."

I bite my tongue so hard that it bleeds.

"Double nothing," Lois adds. "Let's eat. I'm starved."

My ears pick up at the word *eat*. It's a word I rarely hear them say. It shows how desperate they are to stop me from any further shopping.

We trudge past a Little Green Men Pizza franchise that Cortland had sold. We smile but do not stop—we get enough pizza. We finally settle into one of the new Red Rock Cafés.

A waitress approaches. "I'll have the vegetable burger with the vegetables on the side," Lois says.

"Same for me," Becky says. "But I'll have the vegetables with the burger on the side."

"Any dessert?"

"I'll have a Freedom Plan hot fudge sundae with vitamin-enriched carrot ice cream and nutritional supplements on the side instead of the fudge," Lois says.

"Same for me," Becky adds, "but make mine with acorn squash ice cream, put the ice on one side and the cream on the other side, and change the fudge to butterscotch."

*Eaters from hell*, I think.

"And for you, ma'am?" the waitress says.

"Spaghetti with dilled veal meatballs and cognac tomato sauce topped with extra-dried shredded ricotta cheese. I'll also have a frozen aurora borealis for dessert. I understand the recipe is based on an ancient one found in the ruins of a restaurant called Serendipity in old New York called 'frozen hot chocolate.'"

The waitress nods yes.

"Hopeless," Lois whispers to Becky.

"What did you say?" I glare at them and tap my fingers on the table.

"I said I was hopeful we would win the contest," Lois says, whose foot I know is kicking Becky, who is holding her hand over her mouth and giggling.

The girls turn to a screen not far from our table. Becky points and says, "Look," that's her, Solaria Pastrami Andreas, the one who's hosting the Mars Malt contest, standing in front of her home."

The waitress brings their orders. The twins pay no attention.

"Are you sure that's her home?" I ask, adding more grated cheese while the girls' eyes are riveted on Solaria. "It looks like a hotel complex."

"Definitely," they say together. "That's her."

"Shh," Becky says. "I want to hear this. She's telling about how she lost her hand as a child."

"One summer when my cousin Pluto and I were at Cape iPod, I dared him to see which of us could put a hand through a laser fence faster," Solaria says. "But neither of us was fast enough, and both of us had one hand sliced off at the wrist. It took almost a year for mine to grow back."

"Is that why you always wear that beautiful diamond-chip nail polish?" the interviewer asks.

"Yes, and I always favor the hand that was cut off because it's so much smoother and younger than the other." She looks at the camera and holds up her right hand that is dominated by a rare blue-ice sapphire ring.

"Mom." Lois interrupts me looking at Solaria's hand.

"What?" Pause. "*What?*"

"Now that we didn't find anything to wear in Pharaoh City, can we shop with Aunt Flo in New Chicago?"

I nod a weary yes.

# 17

I GO TO JERSEY AND Trenton's home to review the scans of the Candy Universe. Trenton is an independent forensic scientist who works for Mars Yard. Police captain Lamont Blackberry hired him when Trenton solved the mystery of what came first, the chicken or the egg, by reasoning that the egg came first because we usually eat eggs for breakfast and chickens for dinner.

Jersey and Trenton met at a rehabilitation center where Jersey gets her eye implants cleaned. Trenton's body was being rebuilt after a racing car accident. He had accelerated too fast at a ninety degree corner after heading out of a double-S turn and hit a wall faster than a speeding bullet.

When Trenton learned of an experimental procedure that would replace his veins and arteries with wires, his skin with silicone, and his heart with a new red valentine one that blinked "I Love You," his one functioning eye zoomed to a screen over his bed that blinked "yes." This choice was definitely a no-brainer because although he would look different and be considered the first human-android, he would be able to lead a relatively normal life. To quote Trenton, "It sure beats being a brain in a bottle."

When Jersey took off her glasses and he looked into her irises for the first time and scanned them, his neuron-settings soared. Jersey fell hard for Trenton after their first night together, because the first thing he did in the morning after rebooting was look her in the eyes and whisper, "Welcome. You've got mail." She thought that was one of the most exciting things she had ever heard, because she rarely got any mail.

Becky and Lois get hysterical when I use the words *implants* and *Jersey* in the same sentence. "Implants? Yeah, right," they say, rubbing their chests.

"Sorry I'm late," I call, letting myself in. "I stopped off for a litchi smoothie." I peer into a dim room. "How can you see? It's so dark."

"I wasn't aware it's dark," Jersey says. "I had my high beams on, the latest designs copied from bumblebees that see ultraviolet and some freshwater fish that see infrared."

"I'll remember that next time I order honey-roasted fish."

"I have heat sensors," Trenton adds. "I see better than vipers."

We enter the lab. Strange-looking tubes filled with colorful chemicals and gelatinous materials line one wall, and rows of repair parts, exchange parts, and experimental parts line another. Trenton's computer banks bulge with esoteric information and experiments in progress.

Trenton clears three chairs and inserts a scan into a viewer.

"Stop! There! That man," I point. "The one near the perky-looking girl. She seems to be touching the sleeve of her dress. There is something in her hand. Her fingers are covering it. His hand is raised curled into a fist. I remember them because someone said they were on their honeymoon. Too bad the security camera pans away from them just as the warning bell sounds."

Jersey says, "I thought the alarm was activated by low oxygen readings, which later proved to be a malfunction."

"Maybe it wasn't," I say.

Trenton peers more closely. "I'm seeing a heat reflection coming off the man's hand that's a different color than the rest of his arm— meaning it was regrown."

"I saw Solaria Andreas on the holo when I was shopping with the twins. She said that she and her cousin Pluto each lost a hand as children and they had to be regrown."

"Maybe the man *is* Solaria's cousin Pluto," Jersey says.

"When Katie Racket interviewed Drew, she wanted to know if the chocolate could have been poisoned before it arrived at the Candy Universe."

"What did he say?" Jersey asks.

"He said it was possible."

Trenton says, "Congress Drugs is located in the middle of San Andreas Farms. There are public tours of the farms every day."

"But there are no public tours inside Congress Drugs. You have to work there or be a special visitor, like CC was a few weeks ago," I say.

"CC?"

"Colorful Copies, the daughter of Carbon Copies, who just bought Mars Media. I knew her briefly in college. She seduced Drew Barron, who was then my boyfriend."

"Whoa! *The* Drew Barron? Heartthrob Drew Barron? Gorgeous Drew Barron? *You* dated Drew Barron? I can't believe it!" She looks at me more closely. "What was he like?"

"He was different. I don't want to talk about it."

Jersey and Trenton pass significant silent looks.

Trenton walks to a row of computers with alternating blinking red numbers followed by rows of blinking black letters. "Let's see if I can get more on Solaria's cousin Pluto." He sits, sticks his index finger into a slot, closes his eyes, and looks blissful.

Jersey ties and unties the ends of her blue-and-white scarf three times.

"The right side is shorter," I say. She starts to do the process again. "Only kidding."

"No," she brightens. "You're right."

Trenton opens his eyes and removes his finger from the computer. "I used a thermal scan that bounces DNA readings off the clothing of the man at the Candy Universe, and it did match the DNA of Solaria's cousin Pluto."

"And the woman with Pluto?" I ask.

"Name's Breezy Point, and they are not married, related, or on their honeymoon. What's more, police on several planets have been following their activities for years," says Trenton. "If Breezy's father is the scientist Decibel Point, it's a big connection. He developed a drug causing invisibility, but you gained ten pounds for every minute you were invisible. The project was scrapped when the Martians learned of the side effect."

I pat my hips. "I don't think ten pounds is so much. I've gained and lost ten pounds lots of times. I could do a lot being invisible for one minute."

Jersey laughs. "Yeah, like eat all the candy in the Candy Universe." Then more seriously she says, "Why did Congress Drugs make a dangerous product?"

Trenton rises. "I bet no one knew it was dangerous. I read a report saying the testing was incomplete. Decibel probably created the anti-flavonoids for an advanced Freedom Plan product. It's possible that when the testing was slow, he or someone else tried to test it by throwing some in the chocolate vat and seeing the reaction. But that's not likely. He'd never risk ruining his reputation. Besides, Congress Drugs must want him full time instead of as a freelancer because, like all research scientists, he has plenty of opportunities to work in off-planet labs."

Jersey pales. "Don't even think about it, Trenton."

Trenton smiles and pecks her cheek. "Sandy Andreas must pay him plenty so he won't wander off. But someone else could have used the idea."

"Who?" Jersey and I say together.

"My computer keeps bringing up the name *Rocket Packarod* with most pharmaceutical products. His name is linked with Decibel in the Orange Blossom Spray Company, but the partnership was brief."

Jersey pops some gum into her mouth. Like many Martians she loves gum because it's food she doesn't have to eat. "Want a piece?" she offers. I shake my head no.

Trenton continues. "I've analyzed the composition of every type of anti-flavonoid I know. Now I need to analyze a Chocolate Moon."

"Simple," I say, reaching into my pocket and pulling one from the old stash I saved in case I ran out. I hand it to Trenton. "Any chance you would want to eat one?"

"Why would I want to eat it?"

Trenton crushes the Moon. I wince. Then he inserts some into an analysis unit and discards the rest. "Well, nothing wrong with this one." His hands rotate at the wrists 360 degrees. There's a beep. He scans a screen. "The Chocolate Moons found in the bodies of all the coma victims came from boxes with the same packaging code, meaning they came from the same vat, packaged at the same time, and distributed soon after. Hmm…the analysis of the chemical composition of the poison is exactly opposite of the composition of the harmless Chocolate Moon you just gave me, Molly. Of course, I wouldn't be affected if I ate a poisoned one. Maybe I'd find them delicious."

"I wouldn't be surprised," I say. "The people who ate them are lucky they didn't die; you can recover from a coma. I've had a vague feeling about an antidote and a French connection." I reach into my pocket and take the decorative paper from the Candy Universe that the Chocolate Moons sat on. "I scraped this off the bottom of the case. Lamont's got a larger piece, but I wanted your opinion."

Trenton inserts it into the analysis unit. A few seconds later more numbers and letters appear on a screen. "Well, here's no surprise—a small spot matches that in the poison."

"I wonder how long that candy sat in that case."

"Candy moves quickly. Couldn't have been there more than a day." Jersey eyeballs me. "And in some cases only for a few minutes."

Trenton flexes his hand. He picks up a can of WD-4,000 and sprays his hand. "Ah, I could live on that stuff." He opens a drawer and takes out a gray metal box and lifts the cover. "What do you think about my latest generation of listening devices, Molly?"

"Looks like candy sprinkles that top ice cream."

Jersey groans. "Only you would think that. It's obviously electronic devices with nano-nuclear eyes and digital ears."

"But sprinkles are a good name," Trenton says. He closes the box. "Lamont inserted them onto the ceiling of Drew's apartment."

"Drew's apartment! I didn't know he's a suspect."

"Sandy Andreas insists everyone be investigated. Two days ago those 'sprinkles' transmitted a conversation between Drew and Rocket concerning gambling debts. We also heard Rocket switching the Giacometti that Drew bought at Park Bengay with an identical copy. Drew sounded very upset. I'm sure that he'll make every effort to get it back and in the process hopefully lead us to Scheherazade. We suspect she is the one flooding the market with fakes."

Drew and Kandy are having dinner at home. Kandy wears a black bare-backed jersey halter and her latest purchase, a full-length black-and-gold skirt with a dollar-sign pattern. The service-bot rolls toward them with a roasted duck that sits on a bed of macadamia nut wild rice. It stops next to Drew. He says, "Carve and serve." As the service-bot carves, Drew raises a rare glass of syrah, sniffs, and swirls. Then Rocket calls.

Drew turns his chair away from Kandy, who slips off her gold sandals anticipating what she hopes will not be a long discussion. "I know you already asked me about getting you more from Congress Drugs, but it's difficult!"

There is a pause followed by an "uh–huh," followed by a longer pause. He doesn't want to get on Rocket's bad side and risk never getting his Giacometti back. "I am trying harder!" Pause. "Yup, of course Kandy is thrilled to go to the Nirgal Palace Hotel. She's never been to a hotel in space before."

# 18

CC ENTERS CRAIG CASHEW'S PRIVATE dining room. She clicks her open-toed icepick heels on the brown polished floor. Her one-shoulder peach-colored dress is circled with a gray belt. Craig thinks risqué yet conservative like jalapeño chunks in double-dark chocolate.

The room is next to his office. The table sits near a window that overlooks the Culinary's rose garden. It is set with a periwinkle tablecloth and matching napkins. A skinny glass vase holds a sprig of magenta bougainvillea.

Craig slides out a white damask armchair. CC sits. She smiles at Craig, hoping that this lunch will lead to a more in-depth interview and private tour of the Culinary Institute.

"Well, Colorful Copies," Craig says.

"Please, all my friends call me CC."

"Well, CC, I've looked forward to our meeting."

A waiter pours ice water from a silver pitcher. A sommelier approaches and places on the table two tall flutes etched with the Culinary Institute of Mars logo. He pours a small amount of wine into Craig's glass.

Craig sips. He looks at the label. "Ah, 2318," he says. "It was a very good year." He nods to the sommelier who fills both glasses.

Craig and CC look at each other for a minute longer than necessary. "To food," Craig says, raising his glass.

"To *gourmet* food," CC says. They clink glasses. CC puts the drink to her lips. Bubbles tickle her nose. She dabs it with her napkin.

They lower their eyes to the tabletop. There are ten buttons on the top. CC presses the first one and a holograph of a half roasted duck in black cherry sauce appears. She presses the second and the duck is replaced by grilled Dover Sole in lemon butter sauce. A third brings a rack of lamb. "I can't decide," says CC. "Everything looks wonderful. Why don't you order?"

Craig motions with his hand. A waiter places a basket of minuscule golden harbor prawns with a dish of garlicky aioli between Craig and CC.

"Eat while they're hot," Craig says, dipping a prawn in the sauce and popping it into his mouth. CC reaches for one and drops it on her plate. "Ooh, its sooo hot." She picks it up, looks Craig in the eye, and blows on it before putting it into her mouth. "Delicious," she says.

"I hope Sandy Andreas's tour of Congress Drugs and San Andreas Farms didn't wear you out. I saw your interview with Nova Scotia. I heard that Sandy gave you a personal tour of his company."

"Yes, but I was annoyed that I only got to interview two or three of the Congress Drugs scientists and I never completely saw how his Freedom Plan diet foods and supplement pills are made. But when he left to take a call, I got one scientist to show me the products that they've not finished testing. The farms are beautiful, but plants don't talk." She leans closer to Craig. "I'm really more interested in the Culinary." CC blinks her newly dyed rainbow-colored eyelashes.

"Are those eyelashes your natural color?" he asks.

"Is sugar sweet?" she purrs.

Craig kisses her hand. "I'll be delighted to show you the Culinary Institute—our restaurants, our kitchens, the gardens and vineyards, and the Flying Saucer Supermarket. Feel free to interview anyone you want."

"I'm already interviewing someone I want."

Craig smiles.

A waiter approaches. "Have you made your decision, or do you want a minute more?" he asks.

"We'll share the crab bisques with Io mushrooms and the colossal raw-seafood platter," Craig says. He turns to CC. "The seafood arrived fresh this morning from Hellas Planitia Ocean. You need at least two people to finish it."

CC's cornflower-blue eyes look deep into Craig's brown eyes. She reaches out and touches his sleeve. "You're soooo creative. I hear you're going to build a new members-only club."

"Yes, Gramercy Gardens. Why don't I add your name as a charter member? My compliments."

CC oozes. "Wonderful."

"How is Sandy Andreas? I haven't seen him or his wife, Solaria, in a while. Solaria's firm, Sumptuous Solars, is catering and hosting the Mars Malt gala at their home. Did you get an invitation?"

"Not exactly. I'll be there but as part of the Mars Media team."

A waiter places a small green tureen of crab bisque on the table.

"Shall I?" he says, ladling the steaming soup into their bowls. They look at each other, dip in their spoons, and swirl until the pink coral and sand-colored mushrooms fill them.

"Ah," they say together.

"I have to go to Nirgal Palace Hotel for a conference next week. I've never been there." says Craig. "Would you like to join me? I'm told that the room that I booked on Outer Ring 3 is one of their best."

CC says, "Those rooms have the illusion of only having three inner walls. The beds at the far end appear to float in space. A lot of people are afraid, but I'm not one of them." She sips her champagne, takes out her scheduling tablet, and looks. "Maybe," she smiles. "Maybe." One waiter clears the soup. Another places an enormous platter of raw seafood resting on a bed of ice between Craig and CC. "Ah, the pièce de résistance," Craig says, putting several raw oysters on his plate.

CC takes half a lobster and pries its white meat from the pink shell and dips it into a pink creamy sauce.

"Did you ever find that bracelet charm you lost?"

"No. But my father sent me a duplicate." She shakes her wrist. "See, all present and accounted for."

By the time the waiter brings two triple espressos and a chocolate soufflé, CC agrees to go to Nirgal Palace with Craig and accepts his offer of a complimentary charter membership in Gramercy Gardens.

## 19

WHEN I BRING A CHOCOLATE decadence cake, two dozen cinnamon doughnuts, and three pounds of caramel crackles to Lamont Blackberry's office, Jersey says, "I'm embarrassed to be seen with you!"

"But I want to make a good impression."

"You're making an impression, all right. But it looks like a bribe."

"It's a peace offering."

"Bribe."

"Peace offering. The last time Lamont and I met, the day the boys ate the poisoned Chocolate Moons at the Candy Universe, we disagreed about sending the uncontaminated candy into space."

"Bribe," Jersey mutters under her breath.

"Enough," Trenton growls.

Lamont sits at his desk behind a clear glass wall. He rocks back and forth on a beat-up chair that matches his mood and appearance. Three stacked screens, each divided into quadrants, are on the left side of the office, and a large jar of unshelled walnuts is on the right.

From the other side of the glass wall, we see Lamont pick up a walnut and throw it at his partner, Sid Seedless. Sid rubs his head.

Trenton taps on the glass. Lamont looks and buzzes us in. When we enter, Jersey lowers her head because she is embarrassed about all the stuff we are carrying toward his desk.

"What's this?" Lamont asks suspiciously.

"Chocolate Decadence cake, a gift from the Flying Saucer Supermarket. It's an ancient recipe written by a trader named Joe. I hope you like chocolate; I could have brought vanilla."

"Vanilla's good," Sid says, lured to Lamont's desk by the smell of chocolate.

"Shut up. They're not talking to you," Lamont snaps. "And in case you haven't noticed, this case is about chocolate, not vanilla."

Lamont runs his finger around the side of the cake and puts it to his mouth. "Mmm…" Then he does it again.

I poke Jersey in the ribs and whisper, "See?"

Jersey shrugs. "See what?"

"What have you got for me, Trenton?" Lamont raises his eyes from the cake.

"My report proves—"

Lamont slaps Sid's hand as it reaches for a doughnut. The box collapses; doughnuts roll.

"Catch them!" Lamont cries to Sid.

"If I catch them, can I eat them?"

Lamont grabs one before it hits the floor and stuffs it into his mouth. Sid does the same.

Stone-faced, Jersey—who never saw a Belgian chocolate that she liked—picks up the cake with the cold detachment of a lab technician and carries it to a nearby table. Trenton gathers the rest and puts them next to the cake.

Then Trenton places his briefcase on Lamont's desk and says, "Gentlemen!" Then again, more loudly, "Gentlemen!" while clicking the briefcase open. "My report proves how only some Chocolate Moons could become infected and the others left untainted."

Everyone springs to attention.

"Yes, they were all mixed in the same vat, but the composition of the poison was so small that it didn't dissolve but instead bonded with one chocolate nib, meaning only random candies got infected. By the time the Moons reached the packing area, they separated into different boxes and were distributed. I don't think they were targeted for anyone in particular; whoever got a poisoned candy was just unlucky.

"We also studied the Culinary's security holos and saw a man named Pluto Pastrami raising his hand like he was about to throw something into the vat. Turns out he's Solaria Pastrami Andreas's cousin."

Lamont taps the computer and says, "Pluto Pastrami." Several orange and blue lights blink. Lamont's eyebrows rise. "Yes, nephew of Salami Pastrami, owner of Mars Malt Beer, and first cousin to Solaria Pastrami Andreas, Sandy Andreas's wife. She owns the high-class catering firm Sumptuous Solars." He scrolls further. "His girlfriend, Breezy Point, is daughter of Decibel Point." Lamont pauses. "Isn't Decibel Point the same scientist who won a four-flame Bunsen Burner prize?"

Jersey gives my ribs a wincing jab to remind me not to say anything more about Decibel Point.

"He burned down Nero Roma's restaurant with that thing. I loved that place; instead of putting fortunes in cookies they put fortunes in ravioli." Lamont sighs and turns back to his computer. "Aha! Just as you told me, Trenton—Rocket Packarod and Decibel Point were partners in the Orange Blossom Spray Company. A notation claims that Rocket cheated Decibel out of the patent when they were in Las Venus."

I say, "Good thing the listening devices you put in Drew Barron's apartment transmitted what was going on between Rocket and Drew. But it was a close call when Rocket looked up at Drew's ceiling and saw those dots."

"I'm an art history maven," Sid says. "And I think…"

"Art history maven? The only culture you get is in yogurt," Lamont snarls. "But if you are, then you're the perfect person to go to the ABC and round up Scheherazade and recover the stolen items stored there."

"Well, I only got a C," Sid gulps.

Lamont glares at Sid. "Even if Drew is found innocent of taking a poisonous substance from Congress Drugs, if he leads us to Scheherazade, that would be a major accomplishment." Lamont reaches for a caramel crackle and pops it in his mouth. "And while we're at it, what's the name of Drew Barron's beautiful girlfriend?"

Sid brightens. "You mean former Miss Universe Kandy Kane?"

"Enlarge Kandy Kane, Sid. Make a poster-size display. I want to get a better look."

"But she's not one of our suspects," I say.

"A large picture of her right here over my desk will do wonders for this investigation. No one wants to look at a blowup of Rocket Packarod."

Trenton says, "I need a warrant to snoop around Congress Drugs. If they know I'm coming, they'll clean the place up. If there is a discrepancy in their product's weight records, taken near the time of the poisonings, I may be able to find out who was there during those times and who took the anti-flavonoids."

"The warrant's no problem. Are you sure you can get in without being detected?"

Jersey pales. She knows that getting Trenton into Congress Drugs undetected is very dangerous, because the company has vicious trained animals and a tight security system.

It's a sure sign she's very upset when she asks, "Do you have any candy, Molly?"

I hand her the first piece that I grab from my bag. She opens her mouth and quickly swallows. "Was that a Chocolate Moon?"

"No, a Raspberry Swirl."

I'm upset for Jersey. Anyone who can't tell the difference between a Chocolate Moon and a Raspberry Swirl is in big trouble.

## 20

CORTLAND PULLS ME CLOSE. "MOLLY, going to Congress Drugs is dangerous. Everyone knows that the place is a fortress. How will you get in and out?"

"Jersey and I researched the birthdays of their executives and found someone whose birthday is on the day we will go. I'll call ahead and say someone wants to send him a birthday cake from the Culinary Institute and ask if we could deliver it on that day."

"Trenton can disguise himself as a cake?"

"No, he can't disguise himself like a cake, but he can fold himself like origami. Jersey and I are going to hide him in one of the Culinary's large gift boxes and say it's a gift for someone else that we'll bring in with the cake."

The day we go to Congress Drugs, I bring a large birthday cake in a bright blue Culinary box to Trenton and Jersey's home. I place it in their refrigerator while I wait for Trenton to fold himself.

Hearing about the process was one thing; seeing it another.

I cringe watching him roll up his sleeve to the shoulder and collapse his arm until it hangs like a wet cloth at his side. Then he folds it in half at the elbow and in half again until he can tuck it under his armpit. I grab the back of a chair to steady myself because I think I'm going to faint.

"It doesn't hurt, Molly," Trenton says. "If it hurt, I wouldn't do it."

"It looks like it hurts." I lower my head and close my eyes.

"This is so handy when we travel," Jersey says in a cheery voice that only makes me want to run. "I take Trenton in the carry-on case he made for himself and buy only one ticket."

"Two for the price of one," Trenton says, his eye color fading to that of water. I feel nauseous.

Trenton sees my distress. "Why don't you go in the other room while I finish?" he says. "This won't take long." He steps into the box and waves me away with his other arm. I leave.

Soon Jersey calls, "Ready, Molly! You can come in now." She has decorated the box with silver ribbons and golden flowers. And although it is very pretty, I look at it and think of a coffin.

We wheel Trenton to my rover and lift him into the trunk. The box is much heavier than it looks. I get the cake and slide it next to him. Then we attach signs to the side windows of the rover that say "Culinary Institute Deliveries."

We stop at the entrance to San Andreas Farms. Congress Drugs is in the middle of the property. Two security guards find our names on their visitors' list. We show them the beautiful birthday cake and give each two supersize bags of Peanut Butter Moons. Jersey sits rigidly next to me. When no one checks the other box, she relaxes and we roll through.

An apple orchard is on our right; an orange grove with its hypnotic orange smell is on our left. Ahead we can see the chrome yellow three-tiered Congress Drugs. From studying floor plans that we got from Lamont, we know that the bottom and largest floor houses the laboratory. Marketing and sales offices are in the middle. The top, with floor-to-ceiling glass windows with a 360-degree view of the San Andreas Farms that surrounds it, is Sandy Andreas's office.

We park. We take out the cake and place it on the top shelf of a trolley. A guard approaches with a cat on a leash. A sign around its neck says "Kreplach, Vicious Cat of the Day."

"It looks just like a sweet pussy cat." Jersey says. "How vicious can it be?" She reaches out her hand to pat it.

"I wouldn't do that if I were you," the guard warns. He throws Kreplach a can of food. The cat claws it open, swallows the food, and then swallows the can.

"I see what you mean," Jersey says thrusting her hands behind her back.

We show the guard our pass. He looks and nods.

"What's in the other box?" he asks.

"More goodies from the Culinary." Then, with some effort, we remove Trenton's box and put it on the bottom shelf of our trolley. Kreplach sniffs the box. We stiffen. Kreplach moves away. Trenton has no smell.

We are escorted to Congress Drugs' executive floor by another guard. I give him a box of chocolate-covered cherries. Jersey says I am overdoing it, but I tell her that giving candy is not something you can overdo.

The elevator opens. We see a long curving hall lined with clocks set to the local times on various worlds, along with some artwork. Ever since Drew's commercial "Of the People, By the People, and For the People" had sent sales soaring, when Sandy learned that Drew's inspiration had come from a pop song and dance from the United States on Earth called "Do the Constitution," he decided to show off his knowledge of United States history by decorating the halls with important historical paintings.

The first one we pass is of George Washington next to a cherry tree throwing a rock across Delaware Street in Washington that breaks a window. The next one is of Lincoln eating a Gettysburger in a car that has a sign that reads *Made on Mercury*. Finally, outside of the office of the executive we came to see, is a painting of a black man named Jefferson playing the Monticello.

We push the trolley into the office and remove the lid from the cake box. The smell of chocolate rises. A secretary swoons. The smell moves through the open door into the hall. People emerge from their offices and beg for samples.

"For me?" the executive says with wide eyes and a wider mouth. "Who sent this?"

"Can't say. We just deliver," I respond. "Congratulations!" I start to sing "Happy Birthday." Everyone joins in. The executive glows like the child he once was. We hand him a knife. "Cut the first slice?" I say.

While everyone's mouth is salivating and all eyes are on the cake, we turn and roll the cart out the door.

His secretary watches. "Hey, where are you going?" she asks. "Is that another gift?"

"Yes," Jersey says. "Another gift but for a different person."

We open the door and step through. It closes behind us.

"That was close," Jersey says, wiping little beads of sweat from her forehead. We push the cart slowly down the hall. I quickly glance at a floor plan imprinted in my palm and see that there is a storage closet three doors down on my left.

"Quick, Jersey, in here." We open the door and push the trolley inside.

We take Trenton out of the box and cover him with a gray cloth. We take some items from the shelves and scatter them on top.

"Are you all right, sweetheart?" Jersey's voice quivers.

Trenton makes a humming sound that Jersey apparently translates as "All is well."

Jersey's shirt is now drenched with sweat. She doesn't move.

"Are you sure?"

Again another hum meaning yes.

"We have to go. We have to go now! " I beg. I give her a shove and push her toward the door.

Trenton waits. At midnight, he begins his ten-minute process: one minute to roll out flat, three minutes to rev up to a full shape, and another six minutes before he can stand. Every hour there is a security sweep of the laboratory. Existing door codes are replaced with new ones. Trenton knows the codes for midnight through three o'clock, but if the time sequence changes—meaning the hour code is reset for a longer or shorter interval—he may not be able to activate the next code.

He turns on his argon-fluoride laser, which generates ultraviolet light, and sets it to its lowest setting. He shifts his crystalline quartz lens and adjusts his immersion liquids to focus more finely. He leaves the closet and scans the hall. All clear. The stairwell is a few steps away. He enters and descends three steps at a time to the laboratory one floor below.

A double door leads to the laboratory; the outer one has an air lock; the inner door opens into the laboratory. When no one is inside the laboratory, the atmosphere has 50 percent less oxygen, making it deadly to humans. Only those with security clearance are given the code to make it breathable. But as long as Trenton operates on half power or less, this is not a problem.

Trenton inserts his pinky into the laboratory door's keyhole. Nothing happens. He tries his index finger. Same thing. Finally he tries his thumb. It fits but sticks in the lock. Trenton rotates his hand until it separates from his wrist like the tail of a gecko lizard. He turns it with his other hand. *Click!* The door opens. Trenton deflates his thumb and removes it from the lock. He enters. The door locks behind him.

The security office has a hundred viewing screens. Suddenly one buzzes and blinks a red light. A senior guard, eyebrows arched, gazes closely. "I see something moving on the floor in the main laboratory," he says to his junior partner. "It's very strange. I'm getting an organic and inorganic reading. I've never seen anything like it. Did you see it?"

"Maybe a speck of dust on the lens," the younger guard says, trying to hide his annoyance at being interrupted while watching a girl slide up and down a pole on a porn channel.

Trenton detects their reading. He lies down on the floor, shuts down three-quarters of his circuits, and waits. He only needs full power to make measurements and take holograms. His heart beats like a great slow clock.

"Now it's gone," the senior guard says. "I better be on the safe side and reprogram the lock codes. Instead of changing every hour, now they'll change every fifty-five minutes."

The junior guard, now peering at a large nipple on a huge breast, says, "I was just thinking the same thing."

Trenton adjusts his eye cam and scans the laboratory. He slowly moves toward a sign that says "Research Personnel Only."

"It's happening again. I'm getting more readings," the senior guard says.

Trenton hunkers down to half power and crawls along the floor. Then he brings himself to his lowest setting.

"Now it's gone. But you must have seen that," the senior guard says.

"Ooh, ooh, ah…ahh," the junior guard moans.

"I'll take that as a yes. But I think it's a malfunction. Nothing flip-flops from organic to inorganic and back."

Trenton finishes his scans. The fifty-five-minute code clicks. Each code is different from the previous one. He needs another thirty seconds to power up to full. Not enough time before the new series of codes that he doesn't know secures the door.

He sees a large garbage bin and a sofa with several violet pillows. He shreds two pillows, climbs into the bin, and scatters the shreds on top of himself. He deflates himself the way he did getting into the cake box, shuts down 90 percent of his energy, and waits.

"I'm not getting any organic readings now," the senior security guard says. "The time change must have deactivated whatever it was. It sure wasn't a person!"

Jersey checks a home monitor that sends a signal to Mars Yard. "Do you hear what I am hearing, Lamont?" she says through tears. "I'm getting a very weak signal from Trenton, meaning he's all right, but something's wrong. He must be locked inside."

# 21

THE NEXT MORNING, WHEN THE robo-maid enters the laboratory, it collects the garbage bin where Trenton is hiding, brings it to the basement and loads it onto a transport destined for a landfill. It hums exiting Congress Drugs. It gathers speed on the open road. No one sees one container roll off and its contents walk away.

Several days later I press the key code Jersey gave me to let me into their condo. Trenton and Jersey are standing close together peering at something on a table.

"Am I interrupting?"

"No, I was just showing Jersey how I put a nest into an egg. I call it a nest egg. I'm sure if I can market it right it will make us rich."

"Let's go in the kitchen. I have something that many consider a remedy for every condition. I take out a thermal container, put it on the kitchen table, and open it. "It's chicken soup."

"I didn't know you could make chicken into a soup. But I do know how to make soup into a chicken." Trenton reaches for a spoon. He dips it into the soup then brings it to his lips and tastes. "Delicious! Are the ingredients expensive or rare? Is it hard to make?"

"Actually, it's cheap and easy; it recharged the batteries of millions for ages. Want the recipe?" I pick up a stylus and write the recipe.

Trenton scans it with his index finger. "I wonder if I can distill it into supplements."

"It defies distillation. The essence is lost in translation."

Trenton finishes the soup and barrels into his laboratory. We follow. He feeds his readings from Congress Labs into "Analysis" and punches several numeric codes. We hear grinding and whirling noises.

"What's he doing, Jersey?" I whisper.

"Beats me, but he must have found something unusual. Grinding and whirling are serious sounds. Last time I heard them, he had spun gold into flax."

"Can he reverse the process?"

"Are you serious? Would I be standing here if he could reverse the process?"

Finally Trenton turns around. "Hmm, this is very interesting. There is not one weight-loss discrepancy but four! Three were taken from the same batch of poisonous anti-flavonoids at three separate times, one on July 6, a second on July 10, and a third on July 12."

"How can you be sure it was three different people?" I ask.

"I'm sure because each person had to put a check mark next to the sample to release a magnetic cover lock over the substance. Like handwriting, each check is different. All I know is that there are no signs of a break-in. They all had clearance and access, meaning they either worked there or were a guest."

"What about the fourth sample?" I ask.

"The fourth sample was taken a week later, on July 19. It was very different. It looked similar but was harmless."

"Harmless? Why would anyone go to all that trouble and take something that was harmless?"

"If the person taking it was in a hurry, they could easily mistake one white granular substance for another." Trenton cracks his elbows and turns to me. "Have you made any progress with your hunch about an antidote to the poisoned Chocolate Moons? All you said was that you thought it had a French connection."

"I still think it has a French connection. I even called the French Institute. But the operator who answered didn't like how I pronounced *s'il vous plait* and *hors d'oeuvre*s, and put me on hold. Finally I was connected to Dr. D. Gall, who transferred me to Dr. D. Gallstone, who transferred me to Dr. D. Gallbladder before I got disconnected and discouraged."

"Well, keep trying," Jersey says. "New clues, new insights."

I check the time. "I wish I could stay and speculate on who took these substances, but I have to go pack. I finally got Cortland to agree to take me to the Nirgal Palace Hotel. Its way over our budget, but it's our anniversary."

Decibel Point lives alone in a large white loft in New Chicago. His living space is crammed into one corner; the rest is his laboratory. Decibel and his ex-wife, Pencil, divorced ten years ago. She now owns a chain of Freedom Plan ice cream parlors whose specialty is a kitchen sink filled with Freedom Plan ice cream, sauces, and toppings. The entire thing has sixty-two calories.

He is annoyed that she called. "I have better things to do than develop a fifteen-calorie ice cream sundae, Pencil. Besides, I think it would taste like flavored air."

"You're only saying that because even though you developed Freedom Plan foods, you never eat any yourself. You don't care that you've grown so fat that people think you come from Earth. Even being divorced from you is embarrassing!" *Click!* End of conversation.

There's another call. *Oh no,* Decibel thinks, seeing that it's Rocket. "What?" he barks.

Decibel listens and then says, "Of course I know that off-planet labs with their loose regulations are working on edgy new products." Long pause. "Yes, I probably could do the job." Pause. "Pencil is fine. She just called. Wants me to cut the calories from a Freedom Plan ice cream sundae, but I told her it would taste like flavored air." Pause. "What potential as a luxury item? I guess selling it wouldn't be hard for a windbag like you." Pause. "No, I didn't know you bought Titan Drugs." Pause. "Want me to develop another line of anti-flavonoids? We never finished testing the first batch. As you know people were poisoned from Chocolate Moons filled with the stuff." Pause. "My own lab with state-of-the-art equipment? That's tempting. I'll think about it. But I haven't forgotten we still have old business to settle."

# 22

NIRGAL PALACE, MARS'S LUXURY HOTEL that circles the planet, is a bustling showplace of people who parade every hairstyle, cosmetic procedure and fashion. People from Earth are easy to spot because they are the heaviest, shortest and most overdressed.

CC and Craig enter the lobby. Craig stops transfixed by the illusion of the "sky."

"Say something," CC says touching his elbow and edging him to the side while others walk around them.

He points to the pulsating chandelier in the middle that looks like a radiating sun. "It's hard to believe that's an artificial construction."

CC pats his arm. She lowers her eyes. Waves of colors flow into the corridors, creating the illusion of everyone walking on water. She points to a billboard ahead that lists restaurants, bars, ice skating rinks, pools, gyms, a ski slope, theaters, a children's center, library, and levels of duty-free shops.

"This is going to be fun," Craig says.

"Wait till you see the room," CC counters running her hand up and down his arm.

A tall blond man approaches wearing clothes inspired by the costume books depicting the ringmasters at Cirque du Soleil. He smiles, tips his black top hat, and hands CC a lilac-smelling blue rose. She inhales deeply and smiles.

"Welcome to Nirgal Palace. My name is Trapeze. Your reservation is for one of our best rooms, on Outer Ring 3. Your luggage is there, the refrigerator stocked with delicious treats like lobster caviar, the wet and dry saunas with a double-ice mint-splash pool are waiting and keyed to what our medical scan indicated would bring the most relaxing benefits."

Trapeze leads them through a thickly carpeted emerald hallway and pauses in front of a shiny black rectangle set into the wall. His hand passes in front of it. It disappears. He steps through into a moss-green room. CC and Craig follow. The black rectangle reappears. Craig turns and taps it. "Feels solid," he says.

"It is," Trapeze answers.

The room appears to have three sides. A king-size bed supported by nothing visible floats where the room ends and space begins. CC gasps and death-grips Craig's arm. "I don't remember the illusion so convincing the last time I was here."

"We just updated our technologies. Most people are so excited when they see it they immediately go to the bed and lie down. I see you are not one of them." Trapeze walks to a translucent bar tucked into a corner, reaches underneath, and brings up two glass flutes and a pink bottle of Nirgal Palace's private champagne. "Maybe this will help." He opens the bottle, pours, and hands them a glass. CC gulps two large swallows.

"I need to scan your palms." Craig and CC hold out their hands but feel nothing. "I remotely imprinted your right palms with a map of the hotel. Everyone gets lost without it. It fades when you leave. Your left has a key to your room. Just wave your hand in front of the door and it will open and close."

He walks to the door and waves his hand in front of it. The door disappears. When he walks into the hallway and waves his hand toward the empty doorframe, the solid black door reappears.

"That alone is worth the price of admission," Craig says. "Do you really think the bed is in a scary place? Last month when I took you to the New Paris Hilton, you said that you never felt as secure as you did with me." He puts his arms around CC.

"Well, I…"

"Well what?" Craig holds her tighter.

CC pulls back. "This new technology makes it hyper-real. In the past you could see little shadows. Can't we move the bed?"

Craig looks deep into CC's eyes then says the words men have seductively said to women to lower their guard and change their minds, words that go back to the moment pantomime became spoken language, words uttered a microsecond after *help* and *fire*. Craig says, "Trust me."

A few hours later, Drew and Kandy arrive. Drew suspects that Rocket's gift of a weekend at Nirgal Palace was meant as an inducement for getting him another sample of the anti-flavonoid. But he also feared if he didn't play along, he would never get his Giacometti back.

Their room is on Outer Ring 2: first class but not a suite. Drew is disappointed, but Kandy is thrilled to be there. A bottle of champagne chills on the small bar with a card that reads: "To the sweetest sweetheart, Kandy Kane. From Rocket Packarod."

Drew frowns and studies the orange label, knowing it's good but not the hotel's private stock.

Kandy pushes a pad on the side of the closet, selects a perfume from its interior, unpacks her Louie Voo Voo luggage, and places her clothes on the warm silver hangers.

"I love it here, Drew. Do I have time to explore? I want to see the lobby again?"

"I need to make some calls, sweet thing. Come back in an hour." Drew turns and waves over his shoulder.

Kandy wastes no time. She's learned that when she's with Drew, she has time to do half the things on her list or all the things but only halfway.

She enters the lobby and walks toward puffy lime lounge chairs, but all are taken. A man rises and offers her a seat. She thinks nothing of convenient coincidences, like men getting up and giving her a seat just when she needs one. After all, they have been happening since she was six months old and on the cover of *Solar Infant* magazine. She smiles and sinks into the buttery cushions, crosses her long legs, and gazes at the jewel-like comets darting from one end to another of what appears to be the real sky.

"Did you see the look that guy just gave you?" Drew would always ask. "How can you not notice?"

"What look?" Kandy would answer. "Maybe he's reading a sign near me or looking at someone else. I'm not the only person here." It was a charming, disarming, and totally honest answer, and he groaned every time she said it.

Kandy rises and strolls to the gift shop. As she pays for her post-cards, Craig and CC enter. Craig's head turns. Kandy doesn't notice.

Cortland and I enter the lobby of Nirgal Palace just as Kandy is leaving.

"Beautiful girl," Cortland says watching Kandy stride past. "Must be a model or a media star."

"You know, she looks a lot like the woman I've seen with Drew on the society channel. Could she be here with him?"

"She's probably some old rich guy's trophy wife. He looks up. Now if you really want to see something spectacular, look up."

When I look up my jaw drops. I think there is no ceiling, only infinite black sky. I think it's more convincing than the real black sky that I saw when I first came to the Moon with Drew. My sweaty hand grabs Cortland's sweaty hand.

A robotic porter approaches. "Happy anniversary, Mr. and Mrs. Summers. Welcome to Nirgal Palace." It hands me a small bouquet of artificial daisies. "I see you prefer a quiet inner room on Ring 1." I think, *prefer? It's what we can barely afford.* "Please give me your palms so I can imprint a map of the hotel on it." Cortland and I extend our hands. We hear a lot of clicking sounds. "Sorry, it must be out of order again." He hands us two keys. "Here, you can let yourselves in. If you need anything, press 'Robotic Services' on the back of the key."

Nirgal Palace—*Nirgal*, the Babylonian word for *Mars*—is shaped like a doughnut. Our small, clean room has a tiny window that views levels of machinery. If we crane our necks almost to the point of dislocating our spines, we can see the stars.

"Bed's comfortable," Cortland says, plopping down. "Good thing we won't be spending much time in here. And most of the time our eyes will be closed."

"I hope," I say, peering into the gray metal bathroom. "Bathroom's efficient but not enough towels. I'll call Robotic Services."

"If the twins win the Mars Malt contest, they will help attract other talents to the music agency I want to start. I promise when we come back here we'll have a room with a floating bed on Outer Ring 3." Pause. "Molly, did you hear what I said? What's the problem?"

"I wanted more towels. Listen." I hold the card to Cortland's ear. He hears: "For towels, press *one* three times followed by the pound sign followed by the symbol of Saturn above the symbol of a washcloth. For soap, press the square root of...*click*. Thank you for calling Robotic Services. Your call is important to us. Please hang up and try again."

Cortland shakes his head. "You would have thought voice-message hell would be eliminated by the twenty-fourth century." He peers into a mirror and runs his hand through his thinning salt-and-pepper hair. "Let's freshen up and go to the Starbright Lounge for a drink. We can stop at the front desk and ask for towels on our way back."

## 23

THE NOISY, CROWDED STARBRIGHT LOUNGE feels as it always does, like the moment before midnight on New Year's Eve. Rocket sits at a favorite table in the center near the bar. He faces the door so he can see everyone who enters. His fluorescent green suit stands out in a sea of conservative grays. Rocket believes there's no point dressing up if no one notices what you wear.

Kandy and Drew enter. Rocket stands and waves his hands over his head. "Over here, Drew," he shouts. "Over here." Drew touches a blue-and-yellow paisley scarf wrapped artfully around his neck, a small nervous gesture stemming from his insecurities about once being fat.

Rocket takes Kandy's hand bends toward her face and gives her an air-kiss. She wears a crisp pink blouse with a navy blue pleated skirt that ends just above her ankles, showing off black gladiator heels and pink polished toes. Her long dark hair falls straight down her back. A blue-ice sapphire necklace adorns her neck. Perfect.

Rocket pulls out her chair and zeros in on her necklace. "Beautiful blue-ice sapphires." He leans closer and recognizes the expensive smell of Springtime on Venus perfume. "Business must be good, Drew."

Kandy moves her hand to her throat and beams.

"This calls for a Red Spot of Jupiter on the rocks. You've put me in a good mood."

Rocket holds up three fingers, catches a waiter's eye, and points to the table. He gives him the order, picks up the empty dish of macadamia nuts, and waves it in front of the waiter's face. Drew looks away.

Kandy and Drew sip their drinks. Yum. Delicious. Elegant. Hints of ripe raspberry and soft jasmine float on their tongues. Everyone relaxes. Suddenly Rocket, who hasn't taken his eyes off the door except for the few seconds he looked at Kandy, jumps up from his seat, waves his hands over his head again, and shouts, "Craig! Craig Cashew, over here!" Before Drew or Kandy can say anything, Rocket jumps up from the table and starts threading his way through the crowd toward Craig. He waves at a number of people and pretends to ignore their lack of reciprocal smiles but he makes mental notes.

Cortland and I arrive and stand in the doorway of the Starbright Lounge and wait. We watch the head waiter air-kiss his regulars and ignore us. Cortland reaches into his pocket and palms him fifty solars. "Ah, follow me," he says without smiling.

We make our way past clinking glasses, waving scarves, and trays held high to an empty table near the bar. I grab Cortland's arm and pull back. "They're here!"

"Who, sweetheart, Jersey and Trenton?"

"No, not Jersey and Trenton." I turn and hide behind Cortland. "Do you have another table?" I ask the head waiter as he starts to walk away.

Cortland gives me a strange look. "This is one of their best tables and it cost me fifty solars to get it." He nods to the head waiter and palms him another twenty-five. "This is fine. We'll take it."

I move quickly toward a chair where my back faces the other table.

"Well, sweetheart," Cortland says, eyeing Kandy over my shoulder. "Here we are. What's this all about?"

"Don't you recognize him?"

"Who?"

"It's Drew Barron with the woman we saw in the lobby. They're behind me at the next table."

Cortland peers at Kandy over my shoulder again. I put my finger to my lips. "Stop looking. You'll draw attention to us."

A waiter approaches. He gives me the "Flo frown." I pull my long black tunic top over my flabby arms and glare at him. "Greetings," he says changing his frown to a company smile. "I'm your waiter, Bermuda Triangle, but those who are superstitious call me Bernie. You're from Earth or Earth's moon. Right?"

"Is it that obvious?" Cortland asks.

He gives a knowing wink. "You guys look like you could use a light beer. We have over a hundred on tap."

"Two double Kir Royals," Cortland orders.

I finger a small dish of salted peanuts and take out my handkerchief to cover part of my face. I pretend to blow my nose and sneak another peek at Drew whom I have never seen so impeccably groomed and Hollywood handsome.

Craig and CC stand in the doorway to the Starbright Lounge. They look quickly around then enter. Craig sees a fluorescent green jacket zooming toward him. He sucks in his breath. He recognizes Rocket, older than he remembered but nonetheless definitely Rocket. CC senses tension. "Who is that?" she asks. Do you know him?"

"His name is Rocket Packarod, and frankly I haven't seen him since college. Not someone I wanted to meet again."

"You know, I know that name," says CC. Craig's eyes widen. "You're kidding. Where from? A gambling casino or a police blotter?"

"No, really. I did a special for Carbon Copies Media on a community for people with developmental disabilities in Utopia Plantia. I remember there was a Rocket Packarod listed in their highest category, Big Bang Patrons. His son, Zeus Packarod, lives there. Their director told me that Rocket never comes to any of their events or ever visits Zeus but sends a weekly holographic cube with a message and gifts."

Rocket closes in.

"Well, well, Craig Cashew, now big shot and CEO of the Culinary Institute. Long time no see," says Rocket pounding Craig on the back.

Rocket turns and extends a hand to CC. "Rocket Packarod," he says. "And I know who you are. You're Colorful Copies of Carbon Copies Media. Saw your interview with Nova Scotia. Nice work."

CC shakes Rocket's hand.

Craig feels the romance of his weekend melt like an ice sculpture on a hot buffet. Rocket says to CC, "Did you know that Craig and I were classmates at Why U?" He grabs her hand before she can answer and gently pulls till she takes a step. "Come sit at my table. There's someone both of you should meet."

Craig and CC follow Rocket to his table. Rocket waves at more people whose response is suddenly more animated seeing him with Craig and CC.

"Oh my God!" I say to Cortland, drink in hand frozen in midair.

"What now?" he says in a low, dark voice reserved for bad news.

"It's Craig Cashew, my boss at the Culinary, with CC and I think Rocket Packarod. They're headed this way. I wonder why they're all here together. Craig won't recognize me. I'm too low in the Culinary's pecking order for him to pay attention. Rocket and I have never met. And there's a good chance CC won't remember me. You have to help me keep out of Drew's sight, Cortland."

"Relax. No problem. Your back is toward them. Stop being so paranoid. No one is looking at you, not when they have Drew's beautiful girlfriend to look at."

"Meaning?"

"Well, you're beautiful too, sweetheart. But, in a different way."

*Yeah,* I think. Like the difference between the sun and an asteroid. Drew stands, seeing Rocket, Craig Cashew, and CC.

"Drew Barron and Kandy Kane, meet Colorful Copies and Craig Cashew. Craig Cashew is the CEO of the Culinary Institute." Drew looks at Craig and CC. They shake hands. Drew knows who Craig Cashew is and that he outbid him for the Giacometti at Park Bengay. He also knows that CC is his hysterical, jilted former girlfriend.

"Kandy," says Kandy, who does not get up but extends her hand across the drinks and flowers on the table.

"Weren't you in the gift shop this afternoon?" Craig asks. "I thought I recognized you."

"Guess I wasn't paying attention," Kandy says smiling.

Drew stares at her and says nothing. Everyone sits. A waiter replaces the nuts with a better selection in a much larger dish and a plate of mushrooms marinated in aquavit from Ganymede and tricolored sweet olives the size of small plums.

Drew looks at CC. "You look wonderful, CC. Strange meeting here after all this time."

With a smile on her face but a grudge in her heart, CC extends her hand to Drew, who takes it.

"You two know each other?" Rocket asks.

"Drew and I both went to Armstrong U on Earth's moon a lifetime ago," CC explains.

"College? That's where Craig and I know each other from." Rocket extends his arms. "Hey, this must be old-home week!" He snaps his fingers at a passing waiter. "Get us a large tray of shrimps wrapped in wonton skins and a round of frozen Cassini Huygens cocktails."

CC leans toward Kandy and says, "What a beautiful necklace, Kandy. Those are blue-ice sapphires, aren't they? They're very rare."

Kandy nods.

The shrimps in wonton skins arrive. They are deep-fried and crunchy. "Compliments of the chef," says the waiter. They each crackle a small piece in their mouth and leave the rest on a plate.

Except Rocket, who brings out a small yellow bottle. "A little extra vitamin C with a hint of ginkgo biloba." He gives his shrimp a spritz. "Any takers?" He waves the bottle back and forth. "Last chance. Going, going…" He opens his mouth wide, inserts the whole shrimp, makes some noisy chews, and swallows. Rocket puts the bottle back in his breast pocket, gives it a few pats, and turns to Craig. "Drew is executive vice president of sales and marketing for Congress Drugs. He also collects art."

"I know all about Drew and his art collection," Craig replies. "Drew was the one who outbid me for the Giacometti at Park Bengay. Didn't you, Drew?"

Drew lowers his eyes.

"You don't say," Rocket exclaims.

A waiter clears glasses and hands each a Cassini Huygens cocktail. Each has a silver swizzle stick in the shape of a space probe.

Rocket takes the swizzle stick from his glass. "Looks like a listening device. I don't like listening devices." He snaps it, drops it on the floor and crushes it with the heel of his shoe.

Craig gives Drew a serious look and continues, "You must know, that Mars is a haven for stolen art and fakes. I'm sure you got the real thing at Park Bengay. But—and I'm not just saying this because I missed out on the Giacometti—you should have it appraised by an independent appraiser."

Rocket winks at Craig. "Remember Scheherazade?"

Craig gives an icy stare.

"After all these years, she's still one of my best friends."

Craig says nothing.

Rocket adds, "Maybe you've all heard of the ABC, her underground storage facility and art workshop."

No one responds.

"The ABC, Ali Baba Caves," Rocket repeats louder. She sold me a copy of Andy Warhol's *Dollar Sign* and a copy of his *Electric Chair*. They spoke right to my soul."

*Good observation*, CC thinks. Whoever Scheherazade is, she sure read Rocket right.

"And what do you do, Rocket?" she asks.

Rocket crunches a few walnuts. "I'm a wholesale pharmacist." He reaches into his pocket hands her a card and winks. "Good prices. No questions asked."

"Did you hear that, Cortland?" I say, sipping my Kir Royal. "Rocket and Craig Cashew know Scheherazade. I bet Drew knows a lot more than he's letting on."

Cortland signals the waiter. "We'll have a tray of what you just brought to the next table."

"Shrimp wontons. Our most expensive appetizer. Are you sure that's what you want? We have a lovely low fat dip."

"That's what we want," says Cortland, calculating the waiter's tip downward.

We clink glasses. Cortland says, "Happy anniversary, sweetheart." I blow him a kiss.

"What are they doing now, Cortland? I don't want to turn around."

"I see Rocket fingering all the nuts in the dish. Now he's passing them around."

We hear Rocket boom. "Any takers?"

Suddenly the dish slips from Rocket's hand and crashes to the table. The round filberts move with electron velocity into the air. Two land in Craig's drink, two land in Drew's hair, three hit Rocket in the forehead and bounce back to the table and leap toward CC, who raises her hand and swats them away, where they fly over my head and nestle between my breasts like little eggs.

I try to decide if I should leave the nuts alone, pluck them out, or cover them with a napkin. But then they slide lower and drop out of sight.

Rocket rises and looks down at me. "Good catch, sweetheart."

I lower my head. "Excuse me." I head for the ladies' room.

CC glares at Rocket. She gets up and follows me.

"Didn't everyone think that was a good catch?" Rocket says. "Hey, fella," he calls to Cortland. "Would you like to join us when the girls come back from the ladies' room?"

"No thanks," Cortland answers.

I push the door to the ladies' room open. CC is behind me. I hold it for her and she passes.

She turns and looks at me. "You know, you look very familiar. Have we met?"

"No, I don't think so. I look like a lot of people."

"Actually, you don't. Most people are not as heavy as you. Everyone takes supplements and is much thinner. Did you ever live on Earth's moon?"

"Briefly. Very briefly," I say, closing a stall door behind me.

"Well, I never forget a face. I'm sure it will come to me."

CC washes her hands, freshens her makeup, and leaves.

I open the stall door, wash my hands, and peer into the mirror. CC has left her towel on the side of the sink. I take it and jam it into my pocketbook. I saw on the news that she toured Congress Drugs a week before all the trouble at the Candy Universe started—maybe there's a connection. Trenton can scan her biometrics from her towel when I get home.

I walk back to the table. CC waves at me. "I know I know you," she says in a singsong voice. "Sooner or later I know I'm going to remember."

Drew is so busy talking nonstop about Chelsea Clinton, the latest hot artist area in New Chicago, that he doesn't look up.

Rocket, on the other hand, can't resist looking and asking, "Get them out, baby?"

"Let's go," I say to Cortland.

Later, in their room, Craig says to CC, "Rocket and I were just brief acquaintances in college. He was always a character. Drew's more interesting than I first thought. Amazing you knew him at Armstrong U. I really would love to visit him and see the Giacometti."

"What did you think of Kandy?" asks CC. She watches Craig's reflection in a large mirror. His eyes glow.

After a moment, Craig turns and faces CC, whose face twists downward. "What?" he says. And as though she didn't hear, repeats louder. "What? Did I say something wrong?"

CC's brow wrinkles. "No, nothing, but..." She points to the floating bed. "Tonight we're moving the bed."

# 24

Sandy Andreas wears a tie the color of dried blood. It fits his mood. Every day he gets reports that off-planet unregulated labs, like Titan Drugs are planning to make generic versions of his products that will undercut him. Titan Labs and Rocket Packarod's name appear in the same sentence so many times that he doesn't have to draw lines to connect the dots.

Sandy pounds a table and shouts at Drew. "I thought you said that all the tests on our products were successful! I'm still getting cancellations! Sales are flat!"

Drew sweats and swallows. "But Congress Drugs did hundreds of blind tests."

"Blind is the right word. I want answers. And I want answers NOW!"

Drew drags himself home and plops into his favorite chair, his back aching. He stays there a long time. Then he moves to his bed and stays there an even longer time. Eventually he gets up and goes back to the chair. If it weren't for his daily dose of nutritional supplements and reliance on Freedom Plan foods that reduce his caloric cravings, he would binge-drink eggnog.

Kandy peers into a mirror; one hair is out of place. Another day ruined. "You know, Drew," she pouts, "you're always in a bad mood. You work so hard with pills that you're becoming one. Why don't we invite Craig Cashew and CC here to see that Jackie O sculpture? Craig said he'd love to see it."

"Giacometti. There's a big difference."

"Whatever. Just stop being so grouchy! It's bad for my complexion."

A month later the market rallies. Drew's bad mood lifts.

"Hey, Kandy, I have an idea. Let's invite Craig and CC here for dinner."

"That was my idea!"

"Well it's mine now."

"Phone call for you on line three, Mr. Cashew," secretary Vanilla Extract says. "Name's Rocket Packarod. He's not on any list. Do you want to take the call?"

Craig's stomach, which never rumbles, rumbles. "Now that Gramercy Gardens has opened, everyone wants a membership." He sighs. "Put him through, visual off."

Craig takes a deep breath. "Hello, Rocket. What can I do for you?"

"Well, that was direct. No 'How are you?'? No 'Great to see you at Nirgal Palace'? No 'Thanks for the drinks and their best hors d'oeuvres'?"

"So what can I do for you?' Craig repeats in a monotone.

"I thought since I'm your old friend, you would personally invite me to join Gramercy Gardens."

"We were the briefest of college acquaintances," Craig corrects. "Hardly 'old friends.' Besides, it's not just up to me, Rocket. There's a committee."

"Yeah, yeah, there's always a committee. Everyone knows that. But you're the Culinary's CEO."

Craig says nothing.

"By the way, if you're still sore that Drew owns that Giacometti sculpture, I can get one wholesale."

"I'm no longer interested in the Giacometti, Rocket. It's probably a fake, anyway."

"It may be a fake, but it's a real fake. Scheherazade makes such good copies that some trade at higher prices than the original. She told me that she got high-priced lawyers who specialize in art tampering to lobby governments to expand the definition of art forgery by weaving the words *artistic* and *autistic* in a manner so obscure that no one can broach the subject without getting an expensive psychological evaluation from one of the art therapy clinics. She also pays plenty to keep the filibuster of 'Is a copy of a copy of a copy still a copy?' going strong in Congress. Some congressmen said they liked the argument so much that they would give her a discount.

Craig still says nothing.

"Look, old buddy, it would mean a lot to me to join Gramercy Gardens. I'm not getting younger. Time to upgrade the quality of my life. Time to hang with a better crowd." Rocket pauses to gauge Craig's reaction. "Bet you don't think I know the difference between a fish knife, a steak knife, and getting knifed."

Suddenly Craig jumps. "What was that? Was that the sound of a gun?"

"Gun? No, gum. I was just cracking some multivitamin, multimineral gum. You should sell stuff like that at your Flying Saucer Supermarket. I'll get you the best price. Wanna think about it?"

"I'll think about it."

"That's the spirit. Now, I don't want to pull my last ace, but I gotta tell ya, I have a holo of the transaction you helped Scheherazade and me with when you transferred those glass beads off-planet back when we were college pals."

Craig winces.

"Don't worry; I won't chew any gum at Gramercy Gardens. I wouldn't *crack, crack* want to *crack, crack* embarrass such a good old friend. Let bygones be bygones; how about I send you a complimentary case of the gum to show my goodwill. Loosen up, classmate. Live long and prosper."

CC and Craig are delighted by Drew's invitation to come to his apartment for dinner and see the Giacometti.

Craig arrives first; CC follows a few moments later. Drew shakes Craig's hand. CC gets an air-kiss. A hired waiter offers them a Plum Royal: prosecco with a dash of Jovian plum liqueur.

"A house specialty," Drew says. They clink glasses.

"You've done so well at Congress Drugs," CC says. She lowers her eyes and sips. "Sandy Andreas must be a tough guy to work for. When I toured the farms and Congress Drugs, I saw how everyone jumped when he entered."

Drew gives her a long look. "We get along." He turns to Craig, relieved not to talk any more about Sandy. "You've come a long way to see the Giacometti. Well, there it is."

They walk to the gray marble table that the sculpture stands on. Craig peers closely. "As I said at Nirgal Palace, lots of fakes on the market. Have you had this independently appraised?"

"Not yet," Drew lies. "No time." He takes a ginger-infused lobster roll from a passing tray. Kandy, who has just finished dressing, joins them. Drew gives an approving look at her green jersey dress with a slashed neckline, pecks her cheek, and drapes his arm around her.

Then a bell rings and they all turn toward the sound. A hired chef in a white coat and high hat opens frosted-glass doors that lead to a low-lighted dining room. He gestures toward the room.

Everyone enters. Craig walks to three all-white paintings surrounded by soft neon frames that hang on the back wall. "What's this triptych called?"

"*Portraits of the Elusive.*"

"Elusive of what?"

"A continuing process of self-definition."

Craig studies them closely. "I see a lot of veiled aggression. I think I would understand them better in black."

"They look like three white squares to me," Kandy says. "But I like the frames."

The table is set for four. Craig faces Kandy. Drew faces CC. A low row of cream-colored candles runs down the middle.

They dig their forks into a salad of frisée, goat cheese with a small sliced pickled peach, and crystallized wasabi horseradish that makes a sweet heat. This is followed by a rack of lamb with a brandy mint sauce that was aged in kegs floating within the rings of Saturn. The conversation is all small talk until Kandy pushes her hair behind one ear, exposing a blue-ice sapphire earring, looks at Craig, and says, "I hope the food at Gramercy Gardens is as good as this. Drew's membership was just approved."

Craig looks at everyone. He doesn't answer Kandy's question. He puts down his knife and fork and says, "Rocket called me. He wants to join Gramercy Gardens. I've told him it is a committee decision."

There is silence. A waiter clears the main course and places balls of espresso gelato before them. The center is filled with hot fudge spiked with Kahlua and cinnamon. They wait for the waiter to leave the room. Then Craig looks at Drew. "If you brought him as your guest, it would take some pressure off me. I'm not sure how some of my board members would react if he came as my guest."

Drew bristles but keeps his face neutral. He remembers that Rocket still has his Giacometti. He pokes at the gelato until the hot fudge seeps from the center and pools around it.

"I need the favor, and I won't forget it." Craig presses.

Drew wonders what Rocket could possibly have on Craig.

"Sure, Craig," he nods, hoping he won't regret it.

# 25

HEADS TURN. JAWS DROP. SCHEHERAZADE stands next to Rocket and enters Gramercy Gardens. She is a tall woman with dark eyes and straight black hair that falls down her back and stops at her buttocks. Her black dress has more cutouts than fabric. Kandy Kane glowing on Drew's arm in a white body-skimming cashmere-and-silk gown that has the feeling of intimate lingerie enters next.

Sandy Andreas, up front with friends in a corner banquette, sees them and chokes.

Craig Cashew, the evening's host in a perfect white dinner jacket, rushes to his side. Sandy brushes him away, drinks some water, and stops coughing.

Craig accompanies Rocket and Scheherazade to their seats. Scheherazade saunters behind Rocket and slides into the chair Craig pulls out for her.

Drew and Kandy linger at Sandy's table. They avoid Sandy's eyes and air-kiss Solaria. When they look up, they see CC enter wearing a short red number.

CC spots Drew and Kandy at Sandy's table, waves, and joins them. Sandy makes more throat-clearing sounds. He gets up, air-kisses CC, and says how nice it is to see her again and how much he loved watching her on Nova Scotia's program.

Craig returns to Sandy's table, whisks them away, and seats them with Rocket and Scheherazade. Craig notices that Rocket has bags under his eyes and looks exhausted.

Everyone is excited to be at Gramercy Gardens because *Gourmet Galaxy*'s food critic, Alka Seltzer, reported that its polished sandstone walls, tiled floor, and stained glass ceiling are the perfect backdrop for wonderful dishes such as wild Martian buffalo stuffed with *foie gras* and mushrooms.

Sandy turns to those at his table. He has two big things to celebrate. The first is his success in getting a solar clock passed in the United Planetary Council. When there were so many worlds that had days of more than twenty-four hours and just as many that had days of less than twenty-four, the question *What time is it?* had been the number one question. Now, thanks to a solar clock, that debate is finally off the "Easy to Ask, Hard to Answer" list, making the new number one question (tested on senior citizens) *How are you?*

The other accomplishment: standardized currencies. Mars used the solar, Earth used the neuro, Venus used shillings, Mercury used pounds, and so it went. Sandy proposed the starbuck because it was the only currency that made cents. His table celebrated with more champagne, more clinking glasses, and louder laughter.

Jersey and I are at Gramercy Gardens because they need extra staff. We stand in a corner of the kitchen and watch chefs turn food into art.

"I don't know why the head waiter is letting you serve, Jersey, while I only get to refresh flowers and fill salt shakers. I got fitted for an eye cam, so I can take photos."

"They said it was because I fit into the uniform and you don't."

I say nothing, but I know she's right.

"Why do you think they serve such tiny portions on such huge plates? You need reading glasses to eat."

"Tiny? They don't look tiny to me. It's called a tasting menu."

"How come no one ever says they're tasting pizza? Either you eat it or you don't."

"It's about food aesthetics."

"No, it's about economics: skimpy portions, big price tags."

Scheherazade eyes Drew. She removes a thin black leather scarf from her neck, pulls it slowly through her fist, and sets it in her lap.

I watch from a distance as Jersey approaches their table, pours water, and places a bread basket containing bite-size pesto toasts and small cheese biscuits on the table. She lowers the table's background music, Philip Lip Gloss's series of repetitive sounds, so they will not interfere with conversation. A bottle of Rock Crystal is placed next to Drew to chill. I click my eye cam to adjust a telephoto lens and take several shots, hoping they will be clear even though I'm so far away.

Drew says to Scheherazade, "Rocket tells me that you own Ali Baba Caves. I have a large art collection, including a Giacometti sculpture. I might consider storing it with you."

Rocket knows Drew's Giacometti is the fake he gave him and that Drew is just trying to impress Scheherazade. Then Scheherazade pats Rocket's hand. "You just gave me a Giacometti, didn't you sweetheart? I put it on my desk."

Rocket's mouth curls upward.

"I would like to see it," Drew says, leaning closer to Scheherazade. "We should see how much alike they are."

Kandy, not liking the direction of the conversation, asks, "Can I come?"

Drew, as though awakening from a trance, says, "What?"

Kandy lowers her eyes.

CC breaks a pregnant silence. "Carbon Copies Media would love to do a special on you, Scheherazade. Would you consider it?"

Scheherazade raises her glass to her lips, sips, and puts it down. She wipes her mouth with a crisp white napkin, leaving a dark red smear. "No," she hisses.

"Can you hear what they're saying, Jersey? Do they like the food?"

"No one mentioned the food. CC asked to interview Scheherazade."

"What did she say?"

"Either yes or no. I couldn't hear."

After the honey-and-Grappa-marinated poached raspberries, after the Jupiter-chocolate layered cake, after the fig-and-balsamic ice cream, and after the poached-pear soufflé, Kandy and CC finish with double espressos. Rocket asks for a cup of hot water. When it arrives, he adds a packet of beige powder. Craig comes to their table and gives everyone a gold bag embossed with "Gramercy Gardens" in a decorative green script filled with chocolate bonbons and red-rock spices to take home.

Rocket gives his bag to Scheherazade and leaves in a hurry.

I clear their empty table and slide their spoons into my pocket so their DNA can be tested.

# 26

WHEN ROCKET REACHES HERNANDO'S, A hideaway hotel that never asks questions, he knocks three times and whispers low into the callbox. The door opens.

"You don't look well, Number Nine," Velma says from behind the front desk, using his code name. Rocket doesn't say anything. Nor does he look at her long red hair barely covering her right breast as he usually does. She takes his left hand and scans the palm. "You're freezing. Are you sure you're all right?" She rubs his fingers. "Do you want me to call a doctor?"

"No doctors. Don't trust 'em. Just need to sleep." He turns and walks down a hall.

Velma hears a thud. She runs in the direction of the sound. Rocket's door is open. He's on the floor of his room eyes closed and barely breathing.

Rocket is taken to a hospital. When he awakens, he smells hospital smells and gags. He pushes himself up and drinks some water. He hears a knock, followed by a *click*. Rocket slides back down, pulls up his sheet, and faces the wall. A doctor and two interns enter.

"We know you're up, Mr. Packarod," the doctor says, reading the blinking lights behind the bed.

"How long have I been here?" Rocket asks.

The doctor comes closer. Then he says, "You've been here a day. It was touch-and-go until we found the right medication. Fortunately you responded well and are out of danger, although you did some damage to your system. You've taken quite a lot of unapproved alternative food supplements, haven't you?"

Rocket rolls back over and looks at the doctor. He fumbles with his sheet.

"You must be very careful about these so-called health foods. Lots of snake-oil salesmen out there."

"Snake oil? Is snake oil back on the market?" he half jests.

The doctor and his interns glare.

"You of all people should know how dangerous some of that stuff is, especially in untested combinations. We have to do a better job catching the guys who operate unregulated off-planet labs like Titan Drugs. Their products hit the market faster than quarks." He moves closer to Rocket, pulls up his eyelid, and shines a light in his eye. "Get my drift, Mr. Packarod?" He clicks off his light and takes a step back. He pushes a button on his prescription screen and hands the resulting printout to Rocket.

"That medication will continue to reduce the poisons in your blood. Make sure you fill it, or those levels will rise again." He turns to go, followed by the two interns, each of whom frowns the doctor's frown and clicks his light on and off into Rocket's eyes until he sees pinwheels.

Rocket crumples the prescription and tosses it into one of the three baskets that dance before his eyes. Then he calls Drew and tells him what happened.

"Well, are you going to fill that prescription?" Drew asks.

"How do I know what they prescribed won't kill me? I made plenty of drugs in my day— and know every trick in and out of the book." He sips water from a straw in his glass. He coughs and blows his nose. Finally he says, "Come and get me out of here before they hook me up to jumper cables."

Jersey calls. "Come over," she says. "Trenton wants to tell you what he found at Congress Drugs."

Trenton greets me wearing a nifty blue shirt. There's no question that good clothes, one of the few things Trenton splurges on, softens his unusual appearance.

Jersey closes a hall closet, where she just finished arranging cans of the lubricant WD from WD-40 through WD-40,000.

Trenton plops down on his favorite faded chair. "Remember that I told you four people, on four different days, took samples from Congress Drugs? Three took poisonous samples from the same batch of anti-flavonoids and one took a harmless substance. Well, I can trace the first sample of the poisonous anti-flavonoid, taken on July 6, to Decibel Point."

"The same Decibel Point who invented Freedom Plan foods?"

"Yes," says Trenton. "The same."

"Who took the two other poisonous substances that week?" Jersey asks.

"Don't know. Still working on it."

"So why did you call me here?"

"Thought you would like to know who took the harmless substance a week later, on July 18." Trenton cocks his head to one side. "Want to guess?"

"No, Trenton, just tell us," Jersey says shifting from one foot to another. "Stop making this such a big drama."

"The harmless sample, taken July 18, was taken by Drew Barron. The date of his visit matches it. It doesn't match taking poisonous anti-flavonoids."

Jersey's voice drops in disappointment. "I was sure he was guilty."

"But that doesn't make him guilty. Drew must have been so rushed and nervous he grabbed the first thing he thought was the anti-flavonoid," Trenton explains.

"And that's what he probably gave to Rocket," Jersey adds.

I wrinkle my brow and give a quizzical look. "But people were poisoned."

"But not by what Drew Barron took," Trenton says. "Who else had access?"

I say, "CC had access when she did that big interview with Sandy Andreas. She had time in the lab. I remember she told Nova Scotia that Sandy Andreas left her alone for a while in the lab and she talked to Decibel Point, who wasn't happy with how Congress Drugs tested its products."

Jersey and Trenton nod.

"If so," I add, "that would mean the chocolate was poisoned before it arrived at the Candy Universe."

Trenton agrees. "I thought of that too. But even if CC is the third person, there's still a missing fourth sample."

"Does Lamont think Drew should be arrested?" I ask.

"No. He thinks we should leave him alone and let him think he stole the poisonous anti-flavonoids. Mars Yard can still charge him for stealing something from Congress Drugs that didn't belong to him. He's no flight risk—not with his expensive lifestyle and beautiful girlfriend. Lamont thinks that Drew might lead us to Scheherazade. Drew's Giacometti that Rocket switched is probably one of her fakes. And if it is, we can match it and similar art to auction houses and galleries that sell the stuff."

"And Decibel Point?" I ask. "You just told us that he took some anti-flavonoids."

"Lamont wants to wait and see. Thinks he may lead to drug cartels, unregulated off-planet labs, who knows what else."

# 27

Sandy Andreas stands on the curved staircase that descends into the ballroom of his mansion in Redwich, a luxury gated suburb north of New Chicago. He watches as one of the spotlights that the men are trying to affix to the ceiling slip from their hands and crash.

"How much is this Mars Malt gala costing me?" he shouts to his wife, Solaria who removes her hands from her ears she had just covered.

Solaria walks to the bottom of the staircase and meets Sandy. "Mars Malt and my father are paying for this, darling. We're just lending our house."

Sandy glares. "So he says."

"Having the Mars Malt gala at our home is going to bring you such good publicity," Solaria purrs thinly masking her anger at his attitude. "It's a close call between Max and the Planks, Neils and the Bohrs, and the Lunar Tunes, twin girls from Earth's moon. Plus, Marilyn Marzipan has agreed to come and sing 'Happy Birthday' to Earth's ambassador."

"Don't care about the entertainment. Just be in budget."

Solaria Pastrami Andreas is the daughter of Salami and Lasagna Pastrami, who own the Mars Malt Beer Company. She graduated with honors from the Culinary Institute of Mars. At her graduation, Craig Cashew awarded her a prize for her dissertation on the long-forgotten

Martha Stewart, credited with inventing pastels. Now she owns and runs Sumptuous Solars, a successful high-class catering firm.

Solaria has blond hair, a small, straight nose, large blue eyes. She does not look her age. In fact, nobody does. As man's life span increased to over 150 years, Solaria is typical of many who have looked thirty five for the last sixty five years. Many of her friends are wealthy bohemians with an appetite for social causes. The Museum of Charity Parties, where she is the acquisitions chairman, is her favorite. Last month she chose the year's best toothpicks and cocktail napkins for the museum's permanent collection.

Solaria sits on a soft green floral chair, places her notebook on a pink crystal table, and peers at her reflection in an ornate gold-framed mirror. Her palm signals a call. *What now?* she thinks, pushing her hair behind her ear.

Immediately she recognizes Craig Cashew's voice. "Hope I didn't catch you at a bad time."

"As good a time as any, Craig. Sandy's driving me crazy because of all the construction  needed to get this place ready for the Mars Malt gala."

"Need more staff? I'll send some from the Culinary."

"No, I'll get through this. What can I do for you?"

"Is your cousin Pluto Pastrami?"

Solaria's heart sinks. "Well, yes…"

"Ah, then I guessed right. Not that many Pastramis on Mars. And even less who are hot Pastramis."

"Hot Pastramis?"

"Lamont Blackberry from Mars Yard told me that he had reviewed the security holos taken a few days before the children were poisoned at the Candy Universe. They identified Pluto and a woman named Breezy Point standing near the poisoned chocolate vat. Pluto's hand was raised. His girlfriend next to him clutched something in her hand. Later that night I went back to the Candy Universe and found some kind of device. I have a feeling it might belong to one of them. If so, I would like to give him a chance to explain before I give it to the police."

"Why don't you tell him yourself?"

"Please, Solaria, I wouldn't ask if I didn't think this was the best way to handle this."

Solaria clicks off, sighs, and palms Pluto. "I didn't know you were at the Culinary, Pluto. I just got a call from Craig Cashew, who says he found something you or Breezy dropped. Is it valuable?"

"Well, it has sentimental value."

"Stolen. Right?"

"No, it wasn't. Why do you always think everything I do is not on the up-and-up?"

"Well, was this on the up-and-up?"

"Depends on your definition of *up-and-up*. But, no, nothing was stolen.

Solaria says nothing.

"By the way…"

"I'm braced. What?"

"I'm not invited to the Mars Malt gala, but could you could hire me as staff or sneak me in? I saw Max and the Planks at the Pollywood film festival on Pluto. Max is mega deep. I feel so smart not understanding him. Don't worry, you won't even know I'm there; I'll wear one of my disguises."

Two days before the Mars Malt gala, Solaria shows Sandy how she's transformed their home.

"I mixed expensive and inexpensive flowers in unusual arrangements that came in under budget," says Solaria, pointing to one of the large colorful containers.

Sandy nods and smiles.

"And the stage's curtains have transparent layers, providing enough magic for any type of event. The new undulating fiberglass ceiling ripples like the sea. It fits the ballroom so well; we can have it permanently installed for future events. It's way under budget."

"Love it," Sandy chimes.

"Now let me show you the garden."

"The garden? My pride and joy."

Solaria opens the door and they walk outside. Sandy's mouth drops. He looks at the raked Zen rock garden with swirling graveled patterns that replaced his beloved Astroturf and faux Greek statues in compromising positions.

"What's this? A graveyard?"

"It's a Zen rock garden."

"I can't believe you actually bought rocks!"

"But sweetheart, less is more."

"Not where I come from."

"All the nouveau riche will be envious."

"You're sure?"

As much as he hates to admit it, Sandy knows Solaria is right. He knows she endowed his garden with a look of expensive exclusivity and snobbishness that up to this point he had craved but had eluded him. However, he'll never get over how much little gray stones can cost.

The twins arrive in New Chicago to shop for the gowns they will wear at the Mars Malt gala. Flo meets them wearing a casual light-blue-and-white-striped dress with a long flowing scarf.

"I love your outfit," Lois says. "We never see people wear things like that in Pharaoh City. Do we, Becky?"

"Never."

Flo throws her blue scarf over one shoulder. It billows like a sail in the wind. "Has your mother lost any weight?"

"Are you kidding?" Becky says. "Working at the Culinary. Not a chance." She tosses her sweater over her shoulder with limited success.

They get into Flo's rover. "I'm taking you to Ooh Ga Ga, New Chicago's most exclusive shop. When they heard I was coming with two Mars Malt contestants, they couldn't wait to meet you."

The interior of Ooh Ga Ga looks like a glass cube. In one corner there is a small white counter and four white chairs and in each of the other corners, a dress on a black headless mannequin. Two saleswomen in identical white coats that could have passed as lab coats a few hundred years ago and wearing lacy white gloves make a big display of greeting them with air-kisses. Then one pushes a button hidden beneath the counter and a wall slides to the side, revealing two pale gowns suspended from clear Lucite hangers.

"These are our exclusives imported from Titan," she says. "As you can see, they're woven like silver spider webs. Adafruit flora micro-processors are woven into the fabric. When you move rainbows and silver stars will dart out, making you both look like living moon-beams." She flutters the sleeves for effect. "Try them on."

The girls take the gowns and go into the dressing room hidden behind the parted wall. They emerge a few minutes later twirling and bowing. Three women who just entered wave and clap at them. Becky and Lois wave back and blow them a kiss.

"Sold," Flo says to the saleswomen pleased with the choice. She slides her index finger over the charge.

The twins change into their regular clothes and emerge from the dressing room. Flo beams at them. "You can't lose in those dresses, girls. Let's celebrate with a Freedom Plan pizza."

# 28

My family and I are thrilled that the Mars Malt Beer Company is treating us to New Chicago's luxury Heartbreak Hotel. It is a favorite of superstitious people who wouldn't leave home without knocking on plastic and honeymooners hoping that the name of the hotel will help them avoid a divorce. We have the three-bedroom Elvis and Priscilla Suite vacated that morning by bangers from Neptune attending a Bubble and Squeak convention.

Cortland, knowing he will be busy with rehearsals, arranges for me to have a day at Ruby's Spa. And, although he wants me to look my best, he also did it because he doesn't want any distractions.

The next day a cab drops me in front of Ruby's Spa. Two guards, dressed as bottles of Beefeater gin, stand on either side of a bright red door.

I enter a low-lit reception area. Women who make Flo look overweight sit and watch little screens attached to their chairs and view poker-faced models strut on catwalks. The receptionist takes my gift certificate and drops it in a box on her desk. I head toward an uncomfortable-looking chair up front.

"*That* is reserved," she says as my bottom hits the seat. "*You* can wait over there." She points to a low stool in a dark corner. Eyes silently shift from the little screens to me. I feel like a child in a dunce cap. When it is obvious that those who came after me are being taken before me, I go back to the receptionist. "Excuse me. Am I invisible?"

"Shh," she says, hand over mouth. "Are you sure you are in the right place?"

"Yes, I'm sure. I gave you a gift certificate from the Heartbreak Hotel."

"You did?" she chirps. "I don't remember. Sorry, I must have forgotten."

I see the certificate in the "out" box on her desk. I retrieve it and wave it in front of her.

"Here!" I say.

She takes it and holds it at arm's length like a child's dirty tissue.

"I think whoever issued this made a mistake. I think it was meant for Rose's Spa, not Ruby's Spa. We are so overbooked with people attending the Mars Malt gala. You've probably not heard about it. Just a minute," she sputters. "I'll get Ruby."

She disappears behind a pink door.

I hear a lot of murmuring. I hear the words *Rose's Spa* again. Then Ruby appears. Those sitting on the chairs with the little screens look up at her with adoring expressions. She wears a black suit with a black leather belt and a ruby necklace. Her kohl eyeliner makes Nefertiti's look Spartan. High stiletto heels look like they are part of her feet. I know there is no way she could walk in them without having had cosmetic foot surgery.

Ruby gives me a withering look. "I'm so sorry," she murmurs in a voice that would make onions cry. "You've caught us on an extremely busy day. Everyone here is going to the Mars Malt gala. Besides, we don't have any plus-size robes. Now excuse me. I see one of my regular customers." She turns to greet Solaria, who has just opened the door.

"Solaria!" Ruby exclaims, arms outstretched. "Right on time." She takes Solaria's coat and hands it to an attendant who has rushed to her side. Her eyes glare at me over Solaria's shoulder. I hear, "Any last-minutes tickets to the Mars Malt gala, darling? All my clients will be there."

"Sorry, Ruby. All booked." Ruby's face drops.

Solaria looks at me standing next to the desk.

"Pay no attention to her," Ruby coos. "*She* is about to leave."

"Leave? She looks like she's waiting for you to let her in."

At that moment the red door opens and CC, whose complexion is filled with blotches, hair matted to her head and clearly needing all the beauty money can buy, enters. Solaria and Ruby, who know who she is, greet her.

"Right on time," Ruby tells CC. "We can't keep Colorful Copies of Mars Media waiting."

"Thanks for the last-minute appointment, Ruby. So many preparations for the Mars Malt gala. Even the smallest moon wants coverage."

Solaria looks in my direction again, tilts her head, and smiles. "Aren't you forgetting someone, Ruby?"

Ruby glares.

Solaria turns to me. "Aren't you the mother of those beautiful twins, the Lunar Tunes, who are performing at the Mars Malt gala? Wasn't a picture of you, your husband, and daughters on the cover of *Stardust* magazine?"

"That's right," I answer.

All eyes leave the little screens and look at me.

"I knew I recognized you."

Ruby's jaw drops like a high school guidance counselor who finds that a student she tracked to Rockpit Community College got a scholarship to Harvard.

"You have the most beautiful complexion, Mrs. Summers," Solaria says, savoring her zing at Ruby's snobbishness. "Doesn't she deserve a complimentary calobox treatment and two large boxes of your famous Polar Dust for her talented daughters?"

I brighten, raise one eyebrow, and look at Ruby. "*She* just told me there were no large robes."

"Get me one of your deluxe soft silver sheets, Ruby. I'll personally wrap Mrs. Summers in a toga."

Solaria fashions me a Roman-looking toga. She wraps my head in a matching towel creating a stylish looking turban.

CC watches. "I know you. We met at Nirgal Palace. You looked familiar there and you look even more familiar here. What was your name again?"

"Molly Summers."

"That doesn't ring a bell. What's your maiden name?"

"Molly Marbles," I mumble.

"Aah!" CC yelps. "From Armstrong University. You're Drew's old girlfriend. I knew I knew you. How come you never said anything? Didn't you recognize me? Does he know you're here?"

"Yes to the first question; no to the second. I saw no point in opening up the past."

Ruby starts to open the pink door. A client approaches her. "You really should develop a line of togas and turbans called 'The Molly' for your boutique."

Ruby, who won't look me in the eye but doesn't miss a beat, says, "Already on order. How many would you like?"

Once inside, Solaria and CC are given navy blue robes with white collars that are adapted from one worn by Elizabeth of Queens when she went shopping at Parliaments in Manhattan to buy a truss for her hernia. Then three attendants—one with red hair, one with brown hair, and one with blond hair—lead us in three different directions for our individualized procedures.

I am led by the red-haired attendant to my first procedure: foot reflexology. "We believe in starting at the bottom and working our way up. The hairstyle is the last thing we do," she says. "Would you like some vanilla water with a vanilla bean in it?"

I think of Jersey, because it is the only thing I ever ate or drank in her house. "Yes, thanks. Vanilla beans are my one of my favorite snacks," I say facetiously but sounding sincere.

"Then I'll put two beans in it," she chimes.

One client, slightly heavier than the rest, who sits alone, comes over and whispers "Have you ever heard of Rose's Spa?"

"Yes, when I was waiting in the lobby. What is it?"

"It's a gravity-free spa and a retirement community in space for people who love to eat. Some call it Rose's Heaven." I make a mental note.

My foot treatment makes me feel like I am walking on air. Now I'm starved. I look for a table. Then I hear, "Yoo-hoo, Molly! Over here!" in Flo's familiar twang.

Flo sits on a puffy pink cushion, her long twiggy legs with painted golden toenails curled under her. I walk past women drinking water and swallowing pills. "I'm surprised that Ruby let you in. She doesn't let anyone in who's overweight." I sit.

"Well, Solaria Andreas, sponsor of the Mars Malt gala, rescued me. She saw my picture on the cover of *Stardust* magazine. She insisted Ruby let me in."

"That must have gone over big. Ruby is the biggest snob on Mars."

I remove an egg-and-anchovy sandwich on a thick slice of ciabatta bread from my bag and take a bite.

Eyes wide with horror turn in my direction. I take a tiny bite, chew and swallow. One client puts her hand to her forehead and requests smelling salts. I turn away and take a few more bites.

"Did you know that I was at the Andreas mansion yesterday to make sure the food for the Mars Malt gala would be up to code?" says Flo.

"No, I didn't know."

"Solaria called Tasters and Spitters and they sent me. What a menu! It was nonstop spitting. That's why I needed to come to Ruby's. I'm so exhausted I can hardly open my mouth."

An attendant with pea-green hair looking like one limp over-cooked strand of linguini approaches and looks down at me. "Ruby provides lunch. You didn't have to bring..." She pauses and points a bony finger. "...whatever that is." She walks away.

I turn to Flo. "Why are so many Martians obsessed with being so thin?"

"Thin? I don't think I'm thin. Slender maybe. Lean, lanky, stylish. You must mean 'evolved.' No one here is thin. Only people from Earth or Earth's moon think Martians are thin. Earth's moon is the armpit of the solar system, a ball of floating cellulite. It should be liposuctioned out of the sky!"

I restrain a wince, because I will not give Flo any satisfaction.

"How did Martians' attitudes toward dieting begin? We're all from the same stock."

"I guess it started when Mars became independent from Earth and began competing with it. Because of Mars's lighter gravity, we are taller and thinner than Earthlings, and we were winning all the solar-system beauty contests. Our grandparents born on Earth wanted us to keep our edge. They were always dieting and always complaining about dieting."

"I know how they feel," I say, remembering taunts of "Molly Marbles, round as a marble, fat as a moon."

"When Freedom Plan foods were developed, people thought the problem had been solved. But for many, the plan wasn't restrictive enough. People dieted even though they ate Freedom Plan foods. Many rebelled. There were riots. The Capitol was covered in corned beef that was not lean."

"Not lean? Even I know that's bad!"

"People traded calories on the black market. There were illegal trans-fat and triglyceride parties. People binged on junk food. Children threw bagels at schools and cream-cheesed all the windows. It was food anarchy! Times were desperate."

I adjust my toga to cover my Doric column–looking legs.

"About thirty years ago, Dr. Habeas told Dr. Corpus that he had discovered a way to reduce the sense of taste and reduce food cravings. They said taste was the lowest of the five senses and reducing it would enhance the four 'higher' ones. No one waited for studies to be done. Everyone wanted freedom from diet slavery. Everyone here at the spa has been genetically altered except you and that other off-planet person, Colorful Copies."

Just as she says *Colorful Copies*, CC, who is in a cubicle on the other side of the spa, screams. "You people are incompetent! I'm going to sue!"

"What happened?" I shout.

"Her rainbow-colored eyebrows just came off in a facial. No problem. Ruby has experts that have fixed far worse," says a passing attendant.

Then Flo points to the tallest and thinnest woman who sits reading *The Chronicles of Narcissism, Volume One: The Wardrobe.*

"Who is she?" I ask.

"Winner of last year's Miss Skin and Bones award. Isn't she beautiful?"

"Everyone at the Culinary would think she needs a doctor."

"Shhh," she whispers.

"What's the problem? The Culinary serves salads."

"Yes, but just thinking about salad dressing makes my esophagus curl."

I finish my sandwich and hand the empty wrapper to the attendant, who wears latex gloves.

She holds it between two extended fingers and says in obvious pain, "I can't believe you ate the whole thing."

I turn to Flo. "With everyone wanting to be super thin, the supplement businesses must have sent your economy flying."

"My father owns the Sirloin Steak Supplement Co. He believes it's only a matter of time before we evolve further away from our animal beginnings."

"Is that a fact? Well, I think I would rather be an animal than a vegetable or a mineral."

I take a slice of strawberry shortcake from my bag and scoop some whipped cream into my mouth. Flo's jaw drops. "Are you eating face cream?"

"Face cream? It's whipped cream. This is strawberry shortcake."

"Doesn't look short to me. I had a strawberry once. But cake is not permitted."

"No cake? You had birthday cake when you were growing up, didn't you?"

"A large egg-white omelet with candles on top. Except for potatoes I was allowed to choose my own vegetable toppings because it was a special occasion."

I have no words. This is the longest conversation I have ever had with Flo. I understand her a lot better, and my feelings toward her soften. She's really not such a bad egg white.

Eventually I emerge from Ruby's Spa. And I do look great. In fact, better than I have in my life. My skin glows, my hair bounces, and I have two boxes of Polar Dust for the twins. I also have a month's supply of supplements. And since I won't be eating them, I now have the perfect gift for Jersey and Trenton.

## 29

CC WITH NEWLY REFURBISHED EYEBROWS arrives for the Mars Malt gala. Katie Racket, Barbara and Lourdes Bottled Waters, Sensuous Signals of Venus and the Ringling brothers from Saturn Satellites follow. Workmen make last-minute adjustments. Solaria's catering firm delivers enough food to feed Jupiter.

Neils Bohr and the Bohrs are ten minutes early. They are dressed in black and carry black boxes filled with relics and documents, including those left by real estate agents dating from the time of Noah that said after a slight drizzle new beachfront property would become available.

They are followed by Max Plank and the Planks, looking like a marching band of paraphernalia. They were not in a good mood because they had to scrub their opening act with guest performer Marion Brando, the famous transvestite from Venus who does the famous yell for his/her lost poodle, "Stella," because someone forgot to pack his/her desired prop, a streetcar.

Cortland and I arrive with Becky, Lois, Flo, and Billings. Billings, who is not a music lover and can hardly believe the girls have gotten this far, is bug-eyed about being in the Andreas mansion. He embarrasses everyone by dropping cards like Hansel and Gretel's bread crumbs that say "Little Green Men Pizza." He says he's doing it so we can find our way out.

Cortland carries a small green cube containing sound tracks. Flo and I direct two antigravity cases that float next to us brimming with makeup and accessories. Becky and Lois each carry a carefully wrapped gown. Finally we find a sign that points us toward the dressing rooms. We are all relieved to see that the backdrop for the performance, a floor-to-ceiling holograph of Monet's *Water Lilies* superimposed on a painting of Earth's full silver moon, has been perfectly installed.

Neils and Max stand like taut rubber bands ready to twang. "Here comes vacant lowbrow commercialism," Neils smirks crossing his arms and giving the twins the once over. "No edge. Unresolved earwax."

Max puts his hand to his mouth and yawns. "Two blond poems on the interconnectedness of mass and void. Do you think they can sing?"

Neils rolls his eyes. "Not relevant; their work has nothing to do with serious avant-garde art and its politics like ours. All they do is pander to melody."

"Melody? It's the lowest common denominator. Pure ear candy. Our work has higher aspirations. We use the musical scale as a metaphor for man's rise and fall, filled with sound and fury signifying the illusion of everything aimed at the easily intimidated. They aim for the top ten on the hit parade. Serious art critics who are read by important collectors and museum curators are not concerned with the sentimental and melodramatic. They go for the pretentious not the popular."

Neils puffs out his chest. "Well then, we should be a shoe in, we've got plenty of pretention. But they are pretty. Maybe even beautiful."

Max puts his hand to his throat and gags. "Did you just say the *B* word? I can't believe you actually said the *B* word. *Beautiful* has nothing to do with serious art.

"Right! What was I thinking? The judges at the Venus Biennale better not learn we're sharing a stage with them. If they knew we came for the money and record contracts, we would be lucky if we got a gig with Ayn Rand's band. In this context, winning could be as bad as losing."

That evening the guests enter the ballroom. Heels click on a clear plexi-bridge suspended over a pool filled with darting lighted robotic sea creatures and women with flowing hair in topless mermaid costumes. Everyone becomes everyone's best friend for fifteen seconds.

Planetarium Jewelers, "the jewelers to the stars," lent Solaria an emerald necklace that matches her dress, a flowing pale green chiffon gown that shifts with her body. Her blond hair is swept up, with one piece dangling down her back.

She greets Drew and Kandy and leads them to a front table. Sandy would have preferred that Drew sit in the back with the rest of his staff, but he doesn't object, because Kandy, a former Miss Universe, is sitting where everyone can see her. Craig arrives and is seated on the other side of Kandy.

Solaria's parents, Salami and Lasagna Pastrami, are at the head table with other family members.

Sandy sits with the ambassador from Earth, Pontius Nimbus. His wife, Vaporous Nimbus, is seated to his left. Her nude-colored dress matches her skin tone so well, it's hard to see where the fabric ends and her skin begins.

Across the table is Venus's ambassador, who invited Sandy and Solaria to Venus last year because of Sandy's success with the solar clock. Solaria was ecstatic because she got to stay at the embassy's guesthouse and not the Hotel de Milo, where she had once slipped in the hotel's theater before a performance of the *Merchant of Venus* when someone yelled "Break an arm!" and she did.

The meal begins. Everyone gets an amuse-bouche of a warm oyster with hazelnuts and sherry butter on a slice of brioche. The soup is a clear broth with a generous portion of *fois gras* and a large truffle in its center. Sandy turns to Ambassador Nimbus. "Solaria got the chef from Mars's best restaurant, Argon Forty, to make dinner. Critic Sagging Guts gave Argon Forty five mushroom clouds."

Vaporous Nimbus chirps, "Ooh, mushroom clouds! I love mushroom clouds." This gives everyone a chance to stare at her hanging out of her dress.

This is followed by tortellini of skate and crab with lemongrass and crab voluté and a salad of baby bib lettuce with thin crisps of macadamia-nut flatbread. There are "oohs" and "ahhs" when the main course, whole roasted boned duck resting in a broth smelling of smoked hickory, mesquite and cherry wood arrives.

The dessert, a dark chocolate beer mug with "Mars Malt: 200 Years" in white chocolate printed on the side, is filled with a tangy mousse made from Mars Malt's version of Kriek, a sweet cherry beer. Finally the lights dim; a drum rolls and the orchestra plays "Hail to the Chief." An enormous tiered cake with two hundred candles is placed next to Solaria's father, who rises. Everyone sings "Happy birthday, Salami Pastrami." He rises, clutches his napkin, tearfully thanks everyone, blows kisses, and sits.

The lights dim again. The room quiets. A spotlight shines on the MC for the evening, Jamie Faxx. "Welcome, ladies and gentlemen. And now the moment you've all been waiting for." He puts his hand to the side of his mouth and booms, "Heeeeeeeere's Max!"

Max, bathed in purple light, in a croaky battered voice accompanied by sounds from fuzz-toned instruments, sings "Dead No More." Holos of dead animals float around the room like icebergs circling the *Titanic*. People close their eyes because their rocking motion, after such a rich meal, makes them queasy.

When the band members chant "Art, mart, fart," turn their backs to the audience, and let out an unfortunate sound, everyone groans except Ambassador Gingivitis, from Jupiter's moon Io, the only true art lover in the audience, who—being from a world that is nothing but a floating rock, and trying to promote it as a sculpture center— insists it's an offstage bagpipe.

Sandy, who can't stand it anymore, gets up and corners Solaria. He grabs her arm so hard, it leaves fingerprints. "This had better get better!"

Jamie Faxx says, "Fresh from this year's Documenta on Jupiter's moon Calisto, let's hear it for Neils and the Bohrs, who'll perform 'It's More Blessed to Receive than to Give.'"

Women rise and join a ladies'-room line that looks like it began a nanosecond after Eve left the Garden of Eden.

Solaria's assistants bring earplugs and eye masks and distribute them before Niels's finale, "I Ain't Got No Persecution."

Cortland and I are bathed in nervous sweat. Flo and Billings are twisting their napkins. We fear that by the time Becky and Lois perform, the audience wouldn't know the difference between their performance and a kindergarten class singing "The Itsy Bitsy Spider."

Jamie Faxx manages a clever monologue that coaxes people to their seats.

The room dims and quiets.

The twins, dressed in their sparkling gowns, are slowly lowered to the stage on a beam of light. Holographs of Mars's moons, Deimos and Phobos, circle them like angels then move and circle the audience. Harmonic sounds sooth tired ears. Their lyrics contain the word *love* 348 times. They smile and flirt. They blow kisses. By the time they end with the hyperkinetic beat of "Moon Rover," the audience (including high school guidance counselors) can't contain themselves and jump to their feet, twisting and shouting, "Let the good times roll!"

"My IQ just went into a free fall," Max says to Niels. "An intellectual travesty."

It takes a while for the audience to quiet, but it doesn't take long for the audience to press a button on the arms of their chairs that signals a vote. A few moments later, Jamie Faxx teases, pauses, and with a full academy flourish announces, "And the winners are…" Drumroll. "The Lunar Tunes!"

Becky and Lois scream and jump.

"Come up here, twins," Jamie cries. The band plays excerpts from "Moon Rover" as the girls climb to the stage. Jamie put his arms around Becky and Lois and kisses them on the cheeks. "Let's hear it for the Lunar Tunes!"

The audience leaps, claps, cheers, stomps. It's a long snapshot moment.

Jamie hands Becky the microphone. "I want to thank my parents and family for making this day happen, and all the boys at King Tut School of Music for letting us rehearse in their locker room." She hands the microphone to Lois.

And Lois says the words parents wait their entire lives to hear, if ever, "Mom and Dad, you were right! All the hard work was worth it!"

"Stand up, Mr. and Mrs. Summers, and take a bow," Jamie says. The spotlight finds Cortland and me. Teary-eyed, we stand and wave.

Drew moves his chair and cranes to get a better view. He drops his glass. "Oh my God, Molly!"

Everyone at the table says, "Who's Molly?"

"We were students at Armstrong University on the Moon. I almost married her. I haven't seen her in more than twenty years."

The room empties. Becky and Lois thread their way through the crowd, signing autographs. "I love their gowns," says Velveeta Kraftchick, the mayor of New Chicago, to Flo, who is standing next to them. "You must be their mother." Flo points to me, and I wave back.

"Amazing," Velveeta says, narrowing her eyes—a sure sign she is calculating my weight.

Then I feel a tap on my shoulder and hear. "When was the last time you heard 'When the moon hits your eye like a big pizza pie'?" I turn to the voice I remember so well.

"Hi, Molly," Drew says, smiling broadly. "Long time no see. You haven't changed a bit."

I feel myself blush. "Well, you have," I say. "You look wonderful."

Drew lowers his voice. "Takes lots of time and even more money to stay this way. I still love food, but Chocolate Moons, or should I say," he looks deeply into my eyes and whispers, "Chocolate *Chocolate* Moons, are my only indulgence. Freedom Plan ones taste—"

"I know, a little gritty."

We laugh.

Kandy pushes through the crowd and finds us. Drew puts his arm around her shoulder. "This is my girlfriend, Kandy Kane. We're having a party and would love you and your husband to come with the twins. Don't worry; I won't serve any onion rings or green cheese. What do you say?"

My heart skips a beat and I smile. But only for a moment.

CC, who had been circling the room with her cameraman, stops next to us and chimes, "Am I invited too?"

# 30

CRAIG CASHEW CROUCHES IN A corner, hidden behind a mountain of fries and burgers at McMooner, a fast-food shop located as far away from the Culinary Institute as possible. When he sees Breezy and Pluto enter, he rises and waves. They sit and eye the food. "I don't know how anyone can eat this stuff," he sneers pushing the food toward them.

Breezy swirls a few fries in blood-red ketchup, puts them in her mouth, and deliberately makes loud chewing sounds. She glares at Craig suspiciously because she knows he must want something; otherwise, why won't he just give them the remote.

Craig removes the device from his pocket and puts it on the table. "If this is what I think it is, it could link the two of you to the case of the Chocolate Moons. You were both seen on the security holo near one of the chocolate vats." He turns to Pluto. "And you were seen with your arm raised when an alarm sounded." Craig slides the remote back into his pocket.

Pluto stiffens. "Thanks for not going to the police. How much do you want for it?"

"I don't want money. Rocket is blackmailing me with something that happened when our paths crossed in college long ago. Nothing for you to be concerned about."

"You and Rocket went to the same school?" Pluto says finding it impossible to imagine.

Craig continues, "Rocket has an apartment on Titan. There's a transport to Titan, where I'm opening a Culinary satellite. Rocket was always a health-food nut. Back then he actually smoked multivitamins."

"Still does," Pluto quips.

"I heard that he was in the hospital recently because he overdosed on health-food supplements. His system may be very fragile." Craig looks at Breezy. "Your father is a very creative scientist."

"So?" Breezy says wondering what Craig is after.

"So, I'm in a jam with Rocket. And you are in a jam with me, because I won't give back the remote unless you help me do something about Rocket. Maybe your father would consider giving Rocket a little something that could alter how he saw his options. The outcome may help all of us to resolve our problems."

Breezy looks at Craig and stays quiet for a long time. Then she takes another fry and swirls it in more ketchup and says, "I guess I could ask him." She lowers her eyes chews for a long time and swallows.

"Do more than guess," Craig says rising from the table.

Breezy says nothing. Then she points to the food. "Mind if we take the rest of this stuff out?"

Craig sits at his desk eating lunch. He's adding some wasabi mayonnaise to a lobster-salad sandwich when his secretary says, "Decibel Point on line one."

"Let me get straight to the point. You have something my daughter, Breezy, owns and wants back," Decibel says quickly. "Breezy and Pluto are in a difficult situation with you, and I want to help them."

"I'm listening."

"Breezy knows I've had issues with Rocket in the past that I want resolved."

"Welcome to the club."

"I also want to confront Rocket about a nagging feeling that I have had about the poisoning of the Chocolate Moons. I was in the process of testing some anti-flavonoids at Congress Drugs. Next thing I know, someone took a sample of the stuff and people are getting poisoned all over the planet. I have a feeling Rocket may have something to do with this."

Craig slides his plate away with the back of his hand. "What does this have to do with me?"

"Breezy told me that Rocket tried to blackmail you with something that happened a long time ago."

"That's true."

"I understand that Rocket takes the transport to Titan, where he has an apartment and where you are opening a Culinary satellite. Rocket has been after me to work at a lab he just bought on Titan. I want to check it out."

Craig dabs his mouth with a beige linen napkin. "So you are saying that we all have good legitimate reasons to take the Mars–Titan transport. And, we all have good reasons to confront Rocket."

"Right. Seeing us together may unnerve him and make him more receptive to what we have to say. It's not hard for us to book a trip to Titan when Rocket will be on board and not hard to get a passenger list. Breezy can travel as my assistant. Her boyfriend, Pluto, can fit her with one of his disguises. Rocket shouldn't be hard to find. He's bound to show up at their duty-free health-food store."

"And if Rocket is not so receptive?" Craig asks.

"As you told Breezy, maybe I could give him something that would make him more receptive. Nothing long lasting, mind you, just something that would change his perceptions of reality."

"It's as good an idea as any," Craig says, pushing his empty plate farther away.

"Then we're united. Let's fly the friendly skies."

Trenton sits in Lamont's office, going over reports. "Did you know that Molly Summers is the mother of the Lunar Tunes, the beautiful twins who won the Mars Malt music contest?"

Lamont's eyebrows rise. "Molly Summers, that large woman who brings me all that food? Hmm. They must take after her husband."

"She also used to date Drew Barron when they were in college. He has invited her and her family to a party at his apartment."

"Dated Drew Barron in college? You're kidding! What a break! See that she's fitted for an eye cam before she goes."

A week before Drew's party, the twins have publicity shots taken. Becky and Lois look so sophisticated, having taken Flo's suggestion of coloring their bodies the way they did when we arrived—two different colors that meet in the center of their bodies—but instead of using harsh, bright colors they used soft pastels. Cortland and I can't believe they are our formerly gum-cracking, hair-twirling, nail-picking, eye-rolling children.

I drive everyone crazy deciding what to wear. Finally I settle on a black suit with thin vertical silver stripes and silver-and-black open-toed sandals. Flo lets me borrow her expensive watch that beeps the minute food touches her lips. I pin it to my suit, where everyone can see its jewels, and turn off the alarm.

A limo brings us to Drew's building. The driver gets out and opens the door. The doorman peeks in. "And you are?" he says in a manner trained to intimidate everyone but other doormen.

"The Lunar Tunes and their family," Cortland replies.

Becky and Lois extend long legs.

The doorman springs to attention. "The Lunar Tunes! My daughter loves your music. Can I get your autographs?"

Becky and Lois sign with a flourish. "I can't believe this," Lois giggles.

Cortland and I nod and smile.

An elevator attendant, who can't stop staring at the twins, takes us to the tower floor.

Drew and Kandy open the door and introduce us to their guests, who ignore me but circle the girls and smile at Cortland. Champagne glasses clink; small scallops encrusted in crunchy candied nori and water chestnuts wrapped in whiskey-smoked bacon are passed around.

A few moments later, an overly made-up CC in a skintight metallic snakeskin dress arrives. People make flattering remarks about her and how they love to watch Mars Media ever since her father acquired it. When she finally pulls away and starts circling the room, I approach.

"Could you ever imagine this?" I say to CC. "I mean, being here together with Drew."

"No, never."

"Just goes to show you, time heals all wounds."

CC gives me a long cold stare.

"Mind if I ask you a few questions?"

CC leans toward me conspiratorially and says, "About old times, right?"

"No, about your visit to Congress Drugs and San Andreas Farms."

"Oh, that. It was several weeks ago. Did you see me on Nova Scotia's program?"

"I did. Ever find the charm from your bracelet?"

CC holds up her arm. "Good as new. Daddy replaced my lost one."

"What's Decibel Point like? You said you met him at Congress Drugs. I've heard that he's a brilliant scientist."

"Well, he's very fat, which is amazing since he created those Freedom Plan foods."

"Do you think he's right when he said Congress Drugs should test its products more thoroughly?"

"Sounds like a good idea, but I know nothing about that." She starts to pull away.

"One last question. Did you spend a lot of time on San Andreas Farms?"

"Yes. After I left Congress Drugs, I was given a tour of the farms and then I had the afternoon to wander. It is amazing how those chocolate nibs are ground before they send them to the Candy Universe."

Drew, seeing us talking together walks over. "You two thinking about poisoning my drink?"

"Too late for that," CC laughs. She puts her hand on his arm and walks away with him while I head toward the ladies' room.

I enter the bathroom, lock the door, and palm Jersey and Trenton.

"You should see this place. It could be on the cover of *Architectural Indigestion*."

"Take any shots?" Trenton asks.

"Everyone is making a big fuss over the sculpture of a scrawny person and ignoring the beautiful marble table that it sits on. If the sculpture were a Niki de Saint Phalle's colorful fat Nana or a plus-size creation by Fernando Botero, I could understand the fuss, but the Giacometti…Come on! It's a stick figure, totally anorexic. Anyway, I took a picture of it. I also snapped shots of the buffet."

"We don't need any shots of the buffet," Jersey snaps.

"Too late. I already clicked. There are also the latest supplements sitting in a glass bowl. I put some in my bag for you."

"Hmm."

"I spoke to CC and recorded the conversation. But she didn't reveal much that was new. She did spend much more time than I thought at San Andreas Farms after being inside Congress Drugs, and she admitted to being near the area where they grind the chocolate nibs. Kandy is wearing a gorgeous necklace. Becky told me it was blue-ice sapphires, very rare and expensive. Someone is knocking on the bathroom door. Gotta go—I mean, gotta *leave*—now."

Chairs are set up in the wood-paneled den off the living room, with a small raised platform in front. Becky and Lois sing while Cortland accompanies them on the pianolyn.

"You must be so proud of the twins," Drew says, looking at me with affection. "I guess the old saying is true: the moon doesn't fall too far from the planet." I blush and turn away.

"Come back and see us sometime," Kandy says at the end of the night, giving the twins a hug. She turns to Drew and murmurs, "Wouldn't it be nice to have children?"

Drew says nothing. But Kandy already knows his answer and says no more.

## 31

CRAIG CASHEW ANNOUNCES THAT HE and an advisory team will go to Titan to begin the process that opens Culinary Titan. Sandy Andreas and some associates will join them to plan the gardens.

Jersey and I are chosen as security-team advisors.

Jersey is overjoyed because her sister, Asbury, lives on Titan. Her niece, Meadowlands, is getting married and the Culinary will pay for transportation. Best of all, Trenton can travel free as luggage in his carrying case.

But Trenton doesn't want to go.

Jersey makes him his favorite silicone milkshake. "Please, Trenton," she pleads. "Asbury is my only family, and I never see her. Besides, we haven't been off this planet in ages. I even have the perfect wedding gift."

"How much?" Trenton asks with eyes spinning like wheels of fortune.

"My sister tells me Meadowlands and her fiancé love pets and surprises."

"How much?"

"We could give them the Schrödinger Box we got as a wedding present. They'll never know it was used. It's always a surprise when you open it. It will cost us nothing, except for buying a new cat to put inside."

"Well, as long as you put it that way. But don't you think a box that was created to demonstrate how the uncertainty principle of quantum mechanics works is too esoteric to give as a wedding present? Marriage is uncertain enough. Forget the box. Just give them a cat."

When I tell Cortland about my upcoming trip to Titan, he decides to stay home and rehearse with the twins, who are swamped with performing engagements.

Jersey and I wait for the space elevator. Jersey's hand clutches the case where Trenton lies folded like a sheet in a drawer. We scan single round-trip tickets to Titan and enter the elevator.

The elevator rises quickly. At midpoint buzzers blare, announcing a storm. "Rock-a-Bye Baby," the music programmed into the sound system to ease tensions, makes everyone feel worse. We finally weave off and join a long serpentine check-in line at the transport's docking station.

A porter approaches and turns to Jersey. "Want me to help you with that case?" He stretches out his arm.

"I'm fine," Jersey says smiling but her stomach knots. She draws the case closer.

"I see you're very nervous about having Trenton in the carrying case. Is it really worth the worry? Why don't you just get two tickets?" I ask.

"Get two tickets when we can travel two for the price of one?" Jersey pats the case. "I don't think so."

Farther up the line a thin man in a shocking pink suit shifts from side to side. I nudge Jersey and point. "I think that man is Rocket Packarod. See that turquoise tote slung over his shoulder? It says AK-47 Vitamin and Mineral Company: Protection for your digestion."

"Definitely Rocket," she says.

Suddenly from behind we hear a booming voice. "What do you mean you lost my reservation? Do you know who I am? I know the president of your company. Want me to call him?" After a short delay, Sandy Andreas, wearing a dark suit and chunky gold jewelry, marches past us and goes to the head of the line.

I find my room on the transport. It is down the hall from Jersey's. They are identical. Both have a small window, a comfortable bed, a media wall, bathroom and dining alcove.

Jersey wheels Trenton's case to their room. She taps a corner twice. It opens. Trenton raises his head slowly. Heat from the case's walls make tiny tubes in his limbs fill with gelatinous substances. Jersey unpacks and puts on a pink flowered robe while Trenton finishes his process.

Trenton steps out and stretches. Jersey says, "Here, sweetheart, let me give you a good spray with the new and improved WD-40,000." He bends and twists. She puts the can down, goes to the console, and clicks "Passenger-List Information."

"Craig Cashew, Sandy Andreas, and Rocket Packarod are all on board."

"So are nine hundred and ninety-eight other passengers," Trenton says, sitting on the side of the bed checking his toes.

"Craig's and Sandy's cabins are on the upper deck. Rocket's cabin is on our deck but on the opposite side. There's also a D. Point and B. Point traveling together. Could it be Decibel Point and Breezy Point?"

Trenton rubs a lubricant into his feet. "Could be."

"I'll palm Molly and see what she wants to do about dinner."

"I'm exhausted, Jersey," I say when she calls. "I'm going to order something from room service. Their take out menu is encyclopedic. By the way, is your shower as small as mine?"

"I didn't think it was small. I have plenty of room. As a matter of fact, Trenton and I can both fit inside. See you in the morning."

Jersey goes into the dining alcove and reads the menu aloud. "How about sliced sturgeon with saffron, lemon, and fennel, or lobster-and-rock-shrimp ravioli with a white-wine-and-pesto sauce or grilled boned Cornish hen in a blood-orange rum sauce, or leg of lamb studded with black garlic with fresh asparagus? Tonight's special is osso bucco."

"Not interested," Trenton says.

"There's Venusian veal with celery-root puree, porterhouse steak with sautéed Uranium mushrooms in a champagne sauce, and grilled halibut surrounded by miniature baked potatoes stuffed with crème fraîche and red caviar."

"Too boring."

"Their featured dessert is a seven-layer cannoli cheesecake with espresso sorbet followed by dark chocolate truffles and candied fruits. They also have grapefruit and pomegranate sorbet served with thin lacy green-tea butter cookies. Anything tempt you, Trenton?"

"No, not really. What else have they got?"

"A plate of shredded iceberg lettuce, a package of Freedom Plan dried pecans with butterscotch supplements on the side, and Cassini Huygens cocktails."

"Now that sounds delicious. Order that. Makes me feel like we're on a vacation."

The next morning, the first thing everyone sees is that their holo screens are blinking a message. Trenton pushes "Play." A voice says, "Welcome, travelers!"

"This must be important," Trenton says, "because we can understand the words and I don't have to translate it from Garble."

"Also," Jersey says, "you can read the words on the bottom of the screen as they are spoken."

"A minor technicality."

The voice repeats, "Welcome, travelers! Before midnight the transport will pass through one of the relatively empty regions in the asteroid belt known as the Kirkwood Gap. And because Jupiter is so large and has so much gravity, it sometimes accelerates objects floating in this gap into orbits different from the one the ship's computer predicts. We do not anticipate being hit. But you should know that the green cubes that line every hall and are in every room closet contain protective suits good for three days of life support. Each stateroom has its own power source and two weeks' worth of supplies. At the first sign of trouble, your room seals and becomes a lifeboat. You can call our toll-free number just in case. Thank you, and good luck."

"Just in case of what?" Jersey opens a closet and finds several protective suits. "Let's leave this door open."

I catch up with Jersey and Trenton at night. They're in their room finishing leftovers from last night's meal. No one can stretch lettuce like Trenton and Jersey.

"Why anyone eats chips and dips when they can crunch on fresh lettuce is a mystery to me," Trenton says. "Want a bite?"

"No thanks. How about going out for a drink?"

We stroll through a series of malls looking for a cocktail lounge. Jersey and I walk slowly looking in shop windows.

Trenton grabs our hands and yanks us away. "You can shop later," he says, spotting a dark, noisy bar called the Purple Tree Lounge.

32

CRAIG CASHEW BOARDS THE MARS–TITAN transport and finds his room. He unpacks, kicks off his shoes, lies down on his bed, and waits for Decibel and Breezy, who share a two room-suite on the deck below.

Breezy dons a brown wig, takes a skin-color-change pill, inserts hazel contact lenses, sprites herself with Menthe perfume, and slips into a tight low–cut, red dress. She and Decibel take an elevator to the floor above, find Craig's room, and press a buzzer.

Breezy stands in the doorway and looks at Craig. She puts one hand on her hip and twirls around. "If Rocket doesn't pay any attention to me in this, there is something wrong with him."

Craig gives a low whistle.

"We need to review our plans," Decibel says, entering and plopping down in the middle of the sofa. "Breezy is going to find Rocket, who will most likely be at Hogwarts Health Foods and…um…um…"

"The word you are looking for, Dad, is *seduce*," Breezy says.

Decibel looks at Breezy. "But only to lure Rocket back to his room so we can talk to him. We don't want to hurt him. We only want to make him think that we might. We'll wait near his room, and when Breezy and he show up we'll invite ourselves inside."

Breezy goes to Hogwarts Health Foods on Shopping Deck 6 and waits. After an hour of pretending to read labels, Rocket appears, wearing an open orange shirt and black trousers. His hair is damp and slicked behind his ears like he's coming from a shower. He glances at Breezy and walks past her, his eyes focused on the herbal-tea section. Breezy follows him. She slides herself between Rocket and the teas.

"Ooh, rose hips, my favorite," she sighs, patting her hips. "That one has a warning about extra valerian. Nothing like living dangerously. Do you take yours straight or…" She lowers her voice. "…do you add a little St. John's wort?" She turns and bends, reaching for the St. John's wort and pushing her tight ass against him. She rises and turns making sure Rocket sees her bat her eyelashes. Then she slowly slides her hand up and down over the bottle and licks her lips.

"Actually, I love it with bladder wrack and a touch of yerba maté," Rocket says, now torn between Breezy and the new line of yerba maté.

Breezy sees his eyes shift away and cries in a breathy voice, "Yerba maté! Yerba maté! Why didn't I think of that? I love yerba maté. You seem to know so much about health food. I would love to be shown your etchings of health foods." She reaches into her bag and pulls out a pair of licorice handcuffs and dangles them in front of him. "You never know who you'll meet on transports, so I always carry my own licorice handcuffs. They're 100 percent organic!"

"Do you like supplements?" asks Rocket. "I can get every kind wholesale."

"*Supplements* is my middle name. I was raised on supplements. I live on supplements. Life without supplements is a life not worth living." Breezy runs her hand over her breasts. "How do you think I keep my figure?" She picks up a bottle of uterine tonic and strokes it. Her tongue circles her lips. "What a sexy-looking bottle. Ooh! Ooh! There's a bottle of kava kava. Do you think I should buy the uterine tonic or the kava kava?" She puts one on each breast. "I need help making up my mind."

"Personally, I would buy the kombucha so we could do the babushka," Rocket says, finally turning from his passion for health foods to a passion for Breezy. Breezy, who substituted yesterday's Menthe perfume for today's good sprinkling of Brewer's Yeast, leans close to Rocket.

Rocket recognizes the smell and swoons over its distinctive vitamin B aroma, an aroma that resembles school-cafeteria Parmesan cheese that kids call "vomit cheese."

Rocket puts his arm around Breezy and gives her a little squeeze. "I know a great little place called the Purple Tree Lounge. Meet me there at nine. We can celebrate our love of health foods with a Buffered Paregoric Sour or a Newman's Own Omega-3 Fish Fins."

Trenton pushes the door to the Purple Tree Lounge, a pickpocket kind of place: dark, crowded, noisy. "Good thing I'm wearing my high beams," Jersey says blinking her eyes and tilting her head.

I grab Trenton's other arm tightly. "Think we'll get a table?"

We push through the crowd. Trenton bumps into to a woman whose dress is held by one thin strap. She holds her pinky up and away from the rest of her fingers, which are curled around the tall stem of a glass, to balance it, and I see a small rose tattoo on the pinky. "Excuse me," he says.

"Watch where you're goin', junk man, you almost made me spill my drink."

"I would have bought you another if that happened. Sorry."

The woman turns abruptly and walks in the direction of the bar on the other side of the room. We see her take a seat next to a man in a bright cerulean-blue-striped jacket with his back to us. It crosses my mind that it might be Rocket.

We look for a table, but the only one available is one near them. We grab it. The woman sees us out of the corner of her eye and swivels away on her stool. We pick at some nuts and wave frantically at the waiter, who finally sees us and brings us our drinks.

"Listen, they're playing 'Moon Rover' with Becky and Lois," I say. We raise our glasses and clink to the twins.

The woman Trenton bumped into takes the arm of the man next to her and whispers in his ear. He shifts. They see his profile, but it is dark, so nothing registers. But when he gets up and helps his drinking companion push toward the door, we can clearly see that it's Rocket.

"He must be traveling to his apartment on Titan," Trenton says. "I wonder who the woman is."

Jersey adjusts a lens to get a sharper view. "She's hard to see, but I think she looks like the one we saw on the Culinary's security holo with Pluto Pastrami, but her skin and hair's different. Wasn't her name Breezy, or Tweezy?"

"You mean Breezy Point, Decibel Point's daughter," Trenton says. "D. Point and B. Point were listed on the transport's guest list. Decibel may be headed to that new drug company on Titan that scientists are talking about. I can imagine how tempting it must be to work off-planet in a new lab with state–of–the-art equipment free of Mars's rules and regulations."

Jersey takes several deep breaths. "Trenton, I'm not going. Don't even think about it."

We finish another round of drinks and leave the lounge. Trenton wants to find a store that sells butterscotch supplements, which is easy to do, because every place seems to sell them. Then Jersey and I pop into Planet Dior while Trenton, who like most men, android or otherwise, dislikes shopping—especially with two women—and goes back to his room.

The store is having a special sale on items with polka dots. Jersey finds a pink-and-green blouse marked down ten times.

"What's the problem, Jersey? You love those colors, and the price is great."

"Do you think anyone will notice that the right sleeve has fifteen polka dots and the left sixteen?"

I sigh. Shopping with Jersey isn't fun.

Breezy and Rocket leave the Purple Tree and sway together, doing a Mango Tango down the corridor toward Rocket's room. Then Rocket puts a hand in his pocket and takes out some echinacea, fenugreek, and devil's claw-yucca and pops them in his mouth.

"You take too much of that stuff," says Breezy, trying to walk as gracefully as she can on her black platform heels, which is not easy considering she drank a Paregoric Sour, a Fish-Oil Collins, and two double Zombies with extra flaxseed oil. "Are you sure it's all safe? This transport carries a lot of unregulated products."

"No problem, sweetheart. You're talking to a professional."

As they near Rocket's room, Rocket slows. "I think I'm feeling a delayed reaction from some calli tea I drank earlier." He sways, but Breezy steadies him.

"Are you sure it was the tea? You've combined a lot of pills."

Rocket doesn't answer and stumbles on toward his room, breathing hard and sweating. He puts his palm to the door. It jolts open. When he and Breezy go inside, he bends and reaches for his throat. The room circles around him.

Decibel and Craig, who have been waiting in the hall for Breezy to return with Rocket, rush to Rocket just as he collapses and convulses on the floor.

"Oh my God!" Breezy screams.

Craig and Decibel lean over him. Decibel puts a finger to Rocket's neck. "No pulse. He's dead!"

"Dead? How can he be dead? He was just alive," Breezy says.

"It works that way sometimes," Decibel sighs. He opens a bag and takes out a small vacuum that he brought in case he needed to sweep Rocket's room clean of evidence.

Craig's voice shakes. "Do you have to do that?" he asks. "He keeled over without any one of us touching him."

Decibel warns, "But we were here. I touched his neck to find a pulse. The police will find our biometrics."

When Rocket doesn't respond to the transport's attendance check, his room is opened and he is found dead on the floor of his cabin. The ship's security team does a sweep with a tracer spectrum light. No prints or DNA are found, not even those belonging to Rocket meaning someone swept the room clean.

Sandy Andreas sits in his cabin on a clear French Provincial–inspired Lucite chair. The cabin has a large picture window and dark blue carpet dotted with stars. The sheets and towels are monogrammed with his initials so he can take them with him when he leaves, instead of having to steal them. He wears a crisp white shirt and chinos and only one gold chain around his neck rather than the usual four.

He is having a good morning reading the *Robber-Barron's Report* that says the Marsdaq hit a five-year high. Market analysts remain bullish on tech and drug spending, and several new products that Sandy's labs manufacture are being deregulated. He is savoring a walnut brioche with apricot marmalade and mocha java coffee when one of the ship's security guards calls. He motions to an assistant to let him in.

"Please sit," Sandy says without enthusiasm to the security officer. He lifts a finger and points to the sofa. "What's this about?"

"Just routine, Mr. Andreas. We're questioning everyone on board as to where they were and what they were doing last night. Can you tell us your destination and the purpose of your trip?"

"I'm going to Titan to advise Craig Cashew, CEO of the Culinary Institute who is also on board, about the gardens and farms at Titan Culinary. Then I'll take another transport going all the way to Pluto's moon Charon to explore places where I can build all-robotic research stations."

"Your doorway recorded that you left your room last night for several hours. Can you tell us where you went?"

"Can't sleep. I have insomnia. Took a walk."

"Anything else?"

Sandy's face tightens like a clenched fist. "Are you accusing me of something? Because that's all I'm going to say without a lawyer."

## 33

ONE DAY AFTER I GET back from Titan, I sit in Jersey and Trenton's living room. The room has a dozen screens built into a wall. The opposite wall has a holograph of the brain that emerges and floats in three dimensions. It looks like a glowing map of the universe. It is one of the few truly beautiful things they own.

"What's that buttery smell? I thought you never ate butter."

"It's the new butterscotch supplements we bought on the trip. Try one."

"I wouldn't exactly call it food, but this isn't bad," I say savoring the taste. "Promise you won't tell the twins that I ate this, or they'll step up their pace monitoring what I eat."

"Lamont called us," Jersey says changing the subject. "Isn't it amazing that Rocket Packarod died when we were on the transport?"

"I had heard he was a health food nut," I say. "Maybe those of us who love chocolate are in better shape than those who love broccoli."

Jersey rolls her eyes.

"I'm not happy with the forensic report about Rocket's death," Trenton says. "I've asked Lamont to send me samples from Rocket's cabin. Remember that woman at the bar on the transport who bumped into me, the one with the rose tattoo on her pinky? I think I remember seeing such a tattoo on Breezy's pinky. But I'm not sure. Let's view the Candy Universe holo again, where the man had his arm raised standing next to a girl."

I sit on the one comfortable upholstered chair reserved for guests and look at the photos on the table next to it. There is one of Jersey as a child and two of Trenton before his accident. I love those photos, because clearly Trenton was once fat.

Trenton keys the middle screen. We wait a moment, then the holo of the Candy Universe plays.

"Stop," Jersey says getting up and pointing to the woman. "Enlarge the hand." She peers at the image. "See, her pinky has a rose tattoo. No question. It's Breezy. I knew it the minute she called Trenton a junk man."

I take another supplement. "Right before the Mars Malt party, I was walking in the garden area. I saw Craig Cashew talking on his palm. I overheard him say, 'Tell your cousin Pluto that I have what he or his girlfriend dropped.' I think Craig must have been talking to Sandy's wife, Solaria, about her cousin Pluto. If Craig found some piece of evidence that links Breezy and Pluto to the poisoning at the Candy Universe and he didn't give it to the police, he's withholding evidence. And withholding evidence is a crime." I take another supplement. "I wonder what he could want from Pluto and Breezy. Could Craig be connected to the poisoning of the Chocolate Moons?"

Jersey removes the supplements before I can reach again. "I can't see a motive. Craig Cashew made the Culinary what it is today."

The next day, as Jersey is cleaning, she puts a lava lamp on her side of the bed and an identical one on Trenton's side. She stands back and watches the symmetrical swirling patterns. Then she programs a micrometer to make sure they stay coordinated. She fears waking up in the middle of the night and screaming if she sees one lamp bubble up and the other bubble down. Then she puts her shoes in alphabetical order inside her closet.

"How could there be no prints or DNA in Rocket's room?" she asks Trenton.

"Not hard if you can make a scanner-vac. Parts can be packed in separate bags and assembled later. It's not a complicated gadget, and it's small."

"There," Jersey says, standing back and admiring her closet. "Perfect. Now I'll do yours."

Trenton blocks his closet door. "No need to get carried away. You know, I wasn't happy with the police lab results. This morning I received samples Lamont got from Rocket's room. The new features I put on my tracers refined their analysis. Guess whose biometrics popped up on my screen?"

"Whose?"

"Breezy Point's, Decibel Point's, and Craig Cashew's. We may never know why they were in Rocket's room when he died. All of them may have had a motive to kill Rocket, but I think none of them did it."

"Really?" Jersey says wide eyed.

"According to recent hospital records, Rocket's body was on the edge of collapse from self-medicating with health foods and supplements. He was hospitalized earlier and a doctor prescribed a medication that would reduce the effects of all his self-medication, but he must have never filled the prescription because the coroner found none. The coroner also said his system was so fragile that the day he died even a baby aspirin might do him in. The culprit seems to be an enriched health food tea that he may have ordered from room service earlier; harmless to most but dangerous when it interacts with other substances.

"He probably died when Breezy, Decibel, and Craig were in his room and it was just an unfortunate coincidence that they were there at that time. I don't know the reason they were with Rocket, but Lamont needs to pick them up and question them."

Lamont Blackberry walks across his office and inserts two fingers into a vending machine sent by a criminal who thought the police should get their just desserts. Two raspberry cream puffs appear on the tray. Then he calls Trenton.

"It will be easy to pick up Craig," Lamont says. "He's back at the Culinary. And my guess is Breezy is back with Pluto in New Chicago. But Decibel Point's DNA isn't registering on any list from any planet or moon." Lamont keys a few words, including *Rose's Heaven* and *Rose's Spa*. "Got it," he says. "Decibel is at that fat farm satellite. The only one that I know that would fit right in there would be Molly. We have to talk her into going and finding him."

Sid Seedless interrupts. "I'm getting an unusual transmission."

"Trenton, are you on the line? Sid is getting an unusual transmission."

"Still here."

"Make sure you record the conversation, Sid," Lamont says.

"Hello. Is this Drew Barron?" a nervous voice asks.

"Who wants to know?"

"Are you the Drew Barron who knew the late Rocket Packarod?"

"Don't want any. Gave at the office." Drew is ready to hang up.

"My name is Roger Orbit. I'm the director of Far Horizons, the community where Rocket Packarod's son, Zeus Packarod, lives."

Drew listens.

"I'm holding a copy of Rocket's will. His lawyer says that he updated it after he was hospitalized following the Mars Malt celebration. He named you executor."

"Executor? That's a surprise. I never knew Rocket had a son until one night at Nirgal Palace when I learned about him from someone else."

"Rocket's left everything to his son, Zeus, in care of Far Horizons," says Roger, fingering a key. "But everything is stored at the Ali Baba Caves. Would you come with me and help me sort through Rocket's things?"

Drew thinks fast. "Scheherazade runs Ali Baba Caves. I met her at Gramercy Gardens when Rocket brought her to dinner. A lot of people have had trouble retrieving things, even with a key. Scheherazade expects a hefty surcharge to retrieve. I'm told if you ask to see Ali Baba, she puts you in a dark room and you watch someone who looks like the Wizard of Oz give a sales pitch about the place, but I'm told it's her in drag."

"So, is that a yes or a no?"

Suddenly Drew realizes that he could bring the Giacometti that Rocket switched with him and if he sees another one at the ABC he could try to trade them. Finally he says, "Yes, I'll go."

Trenton asks Lamont, "Did you record that conversation?"

"Sid, did you record it?" Lamont asks.

"Record it? Let me check."

"What do you mean, *let me check?*"

"Got it. The light on the right blinking."

"It's supposed to be the light on the left."

"Did I say *right?* I meant *left*—I was looking in a mirror. Sorry."

"Why do you put up with him?" Trenton asks.

Lamont sighs. "He's family."

The next day, Lamont calls Sid into his office. "I'm assigning you to follow Drew Barron and Roger Orbit to the ABC."

"Follow them? Why me?"

"Because I said so, that's why."

"But everyone knows they won't let you in unless you pass some kind of test. What if I fail and end up in a dungeon?"

"Too late. Got you a ticket."

# 34

DREW AND ROGER STAND IN front of the ABC. Drew carries a black case that contains the Giacometti that Rocket switched with him. Roger wears a backpack jammed with documentation about Rocket's request. Two large guards wearing brown uniforms that say "Knight 507" and "Knight 509" are at the entrance. They are seven feet tall, have Mohawk haircuts, necks as thick as bears and crack rubber whips. They are not in a good mood.

Drew and Roger enter an elevator that descends into a dark hallway. Ahead is a high door with a picture of a mushroom cloud and the words "Testing Area." 509 opens a creaking door and points to a table with pliers, nails, small sharp objects and a jar that looks like it is filled with blood.

"Sit!" shouts 507, shoving two chairs in their direction. They sit.

"Could I have a glass of water?" Drew asks.

509 cracks his whip and tells 507 to bring some water. "Don't spill it!" he shouts. "The last guy shook so much, his cup runneth over." He cracks his whip again. "Get my drift?"

"Do you have to shout?" Drew says. "There are only four of us here."

"You the voice of authority? Shaddup!"

Roger bunches a handkerchief and mentally says the words to "My Sweet Lord."

"We have to ask you a few questions to make sure you are who you say you are. We want to be fair," 507 says.

Roger and Drew look at each other, knowing that whenever anyone makes a big deal out of saying how they want to be fair, you know you're headed for big trouble.

"I'll ask the questions," 509 says, "because I went to John Gotti Community College and you didn't."

Then he makes a sound like a volcano springing to life. "Does vitamin A make you smarter than vitamin B? How many Napoleons did Napoleon eat before he drank water from the loo? Are synonyms found in a thesaurus or a brontosaurus? What (if any) is the difference between a hamlet and omelet with ham? Where are the shores of Gitchie Goomie?"

They wait nervously while 507 tally their scores. "Not bad," he says. "You both passed." He turns to Roger. "How did you know where Gitchie Goomie was? Not even Scheherazade knows."

"My mother's family came from there. It's not too far from the big sea waters."

"You don't say."

Then 509 covers their eyes and puts earphones on their ears that play a continuous loop of the Weavers singing "Wimoweh" and marches them through winding halls smelling of burning flesh, down long passages that drip warm liquids on their heads amid sounds of a trapdoor opening and something falling into an abyss nearby. At last they reach Scheherazade's outer office and the earphones and eye coverings are pulled off.

Drew rubs his ears.

"No rubbing," 507 says. "It excites some of the guys who have been here a long time."

"Sit here," 509 says.

"No, there," 507 says.

"Here."

"There."

"Here."

"There."

"Stop arguing with me," 509 says. "You people from Minsk always like to argue." His face contorts into a twisted leer.

"Pinsk. I'm from Pinsk, Pluto."

"Minsk on Mercury, Pinsk on Pluto. Same thing. Whatever."

"But there's only one stool," Drew says.

"Shut up, wise guy! You can stand." 509 yanks the stool away and points to Roger. "And you can sit on the floor."

After a while, Drew walks to the wall to his left. It is lined with portraits. "It's the Thieves family," he says, counting. "Yup, there are forty, all right." He turns to the opposite wall and sees a framed award. He reads: "To Scheherazade, the Seven Deadly Sins award: gluttony, anger, pride, greed, lust, envy, and sloth for all your help founding a charter school for scoundrels." Drew says, "Boy, those Thieves really know how to raise funds."

509 approaches and escorts them into Scheherazade's office. Drew recalls the time Rocket brought Scheherazade to the Gramercy Gardens and he and Scheherazade sat at the same table. He wonders if she will remember.

They enter a dark room with three low-hanging lights over Scheherazade's desk. Her red dress clings to her body like wet dry cleaning. Her long black hair, smooth as seal's pelt, falls down her back. Every finger has a ring. Drew thinks: brass knuckles.

Scheherazade stands behind an elaborately carved ivory-colored desk talking on her palm. There is a Giacometti identical to Drew's on her desk. She motions to a green leather sofa against the opposite wall.

"Be with you in a moment," she growls, obviously annoyed with the person on the other end. She turns her back to Roger and Drew, who hears, "No, *off with your head* is not a figure of speech! When was it ever a figure of speech?" She clicks off and says, "Idiot!"

She motions for Drew and Roger to come closer. "You guys looking for a job? I'm looking to hire another knight, because now I have a thousand, and I need one more as a tiebreaker when their union votes." She sits down at her desk, pushes her hair behind her ears, and leans forward on her elbows, revealing a deep cleavage.

Roger and Drew try not to look at her cleavage. Drew notices she wears a blue-ice sapphire necklace identical to the one he bought for Kandy.

"What a beautiful necklace," Drew says.

She fingers the necklace and gives it a long, sensuous touch. "Got it on the home shopping channel. So you guys want jobs?"

"We're not looking for a job," Roger stammers. "A friend of ours has died and he has storage here. I brought his will and a key to his vault." He takes off his backpack, unzips it, and fumbles for the key.

"And who might that be?" Scheherazade says, drumming her nails on her desk.

"Rocket Packarod."

"Rocket Packarod!" Scheherazade throws her head back and laughs. "Neither of you look like a friend of Rocket's. I'm gonna miss those free supplements and drugs."

She points to the Giacometti on her desk. "I got that from Rocket. Told me it was real but I haven't checked. Could be a first edition from my art factory. Even I can't tell if it's mine or a real one unless I put it through elaborate tests." She turns to a silver screen on her desk and touches several points with a long red fingernail. "Ah, Rocket's storage is in an area called the Waldorf Asteroid, section five, cave four. Let me stamp your hands." She takes out her stamp and inks it up, grabs Drew's hand, and pushes the stamp into the back of it. "This is good for a one-day pass. No exchanges. No refunds. Just hold it under the little light at the door and my knights will let you in."

"Ouch," Drew says, rubbing his hand. "That hurt. Did you have to be so rough?"

"That's nothing compared to what you'll feel if you don't give Ali Baba Caves a token of appreciation when you've finished going through Rocket's vault."

Drew works up his courage and says, "I wonder if you remember me? We met at Gramercy Gardens. You came with Rocket. I was on the other side of the table with Kandy."

Scheherazade's lip curls but she says nothing.

507 and 509 stand in front of the Waldorf Asteroid section, each holding back a growling pit bull ready to pounce.

"Down, Rimsky," 507 says. Reaching into his pocket, he pulls out a piece of raw tofu in the shape of a man's hand. He throws it to Rimsky, who retreats.

"Down, Korsakov," 509 says, throwing him a piece of raw tofu in the shape of a man's foot. Korsakov retreats.

507 scans their hands and gives each a shove toward a long, dark, misty hallway.

"I can hardly see," Drew says with grim apprehension. "Does it have to be so misty?"

"We just got the mist machine. No one was afraid without mist."

Drew and Roger walk through the haze in silence until 507 finally shouts, "Stop here!"

Roger inserts the key into a rusty door and turns the lock. A bolt slides.

Drew hands 507 twenty-five starbucks. When he makes menacing sounds and his face remains twisted in a bad way, Drew hands him a hundred. 507 walks away mumbling to himself.

The storage cave glows with amber darkness. One bulb hangs on a thin twisted wire. Drew pushes through cobwebs and sneezes. "Why am I not surprised it looks like this?"

They start at the front and pick through Rocket's things. There are ten pairs of eyes signed Picasso, six sets of dentures signed Matisse, twenty individual ears signed Van Gough, a photograph of Jeff Koons shooting a loon on a moon, eight identical Giacomettis, three Venuses from Willendorff's cafeteria, a box containing cash and a portrait of Kermit the Frog with Miss Piggy, which Roger identifies because he says he saw a copy on a wall in a mart.

On a dark shelf in the back is a scrapbook with pictures of a young Rocket and a woman holding a baby. "I'll take this with me," Roger says.

Drew and Roger lock the storage cave and make arrangements for its contents to be shipped to Far Horizons with the exception of the cash, which they take with them.

"A token of our appreciation," Drew says handing Scheherazade thirty thousand starbucks.

"And a portrait of Miss Piggy and Kermit," Roger adds.

"Wasn't she the first female president of the United States?" Scheherazade asks.

"I'm not sure," says Drew. "But Kermit was definitely a prime minister."

"Thanks for letting us stop by," Roger says backing toward the door.

Scheherazade waves her hand. "You can go."

Drew starts to retreat. She points to him. "You stay."


Sid calls Lamont. "You shouldn't have sent me. I told you I couldn't get in. I told you I would fail their test."

"What was the question?" Lamont asks.

"To be or not to be?"

"What did you check?"

"I checked 'not to be.'"

"You never check *that*. Everyone knows that."

Sid groans.

"What's the matter now? Where are you?"

"Two guys with rubber whips and bushy eyebrows just put me on a tram back to New Chicago with a tattoo on my butt that says 'Rejected: Return to Sender.'"

35

CORTLAND LANDS A SPOT ON *Katie Racket Interviews* to promote the Lunar Tunes and Molawn, his music agency. The twins and I watch and cheer from home. Katie Racket tells Cortland how lucky the twins are to have him as a father and after the show gives him her private number, in case, over a bottle of wine, he wants to show her how one becomes a father.

He gets so much publicity from being on her show that he decides the best way for the twins to get more exposure and find more talent is to go on tour. Billings begs him not to leave, because he's feeling a pinch from his competition, the Original Ray's Red Planet Pizza. So before he leaves, Cortland blitzes the media with ads that say eating a Green Men pizza helps the greening of Mars. Ecology buffs rejoice. Sales soar. Billings is happy, but Cortland's pizza days are over.

Lamont calls. "Molly, how would you like an all-expenses-paid vacation to Rose's Heaven?"

"Rose's Heaven! When I went to Ruby's Spa, someone told me that it was the spa in space for the plus-size."

"That's right. Decibel Point is there. I hope you don't take offense, but you are the only one I know who would fit right in with their clientele. Would you go and find him and keep him busy until we arrive?"

This is a no-brainer. Ever since I learned about Rose's Heaven and its never-ending buffet, I've been dying to go. "The Culinary owes me time off because I put in extra hours when Gramercy Gardens opened. When do I leave?"

I arrive at Rose's docking station. It's been a long while since I floated in space. Ah, the bearable lightness of being. Lovely music plays. An announcer says it is the "Moonlight Sonata."

"Which moon do you think the composer had in mind?" asks a woman dredging the last drops of her first piña colada.

"Probably all of them," I say.

A sign says, "Welcome to Rose's, where no one asks how much you lost but asks how much you've gained." Three attendants greet me. One wears a smock that says "Rose's Angels Regular" and another wears a smock that says "Rose's Angels Deluxe." The third woman wears a smock that says "Rose's Angels Rehabilitation."

"What's the difference?" I ask.

"Rose's Angels Regular is for people who weigh less than five hundred Earth pounds. Rose's Angels Deluxe is for those over five hundred Earth pounds. And Rose's Angels Rehabilitation is for anyone who wants to reverse the genetics that took away their sense of taste."

"I didn't know you could do that."

"Only a few know about it, but it's our fastest growing area. Most of the people who come here haven't tasted anything fully since infancy, when taste suppressants were put into their food. We have to wean them off very slowly or they'll go into shock.

"We wake up their taste buds by having them eat small portions of something strong—things like hot Mexican chili peppers and fiery Madres curries. When they can taste that we move on to something milder. In the end they can taste egg whites. While they are here we also make it impossible for them to turn off the cooking channel. Tell me now; will you be signing up for Rose's Regular or Rose's Deluxe?"

I give a cold, blank stare. How could anyone think I weigh more than five hundred Earth pounds? Are the twins right? Do I look that bad? For the first time in my life, I am seriously upset about my weight. "Rose's Regular," I mumble.

I am shown to my room by a bouncy round woman. "You can adjust the gravity from Earth level to weightless by pushing a button next to the bed. Some people like to try it out while they are lying down. Earth's gravity gets people depressed. Almost everyone who comes here has forgotten how heavy it made them feel, except of

course for those just released from Jupiter's penal colony." She peers
at me closely. "You're not coming from there, are you?"

She opens a closet door. A mirror on the back looks like it came
from a fun house. "You can also adjust this to show how you look now
or how you'd look if you gained or lost weight. Lots of people keep it
on the lowest, which is the skinniest setting, because they have a good
idea what more weight would look like but have no idea about less."

"I know how they feel," I say.

"There are several restaurants," she continues. "The heart of the
spa is the never-ending buffet. Some guests spend all their time at the
buffet, except to bathe, sleep and change their clothes."

"Are there any exercise classes?"

"Of course. We have classes that teach how to get two hot dogs on
one roll, eat the crumbs off a crumb cake so it doesn't show, pick the
chocolate chips out of cookies without breaking them and triple the
food on your plate at a salad bar. If you need anything, just call. My
name is Jumbo."

She pushes a button and chocolate melts over the door lock and
seals it. "When you want to get back in, just crack it open. You can
eat the lock." Watch me. She taps the lock with the key that she
hands me and chocolate pieces fall into her hand.

*Wow!* I think, What a place. No wonder it's in space.

I decide to explore. The first place I go is the gift shop. There is a
book display up front for touting: *Baby Ruth: The Story of a Ballplayer
Who Became a Candy Bar* and *Yolks Without Whites*, a love story that I
read and cried over last year.

"How about a book on investing in chocolate malteds?" asks the
saleswoman. "They never go down in calories."

"I'll think about it." I thumb a copy of the spa's magazine, *Eating.* I
glance at the guest columnists and jump. Decibel Point has written an
article on sleeping and eating versus bathing and eating. Then I read my
horoscope. It says if I sign up now as a Rose's regular, I'll receive a discount and will gain fifty pounds in the next six months. I'm surprised at
how upset this makes me and vow to watch my weight when I get home.

The buffet is in an enormous crowded room. The ceiling has a
blue sky with white clouds so realistic that if I didn't know better, I

would think it was a sunny day on Earth. There are rows of standing rib roasts, platters of lobsters, clams and shrimps to fill a sea, bowls of pastas that would fill Italy, potatoes that would fill Ireland, fields of green vegetables, and a wall with spigots that pump out every kind of sauce. The smell from the ovens, baking every type of bread from brioche to matzos, makes me swoon. Down a hall is an area called Paradise Found. It is filled with desserts: one area for frozen treats, one for sweet melted choices, and another for cakes, pies and cookies.

I elbow my way toward the center of the main room. "Don't fondle the fondant," someone yells as I eye chocolate-dipped strawberries. I am sinking into a meditative reverie from sensory overload when I spot Decibel. I recognize him the moment he opens his mouth and bites into a large ball of mozzarella cheese as though it were an apple. I blink my eye cam, which Lamont had me wear, and send a holo to Trenton. I back into a relatively quiet corner and wait for their answer. There's a long delay.

Finally Jersey calls. "Sorry I took so long. I was making Trenton lunch."

"Trenton is eating lunch? Since when is lunch important to Trenton? I thought he almost never eats."

"I found a box of Quark's Neutrinos at Stop the Shop. Neutrinos come in six flavors. I bought tau and muon. Trenton can't decide which he likes better, but that's no problem because when they're oscillated, they get a greater mass and can exchange flavors with each other. Now that I think of it, I should have bought only one box."

"You mean if you buy a box of vanilla it could turn into a box of chocolate?"

"And strawberry and lemon, and in time, all the rest of the flavors."

"That's a big bang for the bucks. How many calories do they have?"

"Did I hear you say calories? Since when do you concern yourself with calories? I thought you went to Rose's Heaven to get away from that."

I say nothing, because I don't have a good answer.

"We received the picture of Decibel and forwarded it to Lamont. He's on his way. Do you think you can keep him busy till he gets there?"

I zigzag through the crowd and circle closer to Decibel who is admiring several suckling pigs rotating on spits. Their fat crackles and drips onto mountains of fluffy mashed potatoes below. I come closer. Decibel looks at me and asks, "Are you going to dinner after this?" He doesn't wait for an answer. "Come, join me in the main dining room." He holds out his arm.

My skin grows tight. And, even though I have neither the intention nor the ability to eat another meal after the buffet and, in addition, feel a twinge of guilt accepting a dinner invitation from a man who is not my husband, it is a great opportunity to get the skinny on Decibel. So, I take his arm.

Several banana-and coconut-shaped chandeliers hang from a vaulted ceiling; a fountain of pink champagne splashes on an ice sculpture of Rose on one side of the room and a candy sculpture of Rose emerging from a twenty-layer cake on the other. The gravity is set to the level of Mars's moon Phobos—just enough so the food will not fly off the table but the patrons still feel light. The caterer is a descendent from Earth's Borscht Belt, located in mountains called the Catskills. The waiters, who double as verbal pugilists, put every appetizer from the menu on the table without being asked.

"That's what I love about this place," Decibel says. "They know how we think." He scoops some chopped liver on a cracker and pops it into his mouth. "Delicious. Try the chopped herring." He pushes the plate toward me.

We start by sharing a double order of cream of- matzo-ball soup, followed by several ribs from a standing rib roast with four types of mashed potatoes and vegetables au gratin. This is followed by fettuccine Alfredo. We each get a bottle of white wine followed by a bottle of red wine. I can't finish so Decibel finishes it for me. He orders raspberry mousse and chocolate pudding for dessert and makes a speech about endorphins.

"You must be a scientist. You seem to know the chemical compositions of all the foods. Where do you work?" I ask.

"Here and there. Mostly I freelance."

"I used to know someone at Congress Drugs."

"Everyone knows someone at Congress Drugs. It's the biggest drug company and pays the lowest salaries. The turnover is enormous. I can't stand executive vice president Drew Barron. What a phony snob! Thinks he knows everything." His lips tighten.

"Really?" I smile for a million obvious reasons.

"What does your husband do?"

"He used to run a chain of Green Men Pizzas, but now he's in the music business."

"Green Men Pizza? It's the best. Nine pies with all toppings are my limit though."

Decibel sees me looking at a small amount of chocolate pudding he left in a dish. "My mother told me it was good manners to leave a drop. If I were tortured, all anyone would have to do is lock me in a room with dishes that have one last tiny bit of my favorite foods and not let me eat them."

I laugh. Decibel smiles. "Do you have any children?" I ask.

"I have a daughter, Breezy, but she lives with a guy I can't stand, Pluto Pastrami. He's Solaria Andreas's cousin—you know the one who had that Mars Malt party. Pluto gets nothing from that side of his family and is always scrounging around. I wish Breezy would leave him, but she says every time she thinks of doing so she gets a *ding-dong* sound in her head. Besides, she says she loves it when he tickles her feet." Decibel scoops raspberry mousse into his mouth. "Do you have any children?"

I'm about to tell him about Cortland and the twins, but before I can, a waiter comes over and places a plate of bitter herbs before Decibel.

"What's this? I didn't order this."

"Compliments of the two men over there," the waiter says pointing to Lamont and Sid, who are standing to the side of the room waving their badges over their heads. "They say you would know what these weeds are. I personally would have preferred a glass of port and a dish of after-dinner mints."

Lamont and Sid approach. I blush and lower my head, embarrassed that I misled him. Decibel looks more helpless than a fish on a hook.

"Sorry to break up your little party, Decibel Point," Lamont says. "But we're here to bring you in for questioning concerning the death of your colleague Rocket Packarod."

## 36

SCHEHERAZADE MOVES CLOSE TO DREW. She circles around peering closely. The contrast between her knights, all of whom look like 507 and 509, make her realize how long it has been since she was with someone so handsome. Drew senses passion not danger. He risks eye contact and offers a shy smile. She takes his hand and pulls him toward her desk then reaches under and clicks open a small refrigerator and removes a bottle of perfectly chilled champagne and two tall flutes.

"Shall we?" she says twisting off the cap and pouring. Their fingers curl around the stems.

"To art," Drew says glancing sideways at the Giacometti. Scheherazade sees his eye shift but says nothing. They clink their glasses and look at each other for a long moment.

Scheherazade breaks the silence and says. "I majored in art at college. I wrote a thesis on 'The Moan of Lisa' and why she wore a mustache. But only *Mad* magazine would publish my theories."

"Ah," Drew says. "Brains as well as beauty." Feeling more confident he asks, "Is Scheherazade your real name?"

"No, it's Sondra Audrey Goldwyn. But you need something exotic in the art counterfeiting business." She raises an eyebrow. "I changed it officially on Ellis bin Laden Island. Paid extra for a tattoo of Ellis. Want to see?"

"Depends on the where it is." Drew takes two fingers and strokes her neck. Then feeling no resistance, he slides his hand to her right breast and gently squeezes.

"Oooh," she says in a low husky voice arching her back like a cat. Feeling braver he squeezes the left.

"Ahhh," she says arching further.

"Do you prefer *oooh* or *ahhh?*"

"Why quibble?" she pants.

Drew's hand slides lower. He tugs at her tight black skirt. "Not quibbling," he murmurs feeling the skirt release. "Just getting ready to sign on the bottom line."

After a night of bliss, 509 knocks on Scheherazade's door and wheels in a double order of eggs Benedict, honey-roasted bacon, warm brioche that looks to Drew like two breasts, butter curls, passion fruit marmalade and strong hot coffee.

"The coffee is a special blend from San Andreas Farms. Buy one, get one free," Scheherazade says.

Drew clears his throat and coughs several times.

"What's the matter? Did I say something wrong?"

"No, it's just that Sandy Andreas is my boss and I didn't expect to hear his name. Rocket offered me a job heading a drug company he bought on Titan. Now that he's gone I'm not sure what I'll do. The company is still there even if Rocket is gone." Drew sips his coffee and bites off the top of a brioche. "I asked you this before but you never answered me. Do you remember me from Gramercy Gardens? You came with Rocket."

"Yes, and you came with Kandy Cohen."

"Kandy Kane," corrects Drew. "She was a former Miss Universe."

"A former Miss Nose Job Universe. Kandy Cohen. Definitely."

Drew sighs.

"What's in the case that you never let out of your sight?"

"It's a valuable Giacometti sculpture. I was Park Bengay's highest bidder."

Scheherazade slides out of bed and puts on a robe. "Rocket brought me a Giacometti that he said was very valuable."

"Is that the one on your desk?"

"It is," she says tying the sash of her robe into a bow.

"Let's compare them after we dress and shower," Drew says.

Scheherazade pouts. "If you insist but I'd be in a better mood if we added another activity."

Drew puts his case on Scheherazade's desk and opens it. He takes out his Giacometti and places it next to hers. "It is amazing how much they look alike," he says. Then before she can examine them closely, he puts his Giacometti back in its case. Drew sees that Scheherazade is startled so he quickly changes the subject. "Tell me was there ever an Ali Baba?"

"Of course. He offered me this job because he couldn't take any more dark nights of the soul and clouds of unknowing and wanted a job in Las Venus, a place where the action never stops. He now works for Donald the Twentieth."

"Donald Trump the Twentieth?"

"Who's Donald Trump? Ali works for Donald Duck. Want to visit him? I'm tired of hearing the problems of a thousand and one knights who only want to work days."

Before Drew can answer, she walks to a closet and takes out an expensive Tabriz rug.

"Magic, right?" Drew says. "Does it work?"

"Of course it works. How did you think we would travel? Click our heels together three times and say there's no place like Las Venus and when we open our eyes we'll be there?" She pushes a button on the wall. 507 and 509 enter with a stretcher and place the rug on top. Scheherazade gets on and motions for Drew to sit behind snowmobile style. He wraps his arms around her waist. They lift the stretcher place it on a rover and drive them to the transport.

When they arrive Scheherazade opens her palm and says, "Code forty-three."

"What's code forty-three?" Drew asks.

"Frequent flyer miles."

The minute Scheherazade and Drew enter the Las Venus Casino paparazzi greet them and send a live broadcast to Mars Media's High Society Channel. Kandy, who never watches any other channel, tunes in, jumps, realizes what's happening and packs her bags.

"This way," Scheherazade says threading through the noisy crowd past loud rows of blinking slot machines, roulette wheels and black jack tables. She pushes Drew into a corner of a dark restaurant. A waiter approaches and hands them an oversized menu. "I know this place so let me order. I'll make it simple."

The waiter returns for their order.

Scheherazade looks up and smiles. "Large fresh beluga, large smoked salmon, fresh truffle risotto, a flaming pheasant, two racks of lamb and two bottles of pink champagne."

"You call that simple?"

She grabs his hand and before he realizes what's happening she activates his palm pay. "Simple for Las Venus," she says dabbing her mouth with a white linen napkin.

They exit the restaurant and blink into the casino's bright lights. Scheherazade links her arm through Drew's arm. They pass several gaming tables and head toward a man shaking some dice. His only distinguishing feature is a big nose. Without any introduction Scheherazade thrusts her hand toward his nose. "Ali is going to let us win," she says giving his nose a twist. "Or he knows that I'll send 509 to collect back pay. Isn't that right, Ali?"

Ali rubs his nose. "Good to see you too, Sondra Audrey," he says deliberately to annoy her. Scheherazade winces. He eyes Drew. "I see life at the ABC is agreeing with you."

Drew is taken back by this performance and thinks of sweet Kandy, whom he suddenly misses. He sighs knowing that Kandy would never do anything like this.

The next day, before Drew finishes packing for his trip home, he puts a small mark on the base of his Giacometti and goes into Scheherazade's office. He snaps his case open, removes his Giacometti and places it on her desk next to her Giacometti as he did before. "Las Venus put me in a risky mood," he says. "Why don't we exchange sculptures? Who knows which one is real?"

Before Scheherazade can answer, he puts his hands on both sculptures sliding and switching them around and around playing the three card Monte trick Rocket played on him. His hands move faster and faster.

"Stop!" she shouts. "You're mixing them up."

Drew does one last complicated pass, grabs her Giacometti, throws it into his case. A DNA bolt slides shut. Scheherazade's face twists. She knows that she can't get the case to open without blowing up Drew, whom she no longer cares about and its contents, which she does.

Drew takes the case walks to the door and opens it.

507 and 509 who were waiting outside and heard everything start to stop him.

Scheherazade raises her hand. "Let him go," she snarls. "We'll deal with him later."

Drew walks through the door and starts down the hall. "We're not finished with this!" he hears echoing behind him.

# 37

PLUTO AND BREEZY ARE MAKING love. The holo blinks "Priority: Incoming." The service-bot stops watching them and answers. It's a recorded message requesting that Breezy come to Mars Yard.

"Why me and not you?" she pouts.

"Divide and conquer, baby. I'm sure Mars Yard will get me next." He deletes the service-bot's recent-memory chip.

Breezy rises and slithers into a silky mauve robe that had fallen on the floor.

Pluto continues, "I don't think this is about our visit to the Candy Universe. I'm sure if they had found something connecting us to the poisoning of the Chocolate Moons, we would have already heard from Mars Yard. No one saw me throw any of that stuff Rocket gave me into the vat because everyone was distracted by the alarm. My guess is that this is about Rocket's death on the transport." Pluto picks up a pillow and throws it on the bed. "Let's review."

"I don't need a review, Pluto. I remember as much as you do."

"If we knew that Rocket was going to die, it's too bad you went to all that trouble on the transport, but as it is, we were lucky your father was on the outs with Rocket and receptive to our ideas. Also, we did get Craig to give us back the remote that had your biometrics. It could have linked you to the time and place of the chocolate poisoning."

"What do you mean we were lucky about my father being on the outs with Rocket?" Breezy snaps. "There are a zillion people besides my dad who wouldn't have minded seeing Rocket on a one-way trip to the Andromeda galaxy."

Breezy opens her closet and removes a flashy low-cut yellow-and-black silk crepe de chine outfit that leaves nothing to the imagination.

"Don't overdo it, baby. You don't want to give the wrong impression."

"And what impression is that? I didn't do anything but have a drink with Rocket and walk him back to his room."

"Yeah, and he stopped breathing after you and your father poisoned his ivy."

"How many times do I have to tell you that never happened?"

"Just checking to make sure you get your story straight. The police ask the same question over and over, looking for a chink."

"For all I know, the bartender slipped something into his Paregoric Sour," Breezy says, snapping the clasp of her green sling-back peep-toe shoes.

Breezy is buzzed into Mars Yard. Lamont tells her to sit down; she argues that it will wrinkle her dress. When he insists, she knows he means business and she can't pull the "guilty till proven innocent" card. She waves to her father, whom she sees sitting behind a glass wall talking to Sid Seedless.

Decibel Point admits taking a batch of antiflavonoids from Congress Drugs. He says he took it because he invented the anti-flavonoid and feared that without proper testing it might be dangerous. After the Chocolate Moons were poisoned he knew that he was right. A fresh sample was needed to create an antidote. He took the transport to Titan to be away from prying eyes and prying hands.

"So let me see if I've got this straight, Miss Point..." Lamont says.

"Breezy," she purrs puckering her lips and leaning forward.

"Breezy, you're telling me that Craig Cashew was blackmailing you and your boyfriend with the remote control you dropped at the Candy Universe. But you had no idea what the remote was or what it could do."

"That's right. For all I knew, it was something that could trigger a birthday surprise for that fat security guard, I think her name is Molly, that I saw eating her third box of Chocolate Moons."

Lamont makes a note: *fat security guard.*

"Who gave it to you?" he asks.

"I found it. I don't remember where. I find a lot of things. She opens her bag and pulls out a small blue umbrella. "See this umbrella? Found it on the street." She pulls out a red lipstick. "See this lipstick? Found it on a tram."

"We get your point, Miss Point." Lamont jots down *blue umbrella* and *red lipstick*. "How did Craig Cashew know you had the remote control?"

"How would I know? Ask him. We only knew that because I handled it, my biometrics were on it, and Pluto and I were at the Candy Universe around the time the Chocolate Moons were poisoned." She dabs her eyes with a handkerchief feigning a tear. "If I knew innocent fun-loving people like us, scrimping and saving for the only holiday we have had in five years, could be implicated I never would have gone there."

"Hmm." Lamont jots down *fun-loving*.

Breezy continues, "After the story about the poisoned Chocolate Moons broke, we realized that anything anyone touched there could be used as evidence, and we wanted to distance ourselves from the event. Craig's price for giving the remote back to us was to help him convince Rocket to bury an embarrassing incident that happened to him long ago. We knew that Rocket frequently took the transport to Titan. My father wanted to go there so he could develop an antidote to the anti-flavonoid. Craig was on the transport because he's going to open a Culinary satellite on Titan."

"So each of you had a reason to be on the transport and each of you had a reason to see Rocket. That's very convenient."

"Well before we could talk to Rocket, he keeled over in his room in front of us. None of us touched him." She raises her arm. "Hand to God's ear or two or three."

"God's ear or two or three?"

"Well he's God. Who knows how many ears? Some Hindu Gods have lots of arms. Just playing it safe; I don't want to offend anyone. I'm not that type of girl."

Lamont jots: *God, hand, ears.* He reviews the notes he's taken. Then writes: *A fun-loving fat security guard who walked down a street and sat on a tram finds a blue umbrella and a red lipstick close to one of God's ears but far away from some Hindu's arm.* He turns back to Breezy. "Now the death of Rocket Packarod."

"Didn't Rocket die from an overdose of health foods?"

"That's what the coroner's report shows."

"So there you go: died of natural-food causes."

Breezy takes out the tube of lipstick again and freshens her mouth. She blots it with a tissue and stuffs the tissue into her cleavage so Lamont can see the red smudge. "By the way, how did you know it was us on the transport?"

Then, as though on cue, Trenton opens a door, walks in, and waves to Breezy. "Oh no!" Breezy says. "I remember you. The junk man from the Purple Tree Lounge. You almost made me spill my drink."

Decibel, who finished giving a statement to Sid Seedless, comes in and stands at Breezy's side. "Do you realize who that is?" he says, looking at Trenton. "He was on the cover of *Live and Let Live*. He's the latest android model. Almost human."

"I *am* human," says Trenton. "Of course, more human future than human past."

Breezy frowns. "If that's the future, I'd rather look like Wilma Flintstone!"

"You don't want to look like the Flintstones if everyone else looks like me." He leans close to Breezy, who immediately turns away. She reaches into her bag for sunglasses that cover half her face.

Lamont says to Breezy, "We're going to hold you a bit longer. We have more questions for you and your boyfriend, Pluto Pastrami." He turns to Decibel. "You can go, but don't leave the planet."

Hearing this, Breezy immediately calls Pluto and tells him that Lamont wants to question him.

Pluto arrives with Jack McPloy; a lawyer the Pastramis keep on retainer. Lamont shows them holos of Pluto and Breezy at the Candy Universe with Pluto's hand raised near the chocolate vat.

"Proves nothing," Jack says. "Looks like Pluto was waving his hand. And as far as Breezy, Decibel, and Craig's dealings with Rocket go, nothing happened on the transport except that they saw him collapse."

Lamont releases Decibel, Pluto and Breezy until trial dates can be set.

Drew enters his apartment. The first thing he sees is a flashing message from Kandy. He taps the lock to his carrying case, removes the Giacometti and places it on the marble table. He pours himself a stiff Saturian whiskey and brings it into the bathroom. None of Kandy's things are there. He gulps the drink; adjusts the shower selecting Niagara force; steps inside; air dries, goes back into the bedroom and lies naked on the bed. "Play messages," he says.

Kandy's voice: "I saw you and Scheherazade on the high society channel. No need to say more. I'm staying with Solaria Andreas till I get my own place. You have the number. I left the blue-ice sapphire necklace on top of your desk. I can't bear to wear it."

Drew tries to sleep, but after turning his pillow over every minute with the hope of finding a cool spot, he gets up and eats four packages of Chocolate Moons. Then he sleeps and dreams that he has regained all his former weight, and a descendent of Fernando Botero, an artist best known for painting everyone fat, does a six-foot portrait of him that everyone laughs at and no one wants to bid on at Park Bengay. He jerks awake pounding a pillow on his stomach.

The next day he takes the Giacometti to an appraiser. His stomach twists when the appraiser shakes his head no. Not wanting to burn all his bridges with Scheherazade, he calls her and tells her the results.

"Why should I trust you?" Scheherazade screams. "I'll do my own evaluation." *Click!*

The next day, dressed as sheep in wolves' clothing, 507 and 509 break into Drew's apartment and take the Giacometti. They're angry because Scheherazade just hired one more knight to her thousand, making a thousand and one, a tiebreaker in a winner-take-all vote about joining the Knights of Columbus or the Knights of Vasco de Gama. They leave a card: "507 and 509 Locksmiths: Fixed Locks Broken. Same-Day Service."

Drew calls Roger Orbit.

"Great timing," Roger says. "We're having a memorial event honoring Rocket. I'll sit you with the Big Bang Patrons."

"No thanks, Roger. I'm just calling to tell you that the Giacomettis were fakes. Other artworks could be too."

"I hope they all are."

"Why? I would have thought you would be upset. Far Horizons needs the money."

"Well, I just learned from our generous new donor that there is a brisk market for copies and an even greater market for copies of copies. Anyone can get numbered signed limited editions because it's so easy to get them extended. With unlimited editions no one ever knows how many there are. Adds to their mystery, ergo their value. Unlimited Editions stock is soaring."

"And who may I ask is this new generous donor who has given you this information?"

"Scheherazade. She's going to be our speaker at our next fundraiser. Sorry you'll miss her keynote address: 'How to Fool All the People All the Time.'"

# 38

THE NEXT MORNING, A CALL from Sandy's secretary wakes Drew. "He wants to see you immediately. Be prepared. He's having a tantrum that looks like a prelude to a tornado."

Sandy sits at his desk with micro phones on each finger, talking to ten people at the same time. It looks like he's practicing some new kind of musical instrument except that his voice sounds like scratched glass on gravel. As soon as one of his secretaries lets Drew in, Sandy shakes his fingers disconnecting the phones and charges toward him. He motions for him to sit. Drew sits. Sandy peers at him like a scientist examining a deadly virus.

"The police have been all over me, Drew. They thought I had something to do with the death of that crook Rocket Packarod because we were on the same transport and I walked near his cabin. I didn't even know he was on the ship. And now Lamont Blackberry wants *you* to stop by Mars Yard! Any idea what that's about?"

Drew shrugs. Sandy gives him his most intimidating stare. Drew looks concerned but says nothing, enraging Sandy more.

That afternoon Drew stands in the Mars Yard waiting room under a blinking light that maximizes nervousness. It was designed by a group whose level of nervousness was consistently off the charts: mothers waiting to hear if their child got into an exclusive nursery school. Drew blinks and reads a sign that says "Take a number."

"Do I have to take number? I'm the only one here," he says putting his hands in his pockets and tucking his neck into his collar.

"Yes, you do," the policeman on duty says.

Drew pulls off a number. "How come it says 'Number Two'? No one else is here."

"No one likes to go first. Makes people feel better about being interrogated and tortured."

"Tortured?"

"Only kidding. You have nothing to fear but fear itself."

"Fear of fear is a lot of fear."

Drew sits on a well-worn sofa next to a table with a bowl of fortune cookies, takes one, cracks it, and reads, "Your number is up. You will go on a long journey to a dark place for a long time." He frowns.

"Don't worry," says the policeman. "They all say that or 'Consider the lilies of the field.'" Drew crumples the fortune and throws it toward the garbage. He misses.

"Aren't you going to pick it up? It has your biometrics all over it."

Drew gets up and tosses it in the basket.

The policeman thrusts a clip-screen into his hand. "Fill out this form."

Drew takes it and looks. He sees a series of inkblots and a list of multiple-choice questions. Drew reads: Is this a picture of a man killing a woman with an ax or an ax killing a woman with a man? Pick or an answer will be assigned to you.

"This is ridiculous," Drew says. "I refuse to answer."

"I'm noting that you have a hostile vicious attitude. Is that what you want?"

Drew sighs and picks up the stylus.

Five minutes later, the inner door opens. An android that was hauled in from *Disconnect*, a home for retired androids because the police were short staffed, pushes a walker and shuffles to the center of the room.

"Next number," it shouts. Drew hands it the paper. "We're sorry. This is not a valid number. Please check the number and try again."

"How can the number two not be a valid number?" Drew asks.

The policeman looks up. "Sorry for that. Two is an even number. They sent the odd man out." He pushes his keyboard. The android turns and makes a slow exit. Then an identical android appears.

"Next number," it shouts in the same mechanical voice. Drew shakes his head, makes an annoyed expression and hands it the number two.

"I've learned not to mess with them," the policeman says. "They have a very strong union."

When Lamont confronts Drew about taking a substance from Congress Drugs, Drew doesn't deny it.

"I didn't know why Rocket wanted it nor what he would do with it. You've got to believe me. I swear I'm telling the truth. I'm even willing to submit to Chinese water torture, circumcision—anything to prove it."

Lamont, pausing for maximized drama and not missing a wonderful opportunity to stick it to Drew, looks down at Drew's trousers and lets him think that he is considering circumcision. Then Lamont raises his eyes and says, "But after the poisoning, when the market crashed, people privy to insider information were able to make money selling short. Bet you made a bundle."

Drew's eyes shift sideways. He says nothing.

"By the way, that substance you took from Congress Drugs and gave to Rocket was harmless."

"Harmless? What do you mean, harmless? Didn't people fall into comas after eating poisoned Chocolate Moons?"

"Yes, they did, but not from what you took from Congress Drugs. You must have been in such a rush that you grabbed the first white powder you saw, thinking it was the anti-flavonoid."

"Did anyone else take the real anti-flavonoid?"

"Yes, three other people."

"Three? You're sure?"

"Who are they?"

"We can't disclose the information at this time because we are still in the process of collecting evidence."

"So why am I in trouble if I'm not the one who took the anti-flavonoid?"

"You stole a product from Congress Drugs that didn't belong to you. Sandy Andreas wants to press charges. But if you cooperate we can reduce them."

"Cooperate? What do you want me to do?"

"Help us catch Scheherazade and in exchange we'll give you a sweet deal."

"Done," he says, wondering if he agreed too quickly.

$$\text{(crescent moon symbol)}$$

# 39

CRAIG CASHEW CALLS A MEETING of Culinary Institute security guards and tells us that Sandy Andreas is expanding San Andreas Farms. For the next two weeks, Sandy needs additional personnel until a larger team is hired.

Jersey and I, anxious to get an insider's view of the farms, volunteer to go.

When CC learns that San Andreas Farms is expanding and knowing there will be a lot of digging as part of the construction she freezes. Then she calls Sandy Andreas.

"I hear you're developing new land. I was wondering if you would like me to do a follow-up story about San Andreas Farms."

"News travels fast," Sandy says. "That will be great. I'll also give you an exclusive on our newest project, blue watermelons. I always thought that the insides of watermelons should be blue because they are made of so much water.

"Makes sense. What did you do?"

"When we tweaked the DNA of blueberries and watermelons the inside color looked like blue sky reflected in a lake."

"Wow!" CC says. "They should make a big splash when they hit the market next month. I'll give them a big plug."

I get a few days off before the assignment begins. It has been a long time since I've had people over for dinner and it will give me an opportunity to meet Becky's new boyfriend, a yodeler named Franklin Delano Rosenberg whom Becky calls FDR and Cortland calls a person who can't sing.

Lois will be shopping with Flo, a much higher priority than eating, so I invite Jersey and Trenton who never decline a dinner invitation.

I wear a loose blue-and-gold-striped caftan that hides my bulges and ballet flats so I don't wobble on heels as I serve. Since my trip to Rose's Heaven, and asked if I was in the over-five–hundred-pounds category, I watch what I eat. The bulges are smaller as pounds come off. But no one notices, least of all Cortland, who doesn't see my progress because he travels and is exhausted after searching for new talent for his music agency, Molawn Music. Last week he signed the Bottles, a six-pack of vocalists he found at a recycling plant.

While I'm setting the table, Lamont calls. "I called to tell you we determined the identity of the third person whose biometrics were found next to where the missing poisonous anti-flavonoids should be at the Congress Drugs lab."

"Was it Sandy's wife, Solaria, or her cousin Pluto?" I ask, adjusting the flowers I had put in the center of the table.

"Try again."

"Nooooo, not Colorful Copies!"

"Yup. Her biometrics and time stamp at Congress Drugs match. Remember, after her interview with Sandy Andreas and her tour of their laboratories and San Andreas Farms, she was on Nova Scotia's program."

"Yes, I remember because Cortland wanted to watch Earth's news from Quito, Ecuador, but I insisted because I wanted to see Colorful Copies. We went to college together."

"Were you friends?"

"Definitely not!"

"So," Lamont says backing off, "do you remember she held her arm to the camera to show off her charm bracelet? She thought she had eight charms, but when she counted, she only had seven, meaning she lost one somewhere."

"I also remember that she mentioned talking to a fat scientist at Congress Drugs, who was most likely Decibel Point, as no other scientist is overweight. He told her that he wasn't happy with the way Congress Drugs tested new products. But this doesn't mean she took the anti-flavonoids to poison something. After all she is a reporter. Maybe she wanted to—"

"Reporter or not, it's a theft. I learned that you and Jersey will be spending time at San Andreas Farms this week. Keep your eyes peeled for a clue that might pin her to the case."

Becky's new boyfriend is a tall, thin young man with a dark handlebar mustache. He brings me a gift from the Metropolitan Museum of Art's thrift shop on Jupiter's moon Ganymede that says in big red letters, "Made in Ganymede, home of the solar system's best Chinese reproductions." It's a windup music box with a miniature von Trapp family inside yodeling the Mars national anthem. Cortland examines it and winds it so tightly that he can't stop it from playing. So he stashes it in the freezer, where it plays until it freezes.

We sit at the table. Cortland and I are at the ends. Jersey and Trenton face Becky and FDR. Cortland pours a mid-priced pinot noir that took him an hour to select while wondering if FDR was a future son-in-law. FDR yodels a toast that makes Cortland cringe. When I see everyone enjoying their food and we have discussed possible reasons why CC would take the anti-flavonoids, I say, "Okay, we now know that CC's biometrics match those of the third person who took anti-flavonoids from Congress Drugs, but we still don't know who the fourth person might be."

Jersey guesses. "Rumor has it that Mars Yard might pick up Craig Cashew."

Trenton scoops a large third helping of butternut squash that I tossed with curry powder maple syrup and roasted apples. "As far as we know, Craig hasn't been to Congress Drugs in years."

"It's true that Craig is driven and difficult, but I think he's a creative genius, like when the seven-layer cakes had eight layers and he called it the Seven Plus. Or, when the cakes had six layers and he told the press it was because the Culinary baked cookies for sick children with the flour saved from the missing seventh layer. I can't see any motive. Lamont must want him for something else," I say.

As I speak, a fleeting thought of owning a restaurant and consulting with Craig Cashew surfaces, but I dismiss it as a fun fantasy.

"I would love more turkey," Trenton says. "It's delicious. What's this meal called?"

"Twenty-first-century traditional American Thanksgiving dinner. The diet police outlawed it in the twenty-second century as too fattening but now with all the Freedom Plan foods and supplements, it's been pardoned."

"Good thing," Jersey says reaching for another roll.

My caramelized-apple-pecan cake and pumpkin pie finish the meal. We all make a Thanksgiving groan and leave the table.

"What a meal, Mrs. Summers," FDR says. "Makes me feel like yodeling."

"Not necessary," Cortland pipes, wondering what Becky sees in him and restraining from saying the old adage: those who can sing, sing; those who can't, yodel.

I give Jersey a doggie bag with leftovers that would last Cortland and me a half hour but will probably last six months with them. "Before you both go, can I ask you something?"

"Sure," Jersey says, putting a handful of my favorite after-dinner mints into her pocket.

"How come you have almost no real food in your house and when we eat lunch at the Culinary you order almost nothing, yet you both cleaned your plate and asked for more?"

Jersey glances sideways at Trenton, who gives her a poke. She looks like the cat that swallowed something and it wasn't a canary. "Well," she stammers. "Who can resist free food?"

"Besides," Trenton adds "if I can reduce a meal like that to supplements it might make us rich."

## 40

JERSEY AND I SIT ON a tram that Sandy Andreas sends to the Culinary to bring the extra security guards to his farms. When we pull into the parking lot, Jersey closes her book *Catch the Guy Who Drank the Rye*, by J. D. Scavenger. I remove earphones and click off the twins singing "Lucy in the Sky Lounge with Lucky."

We're greeted by the farm's manager in a red checkered shirt and jeans. He gives us maps and carts that look like ancient golf carts to get around the farms. He also gives us blue caps with peaks whose white letters say "Stolen from San Andreas Farms." He tells us they used to be called baseball caps.

"Talk about cheap," Jersey, an expert on saving money, whispers.

A security guard and amateur sports historian can't resist telling us that baseball was a game where one man wearing a baseball cap in one color throws a little ball to a man wearing a different-colored baseball cap. He holds a big club over his shoulder, and when he sees the ball come toward him, he tries to hit it through a basket. If it goes through the basket, he jumps into his golf cart and flees from the other players, who jump into their carts and try to catch him. If he can make it around a beautifully mowed diamond-shaped park without going into the areas that say "Keep Off the Grass," it's called a touchdown. If he only makes it halfway, it's called a field goal.

"Any questions?" he asks.

No one asks.

Jersey and I climb into our carts. I decide to head north because I want to see the cacao trees whose pods make chocolate. Jersey heads south because she wants to see if Romanian lettuce looks Romanian.

I program the cart's directional panel to "cacao forest," sit back, and enjoy passing through rolling acres of rich growing produce with so many fresh healthy smells that I think I'm breathing a salad.

After a fifteen-minute ride, I arrive.

A friendly worker dressed in the same checked shirt and genes greets me.

"Why are there so many different colored pods and flowers on the trees?" I ask.

"These trees experience different stages of chocolate production simultaneously. They have early flowers and at the same time mature chocolate fruit, so harvesting is done year-round." I see rows of seeds lying on the ground, surrounded by a sugary mucilaginous substance. "All that is fermented off before the seeds are roasted and processed."

"I never realized this was such an elaborate process. Where's the chocolate ground?"

He points to a large brown building.

I walk over and enter. The place is entirely automated. The refiners are large horizontal drums whose blades crush the cocoa beans. I follow a path used mostly by tourists and slowly start circling the room. I am fascinated by the process and seduced by the aroma. Inhaling the beloved chocolate smell so many times puts me in such a dream-like state that I almost don't see what looks like a small colored feather lodged in a crack. Is it what I think it is—a rainbow-colored eyebrow? I put on a pair of protective gloves that Lamont told me to bring, remove the object from the crack, eye-cam it to Lamont, slide it into a bag in my pocket and continue circling.

CC arrives at San Andreas Farms to do her follow-up story and observe the production of the new blue watermelons. Sandy Andreas sends a young attendant to greet her and give her a tour.

After the tour CC says, "This is such a beautiful place. Mind if I stay and continue looking around? The farms and gardens are more interesting than I remembered."

"No problem. Mr. Andreas told me to give you anything you wanted."

"Just give me one of those cute little carts and point me in the direction of the cacao forest. I can't resist seeing those wonderful chocolate-producing plants again."

CC remembers the building that housed the chocolate refinery. She's sure her charm fell somewhere inside. She pulls her cart into a slot and gets out. A worker checking on the fermentation process looks up and says, "You're the second person to come today to see the chocolate refinery."

"Second?"

"Yes, a heavy woman from the Culinary's security team is here inspecting the place until we hire more permanent staff. She went inside about ten minutes ago."

"Really?" CC says springing to full alert. "You're sure she was heavy and from the Culinary?"

"Yes, ma'am. She wore a Culinary Institute uniform. To tell you the truth, I have never seen a person so heavy up close before, so I'm not likely to forget what she looked like."

At first I don't see CC enter through a side door because I'm circling in the opposite direction. She watches me from a distance; my eyes are cast downward as I move closer and closer to the refineries. Then my toe hits a small object. I pick it up. It looks like a gold charm of an ancient computer, from a charm bracelet. I blink my eye cam and send the image to Lamont.

Then I see a shadow of a person to the side closing in. I jerk my head around and jump.

CC holds out her hand. "I'll take that," she hisses.

"No, CC, I don't think so," I glare, spinning and clutching it tightly.

CC pulls my arm. I yank it away and run. "Now, Molly, or else!" she screams.

I run to the nearest exit and close the door. It locks. CC bangs on the door. I go out the other side and run to my cart and get in. CC sees me through a window and runs to a side door and exits. "Wait, Molly, you don't understand!" she shouts.

I start the motor so quickly that instead of turning over and starting, it stalls. I try again. It starts, but by now, CC has caught up with me. "You don't understand," she says again. "Stop!"

"I understand enough, CC. You're not getting away with this." I gun the accelerator and start to move.

CC jumps on the back of the cart. I gun the accelerator again then push the brake, hoping to jerk to a violent stop and she will fall off. But she hangs on. The motor makes more coughing, sputtering noises then quits. CC reaches for my back, but I pull away from her. I jump out and run. Just as I put a little distance between us, my foot gets tangled in high grasses. *Plop!* Down I go.

My heart beats wildly, and for a moment I don't breathe. I pick myself up and start to run again, but I'm winded. CC charges with her arms outstretched. She lunges toward me.

## 41

"Yeah, yeah, what Breezy said is true." Craig says to Lamont spitting out the words. "I withheld a device that I found in the chocolate room that I suspected belonged to her or Pluto. It was the day the schoolboys keeled over from eating the poisoned Chocolate Moons. It was late. Everyone had left the building. I picked it up, slid it into my pocket, and then locked it in a cabinet. I suspected it might be some kind of remote control but wasn't sure."

"You should have called us. It was evidence," Lamont says.

"I didn't know what it was until Decibel Point called me and told me he had a plan to help his daughter, Breezy, and her boyfriend, Pluto. Then I realized I could use it to get their help confronting Rocket about something he was blackmailing me with long ago."

"Breezy's some looker," Sid says showing off his observation skills. "What knockers!"

Lamont rolls his eyes and continues. "But regardless of whether you knew what the device was, you withheld it from the police. And withholding evidence is a crime. You'll have to be arraigned."

Craig Cashew, in his best blue suit, white shirt, and most conservative tie and suspenders, stands and freezes while the judge sentences him to three years of community service at Sang Sang prison, the worst and ugliest detention center in the solar system: a gruesome, repulsive, loathsome place, a true interplanetary eyesore.

News reports say he won't enter the building for health reasons. He pays to have it scrubbed with the strongest possible disinfectant, Lie Sol, and gets an independent committee to give it a lie-detector test. Then he paints the whole place white, endearing him to those individuals inside whose protests about conditions went unheard for decades and who Craig spent most of his life avoiding.

Thin, round-shouldered Izzy Torquemada has been the warden of Sang Sang for twenty years. He is overworked and underpaid. He views Craig's community-service assignment as an obtrusive political appointment. He rejects all suggestions Craig makes because he thinks they are better suited to a spa than a prison.

Finally he lets Craig take ten of the least violent inmates and teach them how to bake. Craig calls Sandy Andreas, who reluctantly takes his call, and convinces him that donating free prewashed produce would be a good tax write-off. He does the same with Solaria, now acting head of the Culinary, who sends Jersey and me to Sang Sang with old pots, pans, decorative molds, used baking ovens and refrigerators.

One month later, Craig invites Izzy Torquemada to tea in a small room that had been a storage closet. The warden comes with an assistant. He barks that he has only five minutes. But before he enters, the smell of old stones and melted wax infused with the perfume of fresh garden herbs reaches his nostrils. He takes a deep breath. His pace slows. He looks up at the golden shafts of light drifting in from two small skylights.

"Welcome to the Monks' Inn," Craig says. He leads them to a colorful round table painted by one of the inmates in a design that weaves the prison's name into an elaborate Celtic pattern that the rich might buy in an expensive shop.

A tall, thin inmate, handsome from one angle and sharp-featured from another, dressed as a monk in a tailored brown bed sheet greets them. He bows. His prison identification number is embroidered in brown buttons that run diagonally across his chest to keep his robe in place. He pours two cups of a liquid that has hints of orange rind, raisins, smoke and wood citrus. He waits as its aroma wafts toward Izzy's nostrils and moves into every sensory site in his brain. The inmate makes a deep bow and retreats. Another places a plate of éclairs filled with delicate vanilla cream next to each of them. Izzy takes a bite and lets the dark chocolate melt on his tongue. Soft cream slides down his throat. He smiles. His mood lifts.

The following month Craig Cashew invites the press and every politician running in and out of office, along with Sandy and Solaria, to a grand opening of the prison's new café. Craig contacts Cortland and asks if the Lunar Tunes would perform. Cortland updates Elvis Presley's "Jailhouse Rock" for the event. The twins wear black and white striped dresses with the red words "Mars Mafia" on the back.

When we arrive we see that Craig has strung blinking lights around the prison's barbed-wire fences, making the barbs look like stars. Everyone drinks tea, eats pastries shaped like little revolvers and knives, munches chocolate handcuffs, and shakes hands with the warden, to whom Craig wisely gives all the credit.

Society columnists report that the Monks' Inn is the charity of the year. They describe sitting on the candy electric chairs as a sweet buzzing experience. Crime rises briefly, since people want to learn gourmet cooking and know that if they go to Sang Sang, they will get a good free education because the state pays for everything. Judges are offered bribes to find ways to extend sentences. Solaria announces that the prison will no longer be called things like the Big House or Sang Sang but will officially be known as the Monks' Inn.

When Craig's community service is over he is hired to run the restaurant permanently. In time, the Monks' Inn overtakes the Culinary Institute as the preeminent cooking school and restaurant complex in the solar system.

## 42

CC LUNGES TOWARD ME, BUT I step to the side. She whizzes past then turns and glares. I hold out the charm for her to see, dangle it in front of my face, then put it in my mouth.

"You wouldn't," she cries. "No! NO!"

*Gulp!* Gone in a swallow.

"I can't believe you did that! Only you would do that!" she screams. "What kind of person are you?" Then she glowers. "No wonder Drew left you!"

I turn and run as fast as I can. I have barely enough energy to move. CC must also be tired because at first I am able to put some distance between us. I make good time, but then the ground becomes hilly and difficult. CC picks up her pace. The gap narrows. I make a sharp right and head for my rover hoping the motor had cooled off. But when I reach the cart and press start, I hear the same sputtering sounds.

Panting and sweating CC grabs the back of my head. She gives my hair a sharp yank and drags me from the cart. She twists my arm so hard that it feels like it's coming out of its socket. We struggle. She shoves me to the ground, gets on top of me, and shoves her fingers down my throat hoping I will gag, hoping the charm will emerge.

I bite down on her hand. She screams and jerks it away. She removes a red shoe, raises it high over her head and zings the heel toward my head. *Thud!* Jagged stars. Another thud. Then nothing.

When I open my eyes, I see Jersey standing over me. "Feel better?" she says looking at my dilated pupils. "You got quite a wallop."

I touch the back of my head. It's damp, sticky, and has a huge lump. When I take my hand away there's blood on it. My voice is barely audible. "What happened? Hey! Were you following me?" Jersey helps me sit. "Not so fast," I caution. "I'm nauseous."

"You probably have a concussion," she says.

I make groaning noises and pull myself to a sitting position. My arms feel like they are in one place, legs in another, and my head split down the middle.

"As a matter of fact, I *was* following you. I had a feeling you were headed for the cacao trees and thought the chances were good that you might spend the whole day there. So I decided the only way you would cover more ground was if I helped you move it along, so I reversed my direction and followed you."

"Good thing," I mumble.

"After you eye-cammed the holos to Lamont, he knew something was wrong because you didn't respond to his next call. Then he contacted me. I got to you right after she knocked you out with her shoe. What an ugly style. If I had her money, I never would have bought it. Did you see that decorative strap? So passé."

"Please, Jersey, then what happened?"

"*Shazam! Kapow!* I gave her a right cross followed by a left hook. When I added a side kick to her lower leg she folded. Too bad you were unconscious; you missed all the action. Anyway, I contacted the head of the San Andreas Farms security team, who came running. CC is beingheld until Lamont arrives."

"I was going to recommend in my report that they get more security cameras," I say. "How often do you think those security holos are reviewed?"

"Glad you asked that question," Sandy Andreas says striding toward us with three people in white coats with a stretcher floating next to them. "I've already retrieved the security holos and sent them to Mars Yard. We'll have the results shortly. Meanwhile, these gentlemen will wheel you to our infirmary and check you out. And, in appreciation for all you and your partner did, I am sending both of you free fresh produce of your choice to your homes every week for a year, starting with a case of blue watermelons."

"I was so worried," Cortland says finding me in the infirmary sitting on a white sofa with a glass in my hand. "Jersey called and told me what happened." He puts his arm around my shoulder. "I'm so relieved you're all right."

I smile weakly.

"Are you drinking a Top of the Ninth?" he asks.

"My third one. It's complimentary. I think I'll have another."

"Is it Passover, Easter, or Ramadan-strength?"

"You're asking? I can't believe you're asking. It's Ramadan-strength. CC is very strong. She could have killed me!"

$$\smile$$

# 43

"You want me to help you catch Scheherazade?" Drew asks Lamont. "We didn't exactly part on friendly terms."

"I'm sure a clever guy like you can think of something that will renew your friendship." Lamont opens a box of Chocolate Moons that has bright red lettering that says *new, pure* and *improved* on the front. He offers one to Drew.

"Thanks," Drew says taking one. "You're sure it's safe." He puts it in his mouth.

Lamont waits while Drew lets the chocolate truffle center melt in his mouth. Then he gives a sideways smile and says, "Depends on your definition of safe."

Drew swallows knowing that Lamont needs him alive rather than dead. "Who were the other three people who took the poisoned anti-flavonoids?" he asks.

"One is the scientist Decibel Point. He says he took it because he created the anti-flavonoid and he knew that Congress Drugs never finished testing it. When people were poisoned, he realized that their symptoms matched the symptoms of animals used for the first early tests. He took it because he needed a fresh sample to make an antidote."

"I've met him at Congress Drugs, but we only said hello. And the others?"

"One other was Colorful Copies."

"CC?" Drew's eyes widen.

"Yes, and we had good help solving this from Molly Summers, her partner at the Culinary, Jersey, and Jersey's husband, Trenton. Molly found a valuable piece of evidence, a charm of CC's plus a rainbow-colored eyebrow linking her to the crime right near a chocolate refining machine at San Andreas Farms."

"Do you have the charm?"

"Yes and no."

"And that means?"

"We know where it is."

"Where?"

"Molly swallowed it."

"You're kidding!"

"Molly and CC fought over the charm. Molly told us that this was the only way she could keep CC from getting it."

Drew tries to imagine his two former girlfriends in a catfight. He can't. But when he thinks of Molly swallowing the charm, he finds it easy to visualize.

"Jersey called us from San Andreas Farms where she and Molly were doing temporary security work and told us what had happened. After CC knocked out Molly, Jersey knocked out CC."

Drew hikes his eyebrows, says nothing.

"We spot-checked the area and found traces of the anti-flavonoid on the ground where Molly found the charm. This definitely links CC to the chocolate poisoning. After we picked CC up and questioned her, she admitted everything because she wanted you to know."

"Wanted me to know what? We had a relationship many years ago. It ended badly. I don't think that had anything to do with this."

"Wrong," says Lamont. "She told us that she did it because she wanted to ruin your reputation. Apparently she never forgave you."

"Ruin my reputation? How?"

"She said that when Sandy Andreas investigated the theft of the missing anti-flavonoid from Congress Drugs, one way or another your name would emerge. And when it did, she, with all her media access, was in a perfect position to give that a big spin filled with innuendos that linked your name with the crime. Even if you were innocent, your credibility as a salesman would be tainted, possibly ruined."

"She suspected that the anti-flavonoids could be dangerous after she was told by Decibel Point, when she visited Congress Drugs, that he felt that there were not enough tests done on some of their new products. But she didn't know exactly what the stuff could do. No one at that point did. She threw it in the chocolate refinery in the hopes that it might contain a substance that would give some reaction that would dramatize the event and got more than she bargained for."

Drew crosses his legs and gives a very serious look. "Well, she was right about that. You said there was a fourth person? Who could that be?"

"Still working on it. Whoever took it left no trace. We only know there was someone else because of the weight discrepancies in the anti-flavonoid between what was reported and what was actually there."

Drew comes home from Mars Yard haggard and distraught. He pours himself a tall Hadron Collider and carries it to his sofa. If he ever needed his particles accelerated this was the time. He stares at the view of River Area below. Then he turns and looks at the copy of the Giacometti on his marble table, admires the craftsmanship, and gets an idea. He codes Scheherazade's number and leaves a message. "I know you don't want to hear from me, but I couldn't help admiring the craftsmanship that went into creating the Giacometti copy. I've decided I would like to buy more art from your factory. Let me know when I can come back and see your complete line. This is strictly business."

Not more than a few moments pass when Drew's palm signals incoming call: "Scheherazade."

"Well, well," Scheherazade laughs. "I can forgive and forget enough for business. After all, my best customer is an educated consumer. Let me send you my catalog? Everything's in the catalog. Check its fluorescent pink toll-free number on the bottom, 1-800-FAKE-IT."

Drew pauses. "Ah," he says, "but there's nothing like seeing the real fake in person."

"That's what everyone says, but they don't know an etching from a lithograph."

"But I do," Drew says, dropping his voice a notch to sound more sincere and less nervous. "I was thinking about a pair of Giacomettis like a Castor and Pollex thing. I'm a Gemini."

"You really are into this," Scheherazade says suspecting that Drew might be laying a trap but decides to play along. "Can I interest you in a trio? Someone just returned a sculpture in brimstone of Shadrach, Meshach and Abed-Nego. I'll give you a very good price."

"Not really my thing."

"Elaine Paginated Pagel's *Art-History Scrolls* were just found in the men's room at the Tate Modern. The cover has a picture of Jesus painting a portrait of Michelangelo. And because I'm willing to let bygones be bygones, I'll let you have it for only twenty thousand starbucks."

Drew considers the offer. If he bought the *Art-History Scrolls*, he would have spent his last twenty thousand solars, but it was something he always wanted to own anyway—copy or no copy.

"Can you do any better than that?" he asks.

"Glad you asked that question. I love a good negotiator. For you, nineteen ninety-nine, but you're pushing the envelope."

"Let me think about it for a few days."

"Well, don't be upset if it's sold. That scroll takes longer to make than a Torah."

Drew pours himself another Hadron Collider and watches the glowing traffic circle River Area. Then he palms Lamont. "I assume you heard the conversation?"

"Every word, recorded loud and clear."

"You must have checked my bank account and know I have a problem with money. You'll have to give me an advance, or I can't buy the scrolls."

Drew can hear shouting and words like *outrageous* and *robbery* on the other end, but finally Lamont says Mars Yard will supply the money. Drew pops one of his dwindling supplies of supplements into his mouth and drains his glass. His mind races as he juggles his options.

Lamont and Sid make plans to meet Drew at New Chicago's Central Station. Drew sends his most treasured things to a storage crater on the side of Earth's moon that is invisible to Earth. It is not far from the shopping center Cortland once invested in that bankrupted him. Drew smiles remembering how Kandy once asked why people on Earth should believe it was real if no one could see it. After all, she argued, land was called real estate for a reason.

Drew takes a picture of himself receiving a Best Salesmanship award from Sandy off the wall. He turns it over and inserts the tip of his pinky into a slot. Out slides a forged identity card saved for an emergency and a thin box holding a syringe of an illegal substance, courtesy of the late Rocket Packarod, that can change his DNA for seven days. He puts it in the false bottom of his travel case then puts clothing and a few personal belongings on top. After, he calls Lamont.

"I need more money to do business with Scheherazade."

"We heard," Lamont says. "Your apartment is bugged, remember? Twenty thousand starbucks have already been wired into your Mars card."

"And expenses? I need more money for expenses."

"Okay, five thousand for expenses."

"Twenty," Drew says.

"Ten," Lamont says.

"Done," Drew sighs.


Drew boards a tram at the River Area station heading to New Chicago. His eyes mist as he whizzes by the luxurious Hotel du Antibodies and other expensive neighborhood haunts. He eats three regular Chocolate Moons.

"Our lunch item today is fettuccini Alfredo and molten chocolate cake for dessert," says a smiling steward. "Would you like Freedom Plan or Regular Plan?"

"Regular. But bring me a double brandy Alexander with real cream first."

Drew's order is placed before him. He unfolds his napkin carefully. He raises his fork and twirls the fettuccini toward his lips. "Ahh," he sighs. Then he thinks, *execution by trans fats. Is there a better way to go?*

44

Everyone teases me about thinking there is some kind of French connection and an antidote to the poison the boys at the Candy Universe ingested. I read everything I can on Sensory Dynamics, the new cultural therapies used to awaken comatose patients.

To enhance my perceptions, I eat lots of escargot and frog's legs, which is not hard because I love fresh garlic sautéed in butter. I dream of the Eiffel Tower, Jean Valjean's silver candlesticks, and Karl Lagerfeld's sunglasses. And most importantly, I take a class that teaches me how to tie one cheap scarf two hundred stylish ways so it looks like two hundred expensive scarves.

Jersey and my family say I'm crazy. But Trenton, hedging his bets, says the closest thing to encouragement: "Hey, you never know!"

When I sing "La Marseillaise," the French National Anthem, my family screams, "Knock it off already!"

I'm obsessed by Marie Antoinette's words, "Let them eat cake." So I savor a double-fudge brownie. Bingo! Knew it! Zest renewed. Told you so!

I'm sure the answer, like the answers to all great riddles—such as "Did the big bang really say bang?" and "Why do the universe's building blocks have an A, B, and a C on them?"—is hidden in plain sight. I think of the rhythm of a wooden spoon clicking on the side of a mixing bowl. First slowly then rapidly, repeating like a mantra promising enlightenment. Then words emerge: *butter, eggs, flour, sugar, chocolate.* I lick my lips, a sure sign that I'm on the right track. I jump in my rover and rush to Jersey and Trenton's home.

Trenton and Jersey are playing their favorite game, Pin the Tail on the Cerebral Cortex on the colorful holograph of the brain that I'm always amazed to see floating in a corner of their living room.

"Hi guys," I say.

Jersey glares at me. "Thanks, Molly, you just made me miss. I hit the thalmus!"

"Sorry," I say. "It could have been worse."

"Yeah, it could have been the frontal lobes," she snaps.

I turn to Trenton, who tallies his winning score and say, "I have an obsession with flour, butter, eggs, sugar, and chocolate."

"You always have an obsession with those things," Jersey replies, rattling the dice. "It's the way of all pastry."

"Want me to distill those ingredients and see if their chemical interactions reveal anything new," Trenton asks wearily.

"Would you? I really think you might find something significant."

"Nothing to lose," Trenton says going into his laboratory and closing the door behind him.

Jersey picks up a few darts and holds them in one hand while she continues rattling the dice with the other. "Do you want to play, Molly?"

"I'm not feeling very cerebral today, but I will have a lemon water."

Jersey gets the water. I take a sip. She peers at me closely. She puts her arms around my waist. "You're thinner!" she exclaims. "Wow! Much thinner!"

In spite of the double-fudge brownie that I ate, I say, "As a matter of fact, I've lost close to a hundred pounds. You're the only one who's noticed. The twins are in their own world, and for the last year Cortland has traveled so much he's barely home."

"You should be showing off, not hiding under those baggy old clothes."

"I guess I'm afraid that if I show my progress, I'll gain it back."

Suddenly we hear knocking and banging, whirling and twirling coming from Trenton's laboratory. Jersey puts her ear to the door. "Now I hear a lot of hissing. Sounds like he's spraying himself with the latest WD. Did you know they were up to WD-4,000,000? He must be having a lot of trouble."

I pace back and forth, circle the room, then circle in the opposite direction. I'm drenched with perspiration.

"Why don't you soak in our new hot tub? It will relax you. This may take Trenton awhile."

We go into the bathroom. I'm surprised to see that there are shelves filled with sea-breeze bath salts, imported from Earth, bitter orange blossom neroli oil, imported from Venus, several products containing aloe vera, a cucumber cleansing lotion, Jojoba oil, Vitamin E oil, essence of young birch tree branches from a Ruby Spa Body Shop and more. Jersey runs the water, adds a generous amount of several products to the tub, hands me a fresh towel and leaves.

As I undress and hang my clothes on a hook, I think Jersey may be cheap about food but she certainly isn't cheap about her beauty products. I step into the warm water, breathe in the perfumed air, put my head back and close my eyes.

"You're right Jersey," I call through the door. "This is wonderful." The swirling jets of water are so soothing that I almost fall asleep. Suddenly, behind closed eyelids, I see a light. It glows brighter and brighter, stronger and stronger, then—a flash of lightning!

My knees jerk toward my chest; my hands push me up. I pop from the tub like a bagel from a toaster.

"Paprika! Paprika!" I yell, running naked from the bathroom. "Paprika! Paprika!"

Seeing me dripping wet and naked, Jersey throws me another towel. I catch it and zap it around like a toga from Ruby's spa.

"I've got it. I've got it," I pant, banging on Trenton's door. "I know what those ingredients mean."

The door opens a crack. Trenton pokes his head through.

"I saw a flash of lightning. The word *éclair* in French means 'flash of lightning.' Try this formula: E equals two éclairs times the speed of swallowing them in the light."

Trenton's eyes sparkle. The door opens wider. "Interesting theory," he says. His eyes spin. He taps his forehead. "But éclairs are off my reference chart." He does some calculations. "You'll have to help me with this one, Molly."

"We have to hurry, because when I did an update on the former cures, the scientists who worked on them discovered that the ingredients that worked best were organic, meaning all had short expiration dates. No preservatives."

We quickly mix a batter, make custard, melt the chocolate, heat the oven, and before you can say "a la carte," voilà: éclairs. This time I do not wince as Trenton takes them back into his laboratory, pounds them into powders, and distills them into liquid supplements that can be injected intravenously. I'm so excited that I don't even salivate.

"This is it," he says with the voice of an anchorman announcing that a storm is over. "This is definitely it! I tested it on ten generations of fruit flies and it worked every time!"

Soon scientists everywhere, especially those who had been working on an antidote, confirm Trenton's results and immediately send him congratulations. Some say he could be nominated for a four-flame Bunsen Burner prize. Jersey celebrates by contacting Groupon and getting a coupon for champagne supplements.

I am relieved and overjoyed that we have discovered an antidote to the anti-flavonoid that poisoned the Chocolate Moons, but I am sad that the patients will be injected with its chemical essence and will not be able enjoy the delicate pâté a choux pastry, custard-cream middle and the smooth dark chocolate topping of real éclairs. But I know the minute the antidote takes effect and they awaken, they will be starved and will immediately ask for one. And they do.

Before I leave I say to Trenton and Jersey, "Excuse me; I have to go to the bathroom."

"You just came out of the bathroom," Jersey says. "In fact I saw you go three times."

"Yes, but I have to go again. It's more urgent. Something feels very different."

"Different?" Jersey asks, concerned that I might be sick.

"I think CC's charm is going to emerge." And emerge it does.

I contact Lamont to ask him to ask CC if she wants her charm back.

Sometime later Lamont tells me that CC declined my offer and said after all it's been through, she never wants to see it again.

## 45

SID AND LAMONT WAIT FOR Drew to exit the River Area–New Chicago tram. They are in plain clothes.

"I could have worn something better," Sid says. "Drew is such a snappy dresser. You make me feel inferior even in front of criminals."

"It's all in your mind."

"No, it's on my back," Sid retorts. "I don't know why you made me wear this old gray velour sweat suit. You just want me out of the loop. And out of the competition for next month's cover of *Diva Detective*."

"Are you finished?" Lamont adjusts his Turnbull and Asser tie, tucks a silk handkerchief into his breast pocket, and angles his fedora over one eye.

Sid frowns. Finally Lamont points and says, "Look, there he is."

Drew is wearing all black. Sid wonders if it's an artist's camouflage or if Drew is just depressed. He slides his jacket zipper up and down and doesn't think he looks so bad.

Lamont and Sid meet Drew. They walk to Lamont's rover.

"Get in the back," Lamont says. Drew moves. "Not you. You sit up front with me so I can keep an eye on you." He thumbs Sid to sit in the back.

Lamont drives to Dr. Scholl's Plaza, an ugly industrial area that lies at the base of the space elevator populated by people down on their heels. It is filled with storage facilities, off-track gaming parlors, cheap hotels, and restaurants with waiters who sing ballads of sad cafés.

He parks at one of the hotels formally used as a 23rd Century Fox B-rated movie set that has never seen better days. Sid pushes the door open into a dim, smoky, foul-smelling lobby. They don't see any door-men or porters, only a vending machine that gives out keys and an empty brown whisky bottle on a desk. Lamont gets keys to two adjoining rooms. He hands one to Sid, who will share his room with Drew. Lamont takes the other. He leaves the door open between the rooms.

No one unpacks.

Drew sits in the dingy hotel room on a faded yellow sofa with Jackson Pollock–like drips that Drew estimates if properly displayed at Park Bengay could sell for a lot of money.

Lamont comes over to Drew. He hands him an unmarked palm. "No time like the present to make the call to Scheherazade to arrange your meeting," he says.

After several rings Scheherazade picks up. A portfolio of etchings of heavy naked women by Lucy and Desi Rubins destined to hang in the lounge of Rose's Heaven lies open on her desk. Rose rejected *Odalisque* by Ingres as sending the wrong message because the woman in the painting was too thin, and as everyone at Rose's knew, you can't be too rich or too fat.

"Hello, Scheherazade," Drew says. "Remember we spoke a few days ago about me coming over and selecting a few more artworks."

"As long as you're coming, can I can interest you in buying some unlimited editions? The market for them is soaring. Even Roger Orbit bought some for the Far Horizons foundation."

"I'll consider it, Scheherazade."

Sid whispers to Lamont, "Maybe that's a good investment. We can make early retirement from the police force."

"Shaddup," Lamont says. "You want early retirement I'll give you early retirement!"

"Did I hear other customers near you? I think I heard something."

Lamont punches Sid in the arm.

"No, just getting my shoes shined," Drew responds.

Scheherazade clears her throat. "I could always use more business. Will that be cash?"

"Of course cash. I'm insulted you asked. I can make it sometime tomorrow afternoon."

Drew closes his palm and says. "I'm going to visit Scheherazade's workshop tomorrow."

"Know that already," Lamont says. "We were standing right here. Ya think we're stupid?"

"Yeah," Sid says. "Ya think we're stupid?"

Drew doesn't answer.

Lamont sighs. "How much do you think you will need this time?" anticipating the question before it is asked.

"At least forty thousand; she thinks I'm loaded."

"You used to be," Sid says.


Lamont thinks the deal he offers Drew is one of the best he ever made. Only a fool would refuse what he considered to be a generous offer of going to a moon of Uranus to work in a toy factory that makes colorful "babushka planets" that fit one inside the other, which children  break and throw at each other.

The next morning Lamont tells Sid to bring Drew down to the lobby and wait with him while Lamont gets his rover. Sid doesn't want to handcuff Drew's hand to his own hand, because no one will be able to tell which one of them is the criminal. So he tells Drew he's using the honor system, and Drew tells him that's a good idea.

Before they leave the room, Sid checks his wrist cam for any messages and reads his horoscope. It says, "Beware the ides of March." Sid thinks hard. But this is July. He presses again. The next message says, "If this is not the ides of March, then just beware." Sid, who was hoping it would say today you will meet the woman of your dreams and win ten million starbucks frowns but then smiles thinking that all this might happen in March.

The lobby is noisy and crowded. Noisier and more crowded than Lamont and Sid thought it would be. Drew tells Sid he has to go to the men's room.

"I'll have to accompany you," Sid says. "As a matter of fact, I have to go myself."

Drew immediately starts pushing through the crowd to the middle of the room. Then he makes an abrupt turn, putting a few people between himself and Sid.

"Slow down," Sid yells.

"It's an emergency," Drew shouts back over his shoulder. Drew pushes the person on his right, who staggers backward into a pile of luggage. Then Drew pushes the person on his left and runs.

"Did you push me?" says the person on the left, retrieving his bearings and making a fist.

"No, it was that other guy," the person on the right says.

"What other guy? You're only trying to make an excuse. I know your type."

"And what type is that?"

Sid yells, "Criminal trying to escape!"

"Who you calling a criminal?" another man cries.

"Animal trying to escape!" a woman standing near them cries.

"Someone's got a dog loose," another person booms.

"What kind of dog? I saw a dog over there," she points to a man wearing a dog costume holding a sign that says, "Eat at Franks."

A man carrying coffee and doughnuts is shoved. His coffee spills. His doughnuts roll. The woman who is talking about the dog slides into the man making a fist. *Pow!* Right in the kisser.

She falls on Sid.

The woman looks down. "It's all your fault! You must be a criminal! Are you the criminal who lost a dog? Help! Police!"

The place is growing more and more operatic.

Sid is pinned under the woman. "I *am* the police," he tries to say. But it does not sound like that. Someone steps on his hand. "Ouch!" Three doughnuts roll near his face. He closes his eyes.

His head throbs. A big guy, with muscles popping all over wearing a Calvin Crime T-shirt with a skull in decorator shades of blood, reaches down and shoves the doughnuts into his mouth. "Next time make them lemon-glazed," he snarls.

Sid gets a hand free and tries to reach for his badge. Now someone steps on his other hand.

"OW!" Sid screams.

The hotel manager finally comes. "Watch it, fella. Don't reach for anything." He flashes his eyes around; his hair is flying. "I'm in charge here." he shouts several times. "Will someone help this woman?"

"What about you?" says the woman on the floor. "You could help me up!"

"That's not my job. My job is to get other people to do things."

A crowd gathers around. Everyone watches as she pushes herself to her feet.

"There you go," the manager says. She gives him a dirty look and kicks him in the shin.

"Where's the dog?" she asks. "Did someone catch the dog?"

Sid, still on the floor, says, "I'm a policeman."

"You shaddup," growls the hotel manager. "Not in those clothes, you're not. I used to have a suit like that. My wife just threw mine out; it was my favorite knock-around wear-at-home. Where'd you get it, big boy?" He peers at Sid closely. "Hey, aren't you number two on the ten-most-wanted list?"

"He's number four," someone says. "Let's make something of it?"

"He's number six," calls another.

"No, number eight," a voice shouts.

Several close in and chant. "Two, four, six, eight who should we incarcerate?"

Meanwhile Lamont, who had been waiting in his rover in front of the hotel, hears all the commotion. He parks his car and goes into the lobby, where someone shoves him in the face and grabs his hat.

"Hey, give that back," Lamont cries.

"Consider it an entrance fee, partner. Take it off ya taxes."

Lamont pushes his way toward the center of the room. A woman's long feathered boa dipped in "kryptonite for blondes" makes Lamont feel weak. He staggers through the room.

Drew makes his way to the back of the hotel and exits. No one stops him. No one follows him. He circles through several buildings, down many alleys, and up a series of staircases until he reaches the base of the space elevator. He finds a dark corner and takes out the forged identity card and presses his finger into it. Then he destroys his old card and places the new one in his wallet. He removes the syringe from the box and plunges the needle into his arm. For the briefest of moments, he feels like he is floating like cracked ice in a glass of vodka. Then he enters the waiting area, looks around, recognizes no one, and strolls casually to a ticket window.

"And where will that be to?" the ticket agent asks.

"Earth's moon. The dark side. Add a shuttle pass to Darth Veda Crater."

"One-way or round-trip?"

"One-way," Drew says.

When Lamont Blackberry visits Sandy Andreas and tells him Drew is missing, Sandy acts like four screaming children in a supermarket. Then Lamont tells him that Mars Yard is at a dead end as to who took the fourth sample of the anti-flavonoid from Congress Drugs.

Sandy brightens. "If I had known you were looking for a fourth person, I could have saved you a lot of trouble." He walks to a tall, thin cabinet in a corner of his office. He opens a door, slides out a tray, and says, "Here it is. I always take a sample of all my products for safekeeping. My biometrics don't appear, because I use my own anti-detection gloves."

As soon as Lamont Blackberry leaves, Sandy calls a press conference. He announces that the substance added to the chocolate, which he readily admits came from Congress Drugs, was never a poison but a potion, and the media better get their act together regarding semantic definitions. No way was anyone ever in a coma; the "victims" were in a restful, rejuvenating sleep. Ingesting it caused a brief metabolic processing delay. So much for the truth.

Then Sandy spends a fortune in PR to rename, reissue, redefine, and repackage all his products. Not long afterward, someone who looks like Sandy Andreas, talks like Sandy Andreas, walks like Sandy Andreas, eats like Sandy Andreas, sleeps like Sandy Andreas and thinks like Sandy Andreas but was not, according to Sandy Andreas actually Sandy Andreas buries all the files containing any information about anti-flavonoids and Chocolate Moons in an unmarked storage area at Ali Baba Caves.

The case of the Chocolate Moons fades into history. Over time it is rewritten as a human-interest piece and later as a favorite allegory clergymen love to tell of man's rise, fall and redemption.

Roses Heaven and Rubies Spa merge becoming "The Ruby Rose." Historians cite this as the definitive end of the battle of the bulge, mankind's final frontier and the marking of a major evolutionary turning point. And when future beings discover a tree that bears a delicious candy fruit, a residual memory, from whence they know not where, wells up inside of each of them and urges that this exceptional tree should have a sign placed next to it. And so one is made. It says: "Low calorie, Guaranteed Fresh, Organic, Nothing Forbidden." Then they ate every one and said it was good.

# Epilogue

CC IS SENTENCED TO FOUR years at a penal colony on Earth picking pineapples in Hawaii. She always felt that what she did was worth it because Drew's reputation was ruined. She returned to the Moon in better shape than when she left because of the workout she got living in Earth's heavy gravity. When her father retired, she became CEO of Carbon Copies Media.

Pluto Pastrami and Breezy Point serve three years for attempted manslaughter. When they're released, Pluto changes his name to Pluto Picasso and opens an art gallery in River Area. He attracts an affluent clientele when he turns a copy of *Nude Descending a Staircase*, by the French surrealist Marcel Duchamp, upside down and says the staircase is a symbol for financial markets, and—since more people make money in bull markets rather than bear markets—*Nude Ascending a Staircase* is far better artwork than Duchamp's original. Copies, and copies of copies, sell out overnight.

Breezy becomes an artist using a medium her father invents, making her a technical virtuoso. She paints *Ode to the Forty Thieves* in a cubist style. Scheherazade ignores the work but her lover, Taliban, considers it a signal to start a war.

Scheherazade remains at her job for life. Her business thrives. She sells several of Mona Lisa's teeth and swears on the head of Medusa, not the supermarket checkout girl, Medusa Feinstein, that they are the real teeth because when she personally took them out of Mona's mouth, Mona moaned.

Sandy Andreas buys a ten-foot copy of Velázquez's *Pope Innocent X* from Scheherazade with his face replacing that of the pope and "Big Sandy Is Watching You" in large black letters on the top, and a copy of Poussin's *The Rape of the Sabine Women* to hang in his home office.

His wife, Solaria, heads the Culinary Institute. She hates the art that Sandy bought, but Sandy says that it is his office and if she didn't like it, she shouldn't go in there, so she never did.

Kandy marries a good friend of Solaria's who is the head chef at Gramercy Gardens. She has a boy and a girl, each of whom look like her and appear every month on the cover of *Beautiful Baby Universe* until they graduate to *Beautiful Teen Universe* and *Beautiful Adult Universe*.

Billings Montana owns the largest chain of pizza restaurants on Mars.

Through middle age and menopause, Flo gains a half a pound that she blames on being related to me.

Decibel Point briefly continues to work for several labs, but as soon as he can, he retires to a community in space where he can eat whatever he wants whenever he wants it and never has to feel the effects of gravity again.

I finally learn that Jersey's last name is Shore. But she says she doesn't want anyone to know, because getting teased about the name Jersey is bad enough. She quits her job at the Culinary and takes a job at a bank because the smell of money is more appealing than the smell of food.

Trenton is given a large space for a laboratory at Mars Yard. Jersey and Trenton continue to live frugally and mostly on supplements, except for the free chicken soup I send them.

Cortland is Mars's biggest music producer. He buys a building in New Chicago and transforms it into a work space and living space. It has a recording studio and offices on the four lower levels; each twin has her own apartment on the middle floors. We live in the penthouse, complete with wraparound terrace, full gym and indoor swimming pool. The entire building rotates maximizing views and light.

In total I lose more than 160 Earth pounds. The twins help me get a new wardrobe and hairstyle. And although I am older, I've never looked or felt better. But my love of food never wanes.

It's a typical morning. I say good-bye to my personal trainer and slide into a hot bath. Friends are coming for brunch tomorrow. I consider "oysters and pearls"—caviar-topped oysters on a bed of tapioca pearls in a sabayon-vermouth sauce that I found in an ancient French Laundry restaurant cook book—but although I love it, I think it too ethereal for the occasion and decide that farm-fresh eggs with pancetta and lobster knuckles on a bed of spinach placed in a hollowed-out brioche is a better choice.

I step from the bath and wrap myself in a peach terry-cloth robe. I go into the bedroom and sit on a soft blue-and-white lounge chair. I reach for the holo's remote and click the cooking channel. Today's guest on *Interviews with Chef Rachael X-Ray* is Pierre Ambrosias, president and CEO of Half Foods, a company that is revolutionizing the food industry.

"Welcome," Rachael says. "Today's guest is Pierre Ambrosias, CEO of Half Foods, a company that combines supplements and nutritional extras such as Growthex and Libido Plus with regular food. His sales have outpaced Congress Drugs' Freedom Plan. This week he will open his first superstore in New Chicago. Please welcome Pierre Ambrosias."

There is applause, whistling, and foot stomping. Lights dim, and a full red-robed chorus walks onto the stage, singing and clapping their hands to an old-time Earth spiritual, "Rocka My Soul in the Bosom of Abraham." Then, as though levitating above the stage in his long white robe, bathed in glowing orange light, on the arms of two young women—one with long green hair called Celery and one with cropped red hair called Tomato—is Pierre Ambrosias.

His image is beamed to a giant screen. I blink several times because I think his image looks like the ceiling at Sistine's Salon in downtown New Chicago where according to the small print next to the image inserted by the CEO of Manicurists Inc. is God holding out his hand to Adam and gives Adam his first manicure.

Rachael points to a light-blue sofa. Pierre and the two young women sit.

"How did you get started, Pierre?" she asks, leaning in.

"I used to work for Whole Foods Luna on Earth's moon. I had also studied Congress Drugs' Freedom Plan. But I had my own ideas and wanted to find a food alternative to the alternatives. And when my wife, Melon, so ripe that she was, died right after eating a cocoanut avocado sundae, I vowed never to rest until I found that way."

His eyes mist. Celery hands him a handkerchief; Tomato wipes his brow. The chorus chants, "Melon, Melon, Half Foods for Melon."

I drop the remote, stand up, and scream. "Pierre Ambrosias is Drew! Son of a..." I realize that I may be the only one in the universe able to recognize him from small inflections in his altered voice.

Drew/Pierre turns directly to the camera.

"I want to introduce my daughters, Lettuce and Tomato. Stand up girls and take a bow." The audience applauds. "See how beautiful and lovely they are, having been raised entirely on Half Foods. My daughters also sing and have their own group, called the Mixed Vegetables. I once knew Molly Marbles Summers, the mother of the Lunar Tunes, and if she is listening, I want her to know my daughters want to be just like their idols, Becky and Lois."

Rachael X-Ray asks her last question: "And what is your best-selling product?

"Half Foods' Chocolate Chocolate Moons. I eat some at the beginning and end of every day because they have real taste but no grit."

I smile, get up and turn off the holo, put my arms out in front of me, stretch, and release. I'm happy that Drew finally found his true calling, albeit a bit theatrical.

We never meet again.

As for me, I have no intention of growing old too fast and smart too late. I have plans.

Stay tuned.

# About the Author

JACKIE KINGON IS A TEACHER, writer and artist. She holds a Master's degree from Columbia University Teachers College in New York City; a Bachelor of Arts from Lesley University in Cambridge, Massachusetts; and a Bachelor of Fine Arts degree from the School of Visual Arts in New York City where she won the outstanding student award.

She has published two articles in *The New York Times* on autism and learning disabilities and one feature piece about her experiences teaching in an inner city school in the south Bronx.

Her paintings have been exhibited in galleries in Washington DC and New York City including the Dactyl Foundation, Washington Project of the Arts, and the United States Embassy to the European Union in Brussels, Belgium. Three works are part of the Estee Lauder collection. She has been a member of the board of the Empire State Plaza Art Commission in Albany, NY and the board of the Friends of Vassar College art museum.

Her short stories have been published in *Flying Island Press-Pieces of Eight, The Fringe Magazine* and *Static Movement Magazine*. Kingon's story for the blind, entitled "A Rose by Any Other Name," was recorded by Voice Needs in League, TX.

Jackie Kingon lives with her husband in Bronxville, NY. Chocolate Chocolate Moons is her first novel.

Check out her web site at: www.jackiekingon.com

21294536R10121

Made in the USA
Charleston, SC
12 August 2013